Cabin Fever
Emma Donaldson

BLACK LACE

Black Lace books contain sexual fantasies.
In real life, always practise safe sex.

First published in 2002 by
Black Lace
Thames Wharf Studios
Rainville Road
London W6 9HA

Design by Smith & Gilmour, London
Printed and bound by Mackays of Chatham PLC

ISBN 0 352 33692 7

Cabin Fever

'If you decide to join us in bed, you can choose one of us as a sex playmate. If you choose me, Emma's allowed to watch. If you choose Emma, I'm allowed to watch.'

Laura suddenly felt very excited. 'And if I choose both of you?'

'That's an added bonus.' Emma beamed. If you choose both of us, it'll be fun for all three of us. What do you say? Are we on?'

'Definitely,' Laura said.

'What about tomorrow night? Are you free, Laura?'

'How about tonight?' Laura said softly. 'I'm free now.'

'Great.' Tom grinned broadly. He disappeared into the bedroom, leaving the girls to undress each other. Emma kicked off her high-heeled sandals and Laura unzipped Emma's white sundress and let it fall to the floor. Emma stood naked except for a minute pair of white panties cut so high that Laura could see the creases of her bikini line.

Her small shapely breasts were already excited, the nipples lengthened and red. 'Here, let me help you, now, Laura,' she said.

Laura obediently raised her arms and Emma peeled off the T-shirt, revealing Laura's white satin body. She pulled down Laura's pencil-slim skirt and took in the glossy flesh-coloured hold-ups with the white lacy tops.

'Wow, Tom'll love these. And I do too,' she added admiringly. 'Let's go and join him.'

He was standing naked in the bedroom, his body just as sexy as Laura remembered it from the other night.

Shangri-la: Where no one grows old,
but at intervals change their bodies.

1

'Yes, certainly, madam. Tuesday, two o'clock. Pedicure, foot spa and ankle massage. Right. May I have your cabin number? I'll give you an appointment card.'

Laura Barnes smiled over the reception desk at the middle-aged café owner, plain but wealthy, who just wanted to rest her legs for a fortnight and be waited on, literally hand and foot, by the cruise staff. This was Laura's sixth cruise and she had become adept at persuading wealthy clients to part with their money, without in any way appearing to be pushy or on the make. Although all the gratuities went into a common fund, Laura's clients always left the biggest tips at the end of every voyage, especially the stressed-out male executives who often just wanted a bit of smoothing and hands-on contact from an attractive young woman. Laura had enough imagination to realise that there were many older men and singletons, having no close family ties, who were never touched by anyone in their everyday lives. This sort of man liked to have his hair washed and blown dry by a pretty young girl, enjoying the sensual feel of her hands caressing his face and head and yet with no wish to take things any further.

Some of them wanted the body massage of course, and revelled in the feeling of helplessness and dependence as they lay out on the treatment couch, submitting to the stroking and smoothing of an expert. Most of them were used to being in charge all the time in their place of work and it was a welcome novelty for them to take such a passive role. None of these clients was in any way threatening or difficult. All left generous tips and flattering comments on the cruise evaluation sheets and Laura had reason to be pleased and grateful at how much they appreciated her skill. She noticed several good-looking guys on this trip, which was quite unusual for the *Jannina*, because most of the passengers were either middle aged or retired. Quite nice too, she thought appreciatively as a tall blond hunk sauntered past the reception desk of the Beauty Spa. He was broad shouldered, slim hipped and handsome, walking with a lazy self-assured confidence that was most attractive.

She nudged her colleague, Fiona. 'There's a bit of body language for you,' she whispered and then bent her head to fill in an appointment card for the café owner, spreading out her slim smooth fingers and very consciously allowing the other woman to take note of her own beautifully manicured, shapely nails.

Then she said pleasantly, 'Was there anything else, madam? Manicures are at a special rate Tuesday and Wednesday, in time for Captain Browning's reception party, of course, and we have eyebrow and lash tinting at half the usual price this week. Can I tempt you?'

She glanced at the older woman's split nails and ragged cuticles. Then she smiled winningly up into the rather careworn face.

'We do warm-oil therapy and silk nail extensions as well,' she said softly. 'It's quite amazing how nicely varnished nails can enhance the shape of your hands. Why not treat yourself? You deserve it.'

The café owner hesitated and was lost. 'Why not?' she said. 'I need a bit of pampering and that's what I'm going to have on this cruise.'

She beamed at Laura as she waited for the extra treatments to be entered on her card and then shuffled off to join her elderly sister and Laura turned to the next prospective customer.

Today was the first morning on board and most of the passengers were waiting for their luggage to be delivered to the cabins. All the stewards and porters were busy heaving trunks and suitcases on to the lifts and directing people to the luxury accommodation that would be their home for the next two weeks. There was a distinct atmosphere of restrained panic as passengers waited anxiously for the luggage which they'd left in the customs shed and which, miraculously, would be delivered to their cabin doors with no delays or mix-ups. There *were* delays and mix-ups of course, but Laura knew that the rows and complaints would all be resolved well before departure time and people smoothed into a good mood at the start of their cruise experience. By the end of the holiday, all problems would have been forgotten and envelopes with generous tips would be passed to grateful cruise staff in recognition of all the services they'd rendered.

But first, every crew member had to heave to and pull out all the stops to make the *Jannina* comfortable and enjoyable for the passengers. Already, the entertainments manager was rehearsing the cabaret acts in the deserted Santorini lounge and the head chef was making the lives of the kitchen staff an utter misery as he contemptuously ordered the youngest commis chef to pour the first batch of fish stock down the sink. In spite of the most careful organisation, there was a lot of bustle and confusion as the *Jannina* staff did their best to find misplaced luggage and to calm worried travellers. Laura knew that many of the more experienced passengers would be coming to book a shampoo and set, manicure or massage while there were still some spaces in the appointments book, but she was well prepared.

As she stood behind the reception desk, tall and poised, a shaft of sunlight bathed her youthful face in a golden glow, highlighting her perfect features and beautiful bone structure. Her blonde hair was piled high on her elegantly shaped head and fastened with a gold-coloured slide. Her full lips were parted in a half smile and her brow was as unlined and serene as always, her feathered eyebrows winging gracefully upwards at the outer edges. This was how she invariably appeared to her cruise clients. She was always attentive and absorbed in what she was doing and seemed totally unaware of what a knockout she looked as she continued to take appointments and reassure unglamorous passengers of her ability to make them beautiful. All the while she was giving off an air of unaffected friendliness as she encouraged them to have something extra, something which cost more money, of course, but which would contribute to their feeling of well-being and the enjoyment of the cruise experience. Her young colleague and cabin-mate was impressed by Laura's technique. Eighteen-year-old Fiona was new to the cruise ship. She was small and pale and anxious to do well, in spite of the fact that her obvious talents as a hairdresser had singled her out above all other applicants for the post.

Both girls were conscious of the cold stare of their manageress, Elinor Brookes, who ruled over the Shangri-la Health and Beauty Spa with a rod of iron. Even her hairstyle was like granite, Laura thought disrespectfully as she carefully avoided Elinor's gaze. The manageress had a dress code which was as rigid as the long-line body-shaper which she always wore under her salon overall. Her staff were not allowed to appear on duty without stockings or tights, however hot the weather, and Elinor's rules applied to all aspects of their lives on board. None of the health and beauty staff were allowed on the upper decks or in the cabins where the paying passengers lived. They were confined to C deck, where the crew common room and the crew cabins were situated. Fraternising with officers or passengers was strictly prohibited, as was the wearing of fashionable thongs underneath the Shangri-la uniforms.

Elinor was a good deal older than the young beauty therapists in her charge and was such a strict martinet that Laura could not resist a grin at the thought that their boss had no idea what brief undies some of the girls got away with under their regulation white overalls. Hairdressers had to wear an elasticated belt of turquoise colour. Beauty therapists had one in pink, but that was where the uniformity ended. In spite of Elinor's best efforts, all the girls at Shangri-la wore what they liked underneath, the briefer the better according to them. Laura herself was often bra-less and wore only tiny bikini briefs beneath her uniform. Elinor's eyes would narrow critically as Laura crouched before a cupboard or bent down to the lower shelf of her trolley and the brevity of her panties showed quite clearly through her white overall. But Elinor felt unable to reveal her prurient interest in girlie underwear and merely tightened her lips disapprovingly at such blatant vpl.

Laura, however, was fully aware of Elinor's beady look and took a mischievous delight in defying her rules. She was twenty-four now, but still remembered vividly her first meeting with her new boss when she was just a student of seventeen.

At the time, she'd been at college in Manchester and had a Saturday job in a hairdresser's. Glancing idly at one of the salon's glossy mags during her coffee break, she'd come across an intriguing advertisement:

HERVEY BEAUTY THERAPY COLLEGE IN LONDON, TRAINING IN THEATRICAL MAKE-UP, SPECIALISED EFFECTS ON DISFIGUREMENT, POST-SURGERY PROBLEMS AND SALON WORK, LEADING TO WORLDWIDE CAREER OPPORTUNITIES, INCLUDING HERVEY CRUISE SHIP SALONS. Write for application forms, Hervey Cosmetics, North Street, NW3 4LL, or telephone Elinor Brookes, (0181) 6530077.

Laura had barely been able to contain her excitement as she raced home that Saturday teatime to send off for the forms. She didn't tell her mother anything about it for the time being, but hugged her secret ambition to herself. Wendy Barnes was divorced and Laura was all she had; the harsh narrowness of her life was only made bearable by her love and devotion to her beautiful teenage daughter. Laura knew this full well and was reluctant to cause her mother any unnecessary pain. After all, she thought, she might not be accepted. In any case, she hadn't even completed her college course yet, she told herself. Better to say nothing until things were definite. No point in upsetting her mum for nothing.

The granddaughter of Beatrix Hervey, the original founder of the firm, interviewed Laura for half an hour and was all well-preserved charm and upper-crust good manners as she offered her tea and chatted gently about Laura's reasons for wanting to try the cruise scene. Then, Elinor Brookes gave her a gruelling five-hour practical and written exam. Even after all this time, Laura could still recite unhesitatingly the five layers of the skin, every single nerve and muscle and all the functions of the cuticle in her sleep. At the end of the exam, Laura was convinced that she'd be rejected in favour of those who'd achieved higher O levels. As it turned out, there were twenty candidates that day and she was the only one chosen. She remembered vividly her feeling of elation when she was congratulated by the sour-faced Elinor and by the other girls, who were all bitterly disappointed. At the same time, she'd been full of anxiety at what her mother might think. Both of these emotions were strong inside her as she finally leaped on a bus at Piccadilly and sped home after her ordeal in the Midland Hotel.

She reflected on how fortunate she'd been to be selected for the beauty salon on the *Jannina* at the age of seventeen, subject to passing her final exams, of course. Wendy had been tearful but proud when she learned of her daughter's success and Laura had spent the next year reinventing herself. Out went the north Manchester accent, along with the cheap and cheerful clothes from the Arndale market. She saved every penny from her Saturday job and washed up at a café three evenings a week in order to buy some decent clothes for herself. She dumped her unambitious spotty boyfriend and had her hair cut regularly at the most trendy hair-dresser's in town. She willingly paid sixty pounds a time to have her hair styled and to add the final gloss on her road to success. Of course, she passed her finals with flying colours and her training at the Beatrix Hervey College in London was just a wonderful dream. When she was just eighteen, she joined the *Jannina* as a qualified beautician.

As she and Fiona continued to take appointments and book clients for various beauty treatments, they smiled at some of the more outrageous clients who seemed convinced that signing up for a hairdo or a skin make-over was going to be their passport to sex and success.

'Shangri-la, where no one grows old, but at intervals change their bodies,' Laura whispered, and both girls started to giggle.

She entered yet another name in the appointments book and glanced up, once again catching Elinor's icy scrutiny. She had a momentary feeling of disquiet, but then stood a little taller behind the reception desk and smoothed down her crisp salon overall. Although she disliked and feared her boss, she had every reason to be grateful to Elinor Brookes for giving her such a golden opportunity; and so too had Fiona, she thought. A little scrap of a girl like that, with no presence or personality to speak of, had been extremely lucky to be chosen for the beauty spa on such a prestigious cruise ship. As I was myself, she mused to herself. But all that was in the past. Laura was now an established member of the crew, determined to take young Fiona under her wing and help her on her way. She was determined that the new girl should make a success of her opportunity. After all, people had been very kind and supportive to *her*, she thought, when she'd been as green as Fiona. The younger girl looked to Laura for guidance and Laura thought how much she could teach Fiona about other things as well as beauty therapy. She smiled to herself as she thought of how much she could show her about sex.

She filled out another appointment card, for an anxious pensioner with badly rinsed blue hair.

'Thursday,' the old woman said shyly. 'It's the Captain's cocktail party and reception.'

Laura consulted the hair appointments book, leaning very close to Fiona and whispering that the old girl would probably be amenable to a quite late appointment, leaving the popular spaces for more profitable clients. Fiona smiled up at her gratefully as she pencilled in 5.30, Thursday. Her green eyes were clear and wide, the whites bright and healthy. She was such an innocent and unsophisticated little thing, Laura thought. Perhaps she wouldn't be able to cope with some of the competitive spitefulness of the cruise scene. Fiona's mousey hair was baby fine and was cut in an extremely short, almost severe style, which on some women would be very butch. On the delicately featured teenager, it looked dainty and refined. Laura felt very protective towards her. The kid was away from home for the first time and it would take a while for her to grow a shell tough enough to cope with the pressures of the Shangri-la and the blatant come-ons of some of the more confident older men that she was bound to meet on the cruise.

Once again, she was aware of Elinor looking at them. She wondered what went on in Elinor's mind. What did she do for sex? Had she a boyfriend? Was there a *Mr* Brookes? She couldn't decide. Probably not, she thought. If there were, he must be the ultimate in wimps. Elinor's flawless make-up and impeccable hennaed hairstyle never seemed less than immaculate. Her teeth were almost American in their white perfection, her lips beautifully coloured, and yet Laura had never heard her boss make a single reference to men or sex. She was only early forties and had a decent figure and gorgeous legs. Surely she must have some outlet. What was it that would turn Elinor on, soften her up, Laura wondered. She'd never seen her even have a drink with one of the guys in the mess. Elinor seemed utterly dedicated to her work.

'Clients bring business,' she would say severely to the spa staff. 'Beauty keeps us in work. Remember that, girls. If we don't get the cruisers to be satisfied with what we're doing, we'll all get our P45s, so don't any of you forget it.'

But these thoughts were cut short by yet another group of women making appointments for the various beauty treatments. There were also, Laura noticed, a couple of fit-looking blokes who wanted an aromatherapy massage and a shampoo and blow-dry. Not the blond one though. Male beauty therapy clients were quite a recent development for the Shangri-la but were proving increasingly popular, and the client list was growing year on year. She and Fiona were kept busy booking shampoos, facials and mud-wrap treatments until, gradually, the queues dwindled and, at 12.30, Fiona disappeared into the staff cubicle. Both girls had the afternoon off and Fiona came out after a few minutes, dressed in her shore clothes. As always, she was wearing trousers and a baby-pink T-shirt. Her face was entirely devoid of make-up except for a slick of pale lipstick.

'Bye, Laura. See you later,' she breathed. 'I'm going ashore to meet James and have a spot of lunch.'

Laura looked at the young girl and smiled, thinking, yes, I guess that's exactly what you're going to have. Can't imagine you having anything more, my love. You'd run a mile if James wanted anything else.

But all she said was, 'Bye, Fiona. Have a nice time now. Don't do anything I wouldn't do.'

Just as if, she thought with some amusement as Fiona blushed and smiled back at her before hurrying off to her lunch date.

Now she moved to her treatment station and began to prepare her trolley for the next day. Each one had its own basin and water spray and she soon had it sparkling and immaculate. She laid out all her manicure things and nail varnishes ready for the next morning, along with her cleansing lotions and aromatherapy oils.

One o'clock. She was pleased to have some leisure time, before everything became too busy. All the passengers on first-sitting lunch were now in the dining room, while the crew still raced up and down in the lifts, delivering trunks and suitcases to the cabins. Elinor would be in charge of the Health and Beauty Spa for the whole afternoon, and that meant she could relax a little. They sailed for the Canaries at 6.30 and Laura decided it would be a nice idea to go and unpack and have the cabin to herself for a few hours. She walked briskly to the door and made her farewells to the young Aussie girl who supervised the Lollipop Club and the Teen Scene Centre. Thelma provided welcome activities and supervision for any youngsters who were cruising with parents and gave a much needed babysitting service during the voyage. They'd been friends for a long time and Laura planned to include Fiona in this friendship as soon as they had some opportunities.

They'd first met in the Shangri-la fitness suite and had one day shared a bench in the steam room. The Aussie girl had a most superb body and when she stood up, the droplets of steam condensing on her glowing skin had made her look like Venus, emerging from her giant seashell. She was so vibrant, radiant with the golden tan that all Australians seem to be born with. Laura thought her stunning, with her smooth and lissom thighs, narrow waist and a magnificently large pair of tits. Laura got excited just looking at her but Thelma herself seemed totally oblivious of her own beauty, seemingly content to play out her days with the children. Her pretty face was open and smiling as Laura said her farewells.

'Cheers, Laura. Have a nice day now. Perhaps we'll meet up for drinky-poos tomorrow night?'

'It'll have to be a quickie then.' Laura smiled. 'There'll be the safety procedures at six.'

'We're on then, sport. See you tomorrow.'

Laura retrieved her bag from behind the desk and made her way to the lift en route to cabin 327 on C deck. In the corridor, she passed their cabin steward, Stanley. He was a tall slender man from Goa, tawny-skinned and incredibly handsome. His short-sleeved white tunic was open at the neck, revealing his strong golden throat and long muscular forearms which were almost as smooth and devoid of hair as a girl's. He had dark sooty lashes and deep-brown eyes and Laura found him very sexy. She often wondered what he'd be like in bed, whether he'd drop his air of distant politeness and display a hidden passionate side to his nature, whether he'd be able to introduce exotic sexual practices to the lady of his choice. The idea of finding answers to these speculations intrigued Laura and she wondered what his reaction would be if she made a pass at him. Probably pretend not to notice, she thought. He was so dignified, she couldn't imagine sex, the great leveller, pushing him off his pedestal.

Nevertheless, he smiled with genuine pleasure when he saw her and said, 'Good afternoon, Laura.'

His teeth were of that almost impossible whiteness, in startling contrast to the dark tan of his face; they looked almost artificial. He was so quiet and aloof that he was a sexual challenge to any red-blooded woman, and Laura thought she'd like to get close enough to him to find out what made him tick sexually. Such an enigma, she thought as she returned his smile.

'Hi, Stanley,' she said, not letting her lascivious thoughts appear in the expression on her face. She fitted her swipe card into the door of 327, taking appreciative note of his shapely buttocks in the white uniform trousers as he walked gracefully away from her.

She saw him every single day and yet she knew nothing about him, except that he sent all his money home to his family and visited his parents in their remote little village every time he was on leave.

There were so many cabin crew members from Goa. Not all of them were as handsome and personable as

Stanley, of course, and many of them were prematurely aged by the stress of the long hours and the need to support extended families back home. By the end of the voyage, Laura knew that she would be heartily sick of the smell of curries and rice, which were served in the C deck canteen morning, noon and night.

Still, Stanley always smelled attractively of some sort of lemony cologne and his hair shone with cleanliness and had an almost artificial blue-blackness. His silky moustache was neat and beautifully shaped. She wondered what his cock was like. Beautifully smooth, she guessed. He gave out an aura of superb good grooming and glamour and yet she'd never heard his name linked to any of the young single women on board. Perhaps he was set to enter into a traditional arranged marriage. Laura continued to watch him speculatively, admiring his graceful loose-limbed walk as he disappeared down the corridor.

She closed the cabin door behind her and threw her bag on to the floor, putting her hands on her hips and stretching her spine luxuriously. The cabin she shared with Fiona was small but well appointed. They even had twin beds instead of bunks and limited, but adequate, clothes cupboards. Stanley always made sure that the tiny bathroom was immaculate and that there were fresh fluffy towels for them every day.

She'd have a shower and wash her hair, she decided, and then she'd be ready in case Steve should call. He'd be busy behind the bar of the Santorini lounge this evening, but maybe he'd find time to see her before work. They'd met on a Caribbean cruise and had been together for two years now and, although Laura loved her job, she felt that Steve was someone she could eventually settle down with. He was as hard working and ambitious as she was herself, but sexy and fun to be with. For the first time in her life, she felt she'd met someone she loved and who measured up to what she wanted from a partner. She recognised that he had shortcomings, that he was quick tempered and prone to jealousy, but was prepared to overlook them because of the pleasure she got in his company. He was, she thought, good husband material.

Sighing, she unhooked the belt and removed her overall, welcoming the release from the tensions of the morning. She unpinned her hair and let it fall on to her shoulders, running her fingers through it and shaking it into a soft golden cascade which felt gossamer light against her skin. Finally, she slipped down her little panties and they fell to her ankles, forming a small pool of black silk around her feet as she stepped out of them and stood completely bare. It felt so good to be without the restrictions of work and clothes and she savoured the feeling of freedom as she ran her hands down her naked body, exploring the contours of her flat stomach and firm thighs, before getting into the shower. She always loved this first voluptuous moment when the warm water cascaded over her head and shoulders and coursed down her breasts and belly. She shampooed and rinsed her thick hair and then soaped her body. Her perfect breasts, in glorious contrast to the slender waist and slim hips, longed to be caressed and fondled.

Her thumbs moved the soap suds in a gentle circular motion on her nipples and then, as the ends puffed up in response, she moved her hands further down over her hips. Her fingers found the soft blonde bush between her legs and she parted her outer lips to let the warm water flow into her cleft. She felt at once sexy and relaxed, as she breathed deeply and let the water run over her for two or three minutes before she finally turned off the tap and wrapped herself in a towelling robe, courtesy of the *Jannina*.

With her hair fastened turban-style in a white towel, Laura stepped into the cabin and gazed at herself for a few moments in the mirror while she blotted her face with a dry flannel.

Even though her full lips were now devoid of lipstick, they were naturally red and moist, her teeth strong and even. Her feathery eyebrows were beautifully arched over the lustrous violet eyes and she only needed to trim the odd stragglers to keep them neat and well defined. Laura's skin was lightly tanned and she took great care of it with toners and moisturisers, just as she looked after her beautiful firm young body by working out regularly in the gym.

She hugged the towelling robe around her and got on to the bed, stretching luxuriously as she laid herself out on the pillows, tipping back her turbanned head and closing her eyes. She was now utterly relaxed and conscious only of the steady regular beat of her heart and her own deep and even breathing. If only Steve could be with me, she thought. Last night had been taken up with the long and tiring journey to Southampton. They'd had little time to do anything except grab a meal and check on to the ship. Today would have been as busy for him as for her. But, maybe later ... perhaps.

She settled herself more comfortably on the bed, closing her eyes and remembering the first time she'd met him on that cruise to the Caribbean. He'd come off duty and was with one of his mates and she was alone, knowing no one, just like Fiona was now, grabbing a sandwich in the mess room and a solitary drink. He'd changed his bar uniform for a pair of tight jeans and a pale T-shirt. His eyes were sparkling and his hair curled crisply, still faintly damp from his shower. They clicked straight away, both of them attracted to the other, not needing anyone else really. And that's how it had stayed from that first meeting. She always made a point of telling him how attractive he was, what a wonderful smell he had, how sexy she found his hard male body and, so far, Steve had never failed to respond. He was always so highly satisfactory in bed, she reflected, although she knew that his ambition for promotion might make him reluctant to settle down yet. But, who cared? On Wednesday, they'd be in Madeira and she and Steve would have a whole day's leave together. Just for now, though, she'd have to make do with her imagination.

She let the towelling robe fall open and touched her nipples gently. They were still sensitised with the hot water of the shower and responded instantly to her pinching and tweaking, swelling and tingling until they ached to be sucked. She spread her legs open and her other hand slid down her body and found the warm wetness of her slit.

Her brain supplied the image of Steve, his lips eager and his cock erect as she thought of him kneeling in front of her, pressing his mouth between her legs and tonguing her lips and her secret little button until it throbbed. In her imagination, she grasped his thick dark hair, using her control of him to heighten her own excitement, pulling his head backwards and forwards as she excited herself with his mouth. Laura's thighs trembled and pulsed as she tried to delay the tremor of her orgasm and to stay on the plateau of its exquisite threshold for a few minutes longer. She squirmed on the bed, holding her legs apart and rubbing herself with the fingers of one hand, while slipping two fingers of her other hand in and out of her pussy. She raised her buttocks as she thought of Steve thrusting his swollen cock in and out, in and out of her willing opening, stretching her and filling her as his balls slapped against her body. She groaned out loud as she imagined him pulling his cock all the way out of her and then driving it in as far as it would go – harder and harder, again and again – until she came in a glorious shuddering climax, her belly fluttering and her thighs twitching as waves of ecstasy swept over her. Now her heart was pounding in her chest and small rivulets of sweat ran between her breasts as she finally lay still.

She leaned back for a few moments and then gave a deep sigh. She felt absolutely fluid and relaxed as her breathing gradually steadied and she moved her wet musky-smelling hands away from her thighs. The air conditioning system in the cabin had cooled her skin and she drew the robe around her naked body, breathing deeply and enjoying the absolute freedom from tension. As she rested on the bed, savouring the aftermath of her satisfaction, she became aware that her turban had come loose and that her hair was still damp. She must rouse herself, she decided. Get out the hairdryer and sort herself out.

Just at that moment, the telephone rang.

2

Laura picked up the receiver.

'Three two seven, C deck,' she said.

'Oh hello, three two seven. How're you doing?'

It was Steve, sounding rather amused at the formality of her reply.

'Oh, hi, it's you,' Laura said fondly. 'Well, things are going quite OK, Steve. We've been taking lots of bookings today, so it's been busy, busy. How about you?'

'The same,' he said. 'But I'm all the better for hearing your voice, my darling. How's old Borstal Betty been?'

'Oh, just as usual.' She knew he meant Elinor. She laughed as she said, 'As frosty as ever; she's the original iceberg. I don't think anyone's ever going to thaw Elinor out. The new girl's nice though. Sort of innocent and unspoilt. I don't know how long she'll stay like that, not with the iron lady in charge. But, see if I care. I'm off duty until tomorrow. Shall we be able to grab a drink later?'

'Won't be able to make any time this evening, love,' he said regretfully. 'But you know I can't wait for Madeira.'

'So it's all arranged, is it? My social secretary's got it all organised, eh?' Laura joked. 'What have you got planned for me then?'

She cradled the phone in her neck and lay back on the bed again, savouring his voice and enjoying the sensation of contentment and relaxation as he continued to chat to her.

'I've fixed us up with a room at the Three Crowns in the Rua dos Ferreiros,' Steve went on eagerly. 'It'll be ours from one o'clock onwards, so I can look forward to making a mess of you.'

'*You*, make a mess of *me*?' Laura laughed.

'Well, perhaps the other way round,' he admitted. 'But just talking to you and hearing your sexy laugh is already giving me the most painful hard-on. I might not be able to last until Wednesday.'

'Tell me about it,' she said indulgently, feeling the wetness between her legs and recognising a stirring of interest again.

'Well, there was no time on the way down and I can't see you tonight, so I'm having to live on my memories at the moment. You were marvellous last Friday at your mum's.'

They'd had to stay overnight before making their way to the ship and Wendy had generously let them have her bedroom, with the big double bed, while she slept in Laura's old teenage room.

'What did you like best?' Laura said softly, as though she were speaking to a small child.

Steve lowered his voice to match her own and said quickly, 'I keep thinking about you stretched out on the bed and me pulling off those tight jeans. I had to practically peel them off you, while you were lying back enjoying it.'

'I just enjoyed making you struggle to get at my knickers.' She wriggled with pleasure at the thought.

'I absolutely adore your knickers, Laura. They're so small and beautifully formed, just as though you were still inside them. I'd like to rub my cock against them till I come. They're just so sexy and silky, it really gets me going.'

Laura giggled. 'You'll have to wait until Madeira,' she

said. 'I hope it's going to be worth waiting for. Just as long as we don't forget the time and jump ship by mistake. We sail at six on Wednesday, remember.'

But Steve was now completely carried away thinking about last Friday when he'd had her laid out in front of him, her lovely slim body spread out and vibrant with her willingness to satisfy him.

After supper, they'd carried a bottle of wine upstairs, and as soon as Steve had finally managed to tug off the said clothes and they were both naked, he made an eager lunge at her, reaching for her pussy with his thrusting tongue. Laura had stretched back luxuriously underneath him, her whole body language urging him to take her in any way that he wanted. She thrust her breasts upwards invitingly, her nipples pointed and ready, and he'd squeezed and pinched them until they lengthened and swelled and she'd begun to roll her head from side to side on the pillows in the throes of her sexual longing.

She lay back, her eyes closed, as he licked moistly at her breasts and then began to nibble and bite them so hard that she moaned and writhed, thrusting her hips upwards towards his hard hot cock, willing him to go further. He slid his hands slowly down her smooth body, savouring every contour of her soft flesh, the hard cage of her ribs, her firm belly and the hollow below her hip bone.

Although Laura's body was familiar territory to him, Steve had made love to her as though it were the first time for both of them. His fingers found her soft bush and then delicately but remorselessly he began to explore the beginning of her slit, probing the warm wet lips until his fingers found the root of her protruding nub, swollen and shining with desire. Passing over it very lightly, forwards and backwards again and again, he'd driven Laura almost mad with longing. Then he moved his hand further to try two fingers inside her dripping opening.

'Oh God, Laura, you're wet through,' he whispered, and Laura just eased herself into a more comfortable position as he slicked the wetness all around her dancing clit and then scooped up even more juice to spread it along the powerful column of his cock. He felt again for the hot swollen lips of her sex, holding them apart with his fingers before pushing in deeply and slowly until he was in her up to the hilt.

She had squeezed his firm arse enthusiastically as they fucked each other harder and harder, his cock grazing her bright red clit with every thrust until they both jerked helplessly to a climax and then collapsed, satisfied.

The images of that night in her mother's double bed were still vividly on his mind as he said dreamily, 'So what are you wearing now?'

Laura laughed again and lied, just to tease him. 'My black satin thong.'

'Oh God,' he groaned. 'If only I could be with you now and lick you down there. I want to kiss and lick you to distraction. Then I want to push my tongue inside you and suck all your juices as you come. I'd like to do it to you while you're still wearing your thong, until it's wet through and too tight for you and you're begging me to rip it off you.'

Laura gave a sudden involuntary intake of breath at this image of the thin black satin rubbing her crotch until she was sore and then the relief when it was finally torn off. She moved the phone slightly to a more secure position under her neck. She slipped one hand into the towelling robe and let it rest softly on her inner thigh. Her nipples began to tingle all over again as they swelled against the soft white fabric.

'So, why is that your favourite, Steve?' she whispered.

'Because you're always totally relaxed,' he answered. 'Because you're lying back and letting me do exactly as I please with you. You're wearing a black satin teddy that matches your thong but the straps are pulled down and your nipples are red and wet through, where I've sucked them so thoroughly that they're like big ripe raspberries.'

Laura loved the way he got totally carried away with his descriptions when he was talking dirty. She moistened her lips and whispered, 'And what is it that you want to do with me?'

'I want to spread your legs and open your pussy lips so that I can see your lovely little cherry. I want you to be so wet that I have to wipe you off before I lick you some more.'

Laura now began to touch her swollen tip, which was still pulsating from her earlier rubbing, and she began to stroke it very lightly and rhythmically while Steve was speaking.

'And do you let me come like that?' she panted breathlessly.

'Oh yes. It's always ladies first as far as I'm concerned, and I can put my fingers inside you one at a time and feel you squeezing them when you finish.'

Laura was now fully abandoned to her own pleasure, but she managed to say huskily, 'So, what are you doing at the moment then?'

Steve answered her promptly. 'I'm standing with my zip open and my cock out. I'm holding it in my hand and I've got such a massive hard-on that it needs your lovely mouth to take it in. I want to slide it in and out, faster and faster as you squeeze it with your lips and lick my tip until I'm desperate to come.'

He broke off for a moment and Laura thought he was about to have his own climax, as she continued to stimulate herself very slowly and gently, but he carried on as before, in the same soft tone.

'Your turn now, Laura. What's *your* favourite? What do *you* like best? Tell me.'

In spite of the two years of her relationship with Steve and the intimacy which had grown up between them, Laura felt almost shy at this question. After all, she usually acted instinctively and wasn't given to any analysis of her sexuality, even the light-hearted sort.

'I don't really know,' she said slowly. 'I suppose my favourite must be the good old bondage scene, where the responsibility is taken off me and I'm totally, deliciously helpless with a man, or even a group of men, enjoying me and giving me absolute enjoyment in return.'

'Oh?' he said somewhat uncertainly. 'You've never confided this one before.'

'You've never asked me,' she said lightly.

'Go on then.'

'Go on then what?'

'Go on about your favourite bondage scene.'

'Well, I ... I meet this ... er ... man ... who gets angry and inflamed if I refuse his come-ons, even though I secretly want him. He's big and strong and determined and if I try to pull away or resist him, he just drags me to him so that I'm helpless, but I'm enjoying the idea of his huge cock entering me, forcing its way in. I like the feeling of vulnerability as I hang from his big powerful hands like a pathetic bundle and then he lifts me off my feet and holds my arms above my head, ignoring my struggles as he fastens my hands together with his leather belt. No matter how I plead or cry out, he takes no notice, but fastens me securely to the hook on the back of the cabin door so that my feet aren't really touching the floor and I can't escape or cover myself up.

'He stands in front of me, watching me, enjoying my resistance and helpless moans as he slowly undoes his shirt and I see his wonderful muscles and glistening tanned body. I'm willing him to drop his trousers so I can see his magnificent cock, but instead, he starts to tear the clothes off my back, one by one. First the thin blouse I'm wearing and then my bra. He just rips them and tears them into pieces, until my top half's completely bare and he can see that my breasts are swollen and aching to be sucked. But he's determined to make me wait and first he pushes off his close-fitting jeans and looms before me with the biggest dick I've ever seen. It's huge and glossy and promising and I can't wait for it to enter me. I want to feel it inside me, a real pussy stretcher, stiff and satisfying.

'Even as I beg him to put it in, he just laughs and torments me a bit further, tugging off my tights and my pathetic thin panties until I'm quite naked in front of him and I begin to heave myself towards him, thrusting my breasts forward, trying to get near him, wanting that hot rod inside me, satisfying me with its length and power.

'He still makes me wait, laughing and watching me struggle, and then he begins in the hollow of my shoulder, pinching the flesh between his lips, sucking at my nipples, working his slow methodical way down my helpless body and caressing the inside of my thighs until I shout to him to do it to me. I can't wait any longer. I want him now. I'm completely at his mercy but he ignores all my pleading and just covers the whole of me with his probing mouth until I hang defeated and passive, letting him do what he likes with me. Only then does he pull my arms down and push me on to the bed, pressing himself against me and rubbing his huge cock into my aching flesh. I'm panting with the relief of having my arms released at last and already wet and ready for him, as he buries his massive cock deep inside me, thrusting slowly and strongly. He pauses to rub me directly on my swollen tip, which makes me jump and buck under his big flattened thumb, as he rolls it over me, teasing and rubbing until I'm mad with desire and I push myself closer towards him so that he fills me up again and lets me come.'

There was silence for a few moments and she realised he was about to have his own climax as she stroked herself into a state of helpless abandon and her orgasm swelled and quaked within her until she groaned out loud with pleasure.

After a few seconds Steve sighed and said quietly, 'Christ, I needed that.'

'I know what you mean,' she said. 'Feel better now?'

'I'll say, but I'd still rather have the real thing with you. I suppose I'll just have to be patient and wait for Wednesday, but you're worth the wait. Oh hell,' he groaned. 'Look, I'm going to have to go back to work, or I'll be late. Love you. See you soon. Bye.'

'Yes. Bye,' she said and quietly replaced the receiver.

She lay back again, thinking languidly that two DIY jobs in one hour were as much as she could cope with. Looking down, she could see that trails of her copious juices were now running freely down her thighs and there was a bright red flush on the skin above her breasts. There was a comforting smell of her sex on her fingers and she'd have to have another shower before Fiona returned, she decided. But it was worth it. She adored her naughty phone calls with Steve. It was the next best thing when they couldn't be together. She suddenly remembered one sad old guy who used to phone the hairdresser's regularly when she worked in Manchester. He always wanted to know what colour knickers the girls were wearing. He always said he was holding his tool in his hand. He was always anybody's if any of them wanted it and the reactions of the girls were always the same. They varied between anger, disgust, amusement and downright disdain. After all, they were young and beautiful and weren't interested in an old perve like him. It was different with Steve though. He was so funny and sexy, always thinking of different ways to please her in bed. She got up, reluctantly, and made her way into the bathroom.

As she came out of the shower all warm and glowing, there was a soft tap on the cabin door. Surprised, Laura opened it to find Fiona smiling up at her in her usual shy manner.

'Hi,' she said.

'Fiona. What's wrong? Didn't you have your swipe card?'

'Oh yes,' Fiona said, holding it up, 'but I thought you might be busy, so I didn't want to burst in on you.'

Her calm green eyes took in the disordered bed and Laura's flushed appearance, but it was hard to judge whether or not she guessed what exactly had been going on.

'That's very thoughtful of you. Come on in,' Laura said. 'But you weren't disturbing me. I washed my hair earlier, and I haven't got round to blow-drying it yet, that's all.'

Seeing Fiona still gazing at the rumpled bed, she added by way of explanation, 'I must have fallen asleep for a bit. Make us a cup of tea, babe, while I put some clothes on and then I can hear all about your lunch with James.'

She dressed hurriedly and Fiona put down her miniature rucksack handbag and filled the travel kettle. The cabin was so small that the two girls had to sit on the beds with their feet up to drink the tea.

'Well? How did it go?' Laura finally asked.

'Oh, all right,' Fiona said diffidently. 'We went to a pub called the Grey Cockatoo and had a nice lunch. James had the Sunday roast and I had pasta with salad. James was driving, so he only had one drink. I'm ... I ... I don't drink at all, so we had some of that fizzy water.'

She took a gulp of her tea and was silent.

She recounts it as though she's a kid who's been on a Sunday School outing, instead of on a date with her boyfriend, Laura thought amusedly.

Aloud, she said, 'So what's he like then, your James? Sexy? Dishy? I bet he's good in bed.'

Fiona moved uneasily. 'He's not my James,' she said quietly. 'But he's very nice,' she added. 'Very quiet and gentlemanly. We were in the sixth form together at school. I've known him a long time.'

She didn't volunteer any more, but Laura grinned and said, 'So what do you do for a sex life then? Is he OK in that department?'

Fiona blushed and stammered, 'It's ... it's not like that at all. I've told you, we're just friends. Nothing else.'

My God, this is like pulling teeth, Laura thought as Fiona sipped her tea and remained silent.

'So you haven't got anyone special?' she persisted.

'No, not really.' Fiona avoided her gaze. 'I suppose I haven't met anyone yet.'

'When we go down for supper, I'll introduce you to one or two people,' Laura promised. 'As well as the dishy officers, there are some nice hunks on this trip, among the passengers as well as the crew. Take no notice of Borstal Betty's stupid rules. A little goer like you should always be able to pull a nice fella. You could soon get yourself fixed up.'

As soon as she'd said these words, Laura heard her own mother speaking and was surprised at herself. There wasn't such a difference in their ages that could make her feel so protective of the other girl. Almost maternal, she thought, and smiled to herself at such an incongruous idea.

But Fiona, misunderstanding the smile and thinking that Laura was taking the mickey out of her, blushed again and said with some spirit, 'It isn't as though I don't get any offers, I just haven't met the right one, that's all.'

Laura looked at Fiona's slender vulnerable neck and guessed that the younger girl was still a virgin. But all she said was, 'Give it time, love. You'll find someone.'

She stood up. 'I'll just wash these mugs and style my hair. We sail at six thirty, so what d'you say we go on deck for a bit and wave goodbye to dear old England?'

The assistant purser had already called for all visitors and non-passengers to go ashore immediately and now the pilot had come aboard. The gangway was lowered on to the dockside and there was an air of excitement and anticipation as the mooring ropes were finally let go.

In spite of the chill breeze, there was a band in green and gold uniforms playing with some enthusiasm on the quayside and most of the passengers were crowding the decks, enjoying the stately progress of the *Jannina*, as she gradually left her berth and slid gracefully towards the Channel. High above them on the bridge there was the usual unhurried administration from the

Captain and ship's officers as they monitored the gleaming, streamlined cruise ship on her way to the Canaries.

Although she'd experienced the excitement of departure several times now, it still gave Laura a little frisson of pride to be part of such a huge undertaking, especially when she knew that she was going to be so far away from home. She could see that Fiona was emotionally affected too, and even the well-seasoned travellers felt the enormous power and prestige of this huge liner, which was only two years old, with her sleek lines and beautiful form. Everyone seemed just as moved and excited as if it were their first time at sea.

Many of the passengers had camcorders and were busy making a record of the *Jannina*'s departure as the bar staff circulated with glasses of champagne. One man in particular, who stood at the very edge of the rail, seemed to be directing his camcorder at every bit of the harbour. Laura had him down as one of those obsessive hobbyists who have to film absolutely everything – no matter how dull – to bore their friends with at a later date. He was stocky and well dressed in a blue sweater, slacks and a padded jacket. They looked like the expensive Gabicci-type clothes which were on sale in the ship's boutique, she thought. Only the lower half of his face was clearly visible and she noticed the thick, rather petulant lips and heavy cleft chin, before he removed his eye from the camera and gazed fully at her. Slightly bulging eyes in a sallow fleshy face. A very bold stare, but he was not as old as he had seemed at first glance, she thought.

Even off duty, crew were expected to be polite to passengers, but Laura mischievously decided to go a little further. She gave her usual friendly smile and pretended to drop her bag. As she bent to pick it up, she made sure he got a good look up her skirt and treated him to a cheeky flash of the pale lemon thong, which displayed her round shapely bum to advantage. As soon as she saw that he'd raised his camcorder again and was directing it straight at her, she dropped a tissue from her bag and crouched again, unnecessarily low, this time giving him a view from the front. She held the pose provocatively for a few seconds, while he took in the little lemon triangle covering her mound, then she leaned over a little so that he could look down at her bra-less breasts. He made no pretence now of sweeping his sights round the deck or recording the scene on shore. His sights were set exclusively on Laura and she gave a cheeky grin as she stood up, realising he was recording her every movement. She turned away as though she hadn't noticed him, pointing out Thelma, the Australian nanny, to Fiona. She was on the deck below and smiled, waving back at them and miming 'six o'clock and drinks' before moving off. Little triangles of coloured bunting stretching from top to bottom of the huge ship waved in the breeze and everyone seemed in holiday mood, in spite of having to wear warm clothes.

Laura ignored the well-dressed stranger with the camcorder and just soaked up the atmosphere of relaxed jollity among the passengers and crew, as she and Fiona took in the sights and sounds of departure. The music of the band was fading somewhat now and was replaced by the first officer's voice on the loudspeaker system, welcoming the eighteen hundred passengers aboard and reminding everyone of the Maritime Safety Drill the next day.

None of the passengers seemed to be taking any notice but continued to drink the complimentary champagne and take photographs as though it had nothing to do with them, and the ship continued to glide smoothly on its way. Laura was still very conscious of the scrutiny of the unknown passenger and gave him a friendly wave.

'Come on,' she said to Fiona, 'let's go and have a spot of supper.'

As they went below, she told Fiona about the way she'd teased the man with the camcorder. 'I bet he won't dare play his holiday video if his wife's watching,' she joked. 'I gave him a real souvenir of his cruise. He certainly got an eyeful.'

But Fiona didn't laugh. She seemed a little uneasy. 'I hope he's not going to make trouble, Laura,' she said.

Laura was experienced enough to know that passengers and clients who were a nuisance or difficult could make life very awkward for the staff, but she just smiled and said jokingly that she could handle Mr Camcorder with both hands tied behind her back and her legs cut off at the knees. This made Fiona smile as well and they were still grinning as they stepped out of the lift and walked along the corridor of the mess deck.

The canteen seemed quiet, not many crew so far, as the two girls went up to the counter to see what was on offer. The mess provided an all-day menu with drinks and bar opening times to match those of the passengers'. Like the public bars, there were tea and coffee dispensers as well as water fountains and the girls had a choice of either these free drinks or paying for bar drinks. Fiona had water, as Laura guessed she would, but when Thelma joined them, Laura ordered a glass of white wine for herself and the Australian girl, signing the tab which she would have to settle up when they returned to Southampton. Tony, behind the bar, made a big fuss of them and was particularly pleasant and friendly to Fiona, as Laura knew he would be, but Fiona continued to be rather shy and inhibited.

In spite of herself, Laura still hoped that Steve would be able to slope off from the Santorini bar and have a swift drink with her, but it was not to be. Instead, several crew members came up to speak to her and Thelma and be introduced to Fiona during the course of the evening, many of them prepared to buy the girls a drink. In spite of Fiona's reserve, it was a very convivial occasion, not only for the renewal of contacts from her last voyage but for the warmth of the greetings from both male and female crew, black and white. Laura sensed that, although Fiona was very low key and didn't drink or smoke, people were prepared to accept her and be friendly, partly because she and Thelma were so popular, and this pleased her very much.

They sat relaxed and amicable, chatting of nothing in particular, and then Laura saw Stanley come into the room. His presence was as tall and impressive as always, his walk as graceful and sinuous as a dancer. Fiona had her back to the door and looked up in surprise as Laura beamed up at him and cried, 'Stanley. Come here and meet someone special. Our latest crew member, Fiona, meet Stanley.'

The result was electric. One minute Fiona was sitting rather passively on one of the wooden canteen chairs, the next she stood up to greet the exotic Stanley and immediately turned a nasty shade of pale. As for Stanley, his liquid brown eyes seemed to overwhelm his face as he gazed with an expression of shocked recognition at the demure young hairdresser.

'You know Thelma already, don't you, Stanley? Fiona's started working with me in the Shangri-la,' Laura said by way of explanation, not at first taking in the fact that there was something of an atmosphere between her two colleagues.

'How do you do?' Fiona said stiffly.

'Pleased to meet you, ma'am,' Stanley said formally and almost immediately murmured an excuse and moved away to the serving counter.

'I wonder what brought that on,' Thelma said. 'I know Stanley's a very reserved and private person, but he's usually prepared to have a chat.'

Fiona made no reply and Laura was destined to remain puzzled by the situation for the time being because, shortly after this encounter, Fiona said that she had a headache and wanted to go to the cabin. Thelma was just beginning to get a party glow on and was sitting close, swapping stories with a fellow Australian, so Laura decided to go in search of Steve and have a goodnight kiss before she turned in. She finished her drink and set off for his cabin.

He was all alone, lying on his bunk having half an hour's break, but he jumped up immediately he saw her; he grabbed her at once and pulled her to him, forgetting even to close the door properly.

'Hi, Steve,' she whispered. 'Just come to kiss you goodnight. Where's Tony?'

'He's still on duty. Won't finish till half eleven,' he said, his breath hot on her neck.

As soon as she heard this, Laura felt her heart begin to pound and excitement fluttering in her belly. She knew Steve already had a hard-on; she could feel it pressing insistently against her. His hands were all over her, squeezing her breasts, rubbing the bare cheeks exposed by the brief thong and holding her mouth, sealing her lips with his own. Laura was on fire now, mad for him, determined to have his rigid tool deep inside her. He pulled back a little, pulling at his zip and she kneeled down in front of him, cradling his lovely long cock in her hands.

'Take it in your mouth,' he begged hoarsely, and Laura

33

needed no prompting. He leaned back against the wall, holding her by the hair as she smothered his iron-hard cock with her lips. She drove up and down the length of his shaft, kissing and sucking, easing her tongue under his foreskin and then pressing it harder and deeper into her mouth, while he rolled his head wordlessly.

She put her hand between her legs. The minute lemon thong was soaked and had pulled so deep into her crack that it offered no barrier to his huge dick.

'I want you inside me,' she panted at last, and she pulled her skirt down, stepping out of it and putting her hand back on to her hot sex, feeling her pussy all puffy and oozing with juice.

Steve pulled her to her feet and clamped his mouth on hers once more. He pulled her blouse open and cupped her breasts, gasping his pleasure at the firmness and texture of her bare flesh and scraping each nipple gently with his thumbnails. Laura was sighing with lust as her nipples swelled and ripened under his touch. He took a nipple between his teeth, rubbing the red end with his hot tongue and moving from one to the other until she quaked with pleasure, trying not to cry out, but hardly able to hold off her climax any longer.

He knew she was ready and slid his hand down, parting her lips and ignoring the soaked thong. His hard prick was pressed against her and she arched her back, wanting to come. He lifted her up and eased his cock into her, filling her completely and making her cry out with pleasure as he found her love button with his fingers. She held on to him, urging him to go faster and deeper as he thrust into her. His eyes closed in ecstasy as they moved together in a hard, brutal rhythm and Laura came gloriously, thrusting and arching until Steve's body went rigid, shuddering as he climaxed, pumping his cream inside her.

His arms were trembling with the strain of holding her up, and then they both collapsed on to his bunk in a satisfied silence.

Steve noticed too late that the door was still slightly open and he hadn't time to get up and close it before they were interrupted by an unexpected visitor. It was one of the fanciable guys she'd seen earlier – the blond one. His confident smile told them that he'd seen everything.

While Laura tried ineffectually to rescue her skirt, Steve leaped up and said angrily, 'What do you think you're doing? Passengers aren't allowed in the crew's quarters.'

'Neither are nice young ladies from the beauty salon.' The visitor grinned. 'If I tell your boss, who knows what will happen. A passenger might get lost and go to the wrong cabin by mistake. Crew know their way round the ship blindfolded.'

He looked at them mockingly. He was devastatingly attractive, lightly tanned and fair with a wide sexy smile and blue eyes as bright as a cat's. Steve was furious now and Laura was convinced he was going to throw a punch at their visitor. That *would* be the end, she thought. She could imagine how Elinor would make a meal of it.

She smiled at the hunk, hoping to somehow rescue the situation, while Steve stood glaring helplessly, his fists clenched.

'Can't we come to some arrangement?' she suggested, her voice low and sexy. She stepped a little closer to him, so that he could smell her sex scent, mixed with Dior perfume.

'What sort of arrangement?' he asked suavely, and gave his slightly mocking smile, his bright eyes holding hers.

'Well, what had you in mind?' Laura purred, and she glanced pointedly at the hard bulge in his trousers.

'Why not?' he murmured, and opened his zip, releasing his raging cock. 'That sounds a very good arrangement to me. I want to come in your mouth though.'

Steve was intrigued now; either struck dumb by confusion as to how to react or silenced by impotent rage – Laura wasn't sure. But she was beginning to enjoy her little game of power. Steve sat on the bed staring at the two of them as Laura kneeled down and took the guy's cock into her mouth. She sensed, rather than saw, Steve leave the bed and kneel at the back of her. She sucked firmly on the stranger's prick and at the same time cocked her arse a little higher, parting her pussy lips and opening herself up to Steve's willing tongue. He grasped her round the waist and licked up and down her crack in long slow sweeps, lingering on her clit and sucking her juices before moving to her bumhole. He licked hard, juicing it and teasing it with the end of his tongue and then moving right into her until Laura was ready to come again.

The hunk was pumping hard, fucking her mouth slowly and thoroughly with long vigorous thrusts, his fingers pinching and tweaking her swollen nipples until she gasped with the pleasurable pain of it. She could taste his male juices on her tongue and lips and could feel his shaft straining powerfully as he grew desperate to come. Both men were moving faster now and Laura cried out as she climaxed. The hunk came at the same moment, shooting his thick spunk into her mouth and throat and shouting his pleasure.

There was no post-coital lassitude. They all got dressed quickly and the visitor faded quickly along the corridor. Laura was still tingling with the evening's action when she and a shell-shocked Steve finally had their goodnight kiss and he hurried back to work. She realised as she sped to her own cabin that she didn't even know the guy's name; it had all happened so spontaneously. And as for Steve ... well, she was sure he'd have something to say about it all after he had sobered up from their surprise lustful encounter. And Laura suspected that, at the end of the day, he would be feeling guilty and looking to blame her for what had just happened.

Fiona was still up but refused Laura's offer of a cup of tea before bed and began to undress, without saying anything. She sat on the bed and kicked off her shoes and slipped off her top and bra, exposing her absurdly small girlish breasts. They were so tiny as to be almost non-existent and when she raised her arms, they flattened out and disappeared altogether. Just mossie bites really; she must only need a teen bra, Laura mused sympathetically as she quickly stripped off her own rather crumpled clothes.

What a frail-looking little thing Fiona was, thought Laura. Her nipples were small and peachy coloured, so tiny they were almost flat. Her thin arms and shoulders were delicate and blue veined, transparent even, as she pulled down her black ski pants and hung them on the chair. And yet she seemed to have the same wiry strength in her legs as a little mouse, Laura observed. When Fiona slipped out of her tights and panties, she revealed buttocks and thighs that were surprisingly well developed and muscular for one so slight. Her skin was smooth and creamy, her soft pubic hair sparse and light, just the colour of mouse fur, and her feet were small and soft. She put on satin pyjamas and went into the bathroom quickly to do her teeth, as though she found Laura's observation of her rather embarrassing.

Laura showered and changed into her Scooby-doo nightshirt and got into bed, thankfully. After such a busy and emotional day, she was grateful for a rest. Two images remained in her mind as she lay back and closed her eyes. One was the encounter with the handsome blond stranger in Steve's cabin, thrusting his magnificent prick in her mouth, and the other was Stanley, shocked and surprised at his encounter with Fiona. She was too tired to make sense of any of these impressions. She just sighed and switched out her bedside light; the ship's engines pulsed rhythmically and steadily with a reassuring and soporific throb as she drifted off to sleep.

3

There was a knock on the door and Stanley opened it silently with his swipe card. He carried in coffee and croissants which he placed noiselessly on Laura's bedside table.

'Good morning, Laura. Your breakfast,' he said politely, and he wiped his hands down the hips of his trousers.

'Thanks, Stanley,' she yawned sleepily. 'Good morning. You couldn't do us a favour, could you?'

He nodded. 'What is it?' he asked in his soft voice.

'Could you be an angel and bring our uniforms, Fiona's and mine. They're in the utility room. They're already pressed, so nothing needs doing.'

'Certainly. No probs,' he said, and his eyes flicked towards Fiona, lying apparently deeply asleep in the next bed. He appeared a bit nervous, Laura thought. Then he turned with his usual feline grace. 'I'll leave them outside your door,' was all he said, and he went out as noiselessly as he'd entered.

Laura sat up as soon as he'd gone and looked across at Fiona. She appeared to be still dead to the world, but there was an unwritten rule among the crew never to leave a fellow cabin-mate to oversleep and so be late on duty. She poured out two cups of scalding hot coffee and walked round to Fiona. They had an inside cabin so it was impossible to guess what sort of day it was outside and she hadn't thought to ask Stanley. She placed a coffee quietly at the side of the sleeping girl and gazed down at her. She still seemed to be crashed out, but Laura imagined that her eyelids were fluttering a little. Perhaps she was only pretending, Laura thought. But why should she do that? Genuine exhaustion after her first day on board? A wish not to have to speak to their cabin steward? Embarrassment at having to share the bathroom and dress in front of someone else who was a stranger? It was true that there was very little privacy on board ship if you had to share a cabin, but most of them seemed to adapt to it.

Or was it something to do with the fact that it was Stanley who'd brought in the breakfast? It had certainly been a bit weird last night, Laura thought, when she'd introduced them for the first time. Maybe they'd met before? She bent over the sleeping girl.

'Good morning, Fiona,' she said softly, and Fiona immediately opened her green eyes, with no trace of reluctance or sleepiness. Almost as if she'd been waiting for me to speak, Laura thought, but she said nothing except, 'Breakfast's here. Can I butter you a croissant?'

'Oh no, thanks. I'll grab one later. I'll use the shower first and then you can have it to yourself.' Fiona got out of bed hurriedly and went straight to the bathroom.

Laura stretched voluptuously, raising her arms above her head and thrusting forward her firm breasts to the extremities of the Scooby nightshirt. She rubbed both hands over them, massaging them comfortingly and reassuringly, and then she turned her attention to her breakfast. Space was so tight in the tiny cabin that it was difficult not to get in each other's way, so she finished her coffee and wiped her sticky fingers on the paper napkin before putting the tray outside in the corridor. True to his word, Stanley had hung the white salon overalls outside the door and she brought them inside and laid them carefully on the bed.

Both girls were silent as they concentrated on getting ready for work, but then Laura asked curiously, 'That was a very funny look Stanley gave you last night. Are you sure you two haven't met before?'

She deliberately looked into her mirror as she asked the question, applying her lipstick with exaggerated care.

'N ... No – not that I remember,' Fiona stammered, and a slow flush crept up the pale neck and suffused her cheeks.

'Well, I'm sure you wouldn't have forgotten,' Laura said. 'He's such a handsome specimen, quite a dish. You'd have remembered him.'

Fiona volunteered nothing else and they left the cabin together and went to the Shangri-la. Both appointment books were full for the whole day and they were kept busy all morning with the various clients wanting different beauty treatments and hairstyling. Even the space outside the salon seemed to be full of people milling around as clients tried for appointments.

Laura noticed one woman in particular, Mrs Grimshaw, who'd asked for a facial and before she'd even taken her place on the treatment couch had stopped at the desk and booked a further appointment, this time for a manicure.

She seems determined to look all-over beautiful, Laura thought. And she's got a fairly good skin. But, as she lay down on the couch and looked up at the beauty therapist, the woman's expression was drawn, almost miserable, as though she were very unhappy.

Laura put the protective headband in place and said pleasantly, 'The biotherapy facial takes fifty-five minutes, Mrs Grimshaw. All the Hervey beauty products are made from nourishing plant extracts and rich moisturisers to cleanse and feed the skin. None of our preparations have been tested on animals and you can buy them either in the salon or in the ship's boutique.'

Eileen Grimshaw just nodded. Her face didn't change and in fact her tense unhappy expression deepened even further and two strong lines appeared between her eyebrows. Not a happy lady, Laura thought. Now, I wonder what the problem is. Women's problems? Man trouble? Difficulties with hubby? She had a bet with herself that it was the dreaded menopause. But who knows? I could be wrong, she thought ruefully.

Laura had done her sales patter so many times that it was almost automatic, so she was able to observe the effect of her words on the clients and was good at giving them the confidence to say what they wanted and hoped for from the beauty sessions.

Eileen Grimshaw was no exception and, as Laura began to gently apply the biotherapy face peel, the older woman almost visibly relaxed and the frown lines gradually disappeared under the beautician's skilful massage.

All the while, Laura continued with her sales chat, explaining the purpose of all the procedures as precisely as a surgeon about to perform an operation.

'This removes any dead skin cells and makes the skin receptive to the active ingredients in the moisturiser,' she said, bending over her willing victim and observing her closely. 'At the end of the treatment, you'll definitely notice a firming of the skin and a radiance in your complexion.'

Eileen Grimshaw looked up into the face of the lovely young therapist and whispered, 'I used to go regularly to the beauty parlour at home, but I've been neglecting myself lately.'

The sad expression came back momentarily and Laura hastily peeled off the mask before her face could set into its lines of misery and despair once again.

'You've got quite a nice skin though,' she said encouragingly. 'And the next stage of the treatment is the facial massage, which drains the impurities from your skin and leaves it looking definitely radiant.'

For the first time, Eileen Grimshaw smiled and Laura said quickly, 'I'm going to use a rich nutritious gel, which feels nice and cool on the skin and which you can purchase for yourself if you like it.'

Very gently, she began to massage the older woman's face and neck, while Eileen lay back with closed eyes.

'This is specially formulated for mature skin and is particularly good for the neck and decollette area, so you'll be able to get out your low-cut gowns, Mrs Grimshaw.'

Eileen opened her eyes. 'That's what I want,' she said feverishly. 'To wear my new dress at the Captain's reception party and to look a bit glam, for my husband Reggie, you know.'

Now that she'd started, Eileen seemed unable to stop. 'This cruise is for Reggie's retirement, you see,' she said. 'He's sold out his business to the Maynard Fine Foods chain. Had a little op. last November and needs a good holiday. And, of course, being the generous boss he is, he's booked a few cabins for some of the other directors. Reggie always rewards loyalty.'

Laura made little noises of agreement, only half listening, but even so, she picked up on the almost desperate vibes of Eileen's unhappiness. Deftly, she applied the final treatment moisturiser and removed the towelling hair-band. Then she helped Eileen up and produced a mirror to show her the improvement in her appearance.

'Definitely more radiant,' she said encouragingly.

'Definitely,' Eileen agreed and, as she got down off the couch, she pressed a handsome tip into Laura's overall pocket. 'Thank you, dear. You don't know how grateful I am for this. A lovely young girl like you, helping me, showing me the way. Perhaps I ought to have my make-up done for Thursday's party. What do you think, dear? Is there hope for the old girl yet?'

Laura was inexplicably affected by the mixture of hope and despair that Eileen was giving out and was moved to want to help her.

'I'll just check for you that we've got a space,' she said. She knew that Thursday was fully booked but went through all the motions of finding the appropriate day and let a beautifully manicured forefinger hover over the page, before saying, 'Twelve thirty all right?'

This would mean using up her own lunch break, but she knew it would be worth it.

'Lovely,' Eileen said.

She then proceeded to buy eighty pounds' worth of the creams and gels that Laura had been promoting during the beauty session, before going off seemingly a little happier.

I don't mind using my lunch hour for clients like her, Laura thought as she entered Eileen's appointment in the book.

Her next client was a Mr Evans for an aromatherapy back treatment. Laura noticed he'd booked eleven-thirty appointments for two days running and wondered fleetingly if, actually, it was physio he needed. She tidied up her trolley and replaced the paper sheet on the couch, prepared her oils and washed her hands. Then she went to the waiting area. 'Mr Evans?' she asked.

She was surprised when the man who stood up and said, 'Yes, that's me,' turned out to be Mr Camcorder, who'd been so noticeable on deck yesterday.

'This way please, sir,' Laura said, and tried not to notice the red moist tongue licking the heavy sensual lips as he followed her into the salon.

Remembering the cheeky flashing she'd treated him to, Laura was all cool efficiency as she indicated the little tray of aromatic oils on her table. She deliberately avoided eye contact and directed her gaze to the neck band of his sweatshirt as she said calmly, 'What sort of treatment did you require, sir?'

He obviously was at a loss about making a decision and stood staring greedily at the shapely breasts outlined under her salon overall. Laura prompted him a little further, giving him a bit more of her sales patter.

'All the products are the finest natural essential oils and are used with a light blender oil. The choice of treatments is either refreshing, relaxing, sensual or stimulating.'

She knew as soon as the word 'sensual' was used that this was the one he would choose, and she was quite correct.

'Oh. Right. I'll kick off with the sensual and try out your stimulating one tomorrow,' he exclaimed as he peeled off his sweatshirt and shorts eagerly. 'How do you want me, darling?' He grinned.

No way at all at the moment, Laura thought to herself, but aloud she said, 'If you could lie on your front, Mr Evans, I'll explain the treatment as we go along.'

He was wearing the most old-fashioned of chain store Y-fronts, with an elasticised band which cut into the collapsed flesh under his substantial belly. He climbed heavily on to the couch and, panting a little, lay down obediently on his stomach. Then, utterly irrepressible, he said, 'Do what you like with me. I'm anybody's.'

I'll bet you are, she thought, but just smiled and decided to ignore him. From the outside of the Beauty Spa, it was impossible for anyone to see in and know what was going on. From the inside, though, the people passing by on the promenade deck could be seen quite clearly. She saw Thelma, her Aussie friend, pass by with a little group of young children on the way to the pool reserved for the under-sevens. All of them were excited. All wore bright-red T-shirts with little white anchors and *Jannina* written on the front. She saw the blond guy stroll by, this time arm in arm with a small slim brunette, and wondered if he were married.

Well, she thought, at least there's help nearby if this randy old fart tries anything. But he lay quite passively face downwards as she warmed her aromatherapy oils and mixed them with the blender oil.

'Before I start the massage, I use a specialist lotion to deep-cleanse the area and drain away any impurities. The skin on the back can become clogged, causing acne and open pores. The lotion helps remove blackheads and pimples. After your massage, I use a purifying mask to sterilise the skin and close the pores again.'

Laura gave him the usual explanations and sales talk while she got out the cleansing milk from the little basket on her trolley. Bob Evans didn't answer but merely grunted contentedly, and Laura spread a towel across the top of his underpants and buttocks, tucking it in to protect them from the oil. She was conscious that he raised his hips slightly, as though to accommodate his prick more comfortably, and she could tell he'd already got a hard-on.

She proceeded calmly with the treatment, spreading the cleansing milk lightly along his shoulders and the back of his neck and then down the middle of his back to his waist. He suddenly gave a groan.

'Oh! Aah! Do that again,' he moaned.

'Do what?' she said rather more sharply than she'd intended.

'Caress the back of my neck again,' he said in a muffled voice. 'It was lovely. I could stand that all day.

You've got a wonderful touch, sweetheart, do you know that?'

But you haven't got a wonderful skin, she thought. His back was blemished and quite rough, not only with dry skin but with various bumps and moles. It was such an unattractive sallow colour and was pitted with old acne scars. I'll bet he was a teenage werewolf when he was sixteen, Laura thought as she wiped off the cleansing milk with cotton wool. He was wriggling and making little growling noises of contentment as though he were rubbing himself against the surface of the couch, but she let her thoughts drift back to her encounter with the sexy stranger the night before and didn't really care what he was up to. He wasn't bothering her and she merely poured a little massage oil on to both palms and began to smooth the coarse discoloured skin with long rhythmic strokes, pressing and kneading the flaccid muscles in his shoulders and stimulating the deeper layers of his skin with the pressure of her thumbs.

She wished it could be Steve she was stroking. How different his smooth young skin would feel. If only he was lying here instead of this ugly old creep. Never mind, she thought, tomorrow she'd have all afternoon to explore Steve's beautiful body and to play with him to her heart's content. At least Evans hadn't been too 'hands-on' as yet although, after he'd had his purifying mask and she'd wiped it off with a moistened tissue, he asked her if she did 'anything special'.

'No,' she said shortly. 'We specialise in aromatherapy, recreational massage or therapeutic massage for sports injuries. Right. All done, Mr Evans.' She took away the towel and handed him his sweatshirt. She left him while he got dressed and she went to the reception desk to check on the next appointment.

He stood up. 'See you tomorrow, darling.' He grinned and lurched off without leaving a tip.

'Yes, worse luck,' she said to herself and then, as she moved towards the couch, she noticed a nasty little pool where he'd spurted on to the paper sheet.

Laura was glad when the afternoon was over. The Beauty Spa closed dead on the dot of four thirty because of the safety practice and she hurried down to the cabin to pick up her life jacket. Perhaps she and Fiona might manage to get a cup of coffee before everything started, she thought as she went swiftly along the corridor, hoping to see her cabin-mate on the way to their respective muster points. Instead, she saw Stanley, who'd materialised noiselessly from one of the lifts and was looking very smart in a white tunic and black trousers.

'Hi, Stanley,' she greeted him. 'Don't suppose you've seen Fiona, have you?'

'No, sorry,' he said and made to pass her, but Laura stood squarely in front of him.

There was something very intriguing in the situation between the handsome Goan and the virginal young hairdresser and she was interested in getting to the bottom of it.

'It seemed to me that when I introduced you to her, you and Fiona had met somewhere before. Am I right, Stanley?'

His deep-brown eyes slid away momentarily and he took a step backwards, but then, aware of her intent gaze, he looked her in the eye and said simply, 'Not met exactly.'

She cocked an eyebrow at him and he went on carefully, 'But yes, I had seen her before. That is, when the ship was in dock and was being turned round for the trip to the Canaries. Only the stewards and cleaners were on board, but Fiona was having her preliminary interview with Miss . . . Miss Brookes.'

'So?'

'So . . .' He paused and rubbed his palms down the sides of his smart trousers. A typical gesture, which denoted the extent of his tension.

'Well,' he said carefully, 'they were in the beauty salon. By the jacuzzi. Both of them were absolutely stark naked.'

Laura almost laughed at the intensity of his disapproval. 'So, what were they up to?'

He licked his lips nervously. 'I don't have a clue, Laura. And it's none of my business, ma'am. If you'll excuse me . . .'

He walked away, the ties of his life jacket trailing on the floor.

Laura was even more intrigued at these revelations and determined to quiz the innocent little Fiona about her unusual job interview with the formidable Elinor, but Fiona was nowhere to be seen so just for now, she thought, better to concentrate on the job in hand. She finally caught up with her on the way to their muster station.

'What's the secret between you and that spiteful cow Elinor?' she whispered as they took their places for the safety drill.

'What do you mean?' Fiona muttered, refusing to meet Laura's eyes.

'I mean that you were seen in the nuddy with our dear manageress when you were being interviewed for the Shangri-la.'

Fiona's face went from bright red to chalk white and then back to red. 'I don't know what you're talking about,' she said defiantly. '*Who* saw us?'

'I have my spies.' Laura laughed. 'You must have been up for a bit of fun if you were stripping off for the iron lady.'

Fiona pressed her lips together and refused to answer, so Laura got no further.

For the passenger Maritime Safety Procedures, all officers, staff and crew had carefully designated positions and were expected to be at their stations within a few seconds of the alarm going off, so the two of them were soon separated. Their task was then to help passengers with their life jackets and escort them to their particular muster points where the officers would be on hand to organise the lowering of the lifeboats if the order came to abandon ship.

There was a sort of inevitable pattern about these exercises. Some of the more blasé passengers ignored it altogether and lurked in their cabins, hoping it would all go away, but most did what was required of them and assembled in the various lounges, self-conscious and giggling, with their bright-orange Mae West life jackets. The crew had to circulate and be nursemaids to the elderly, inexperienced or doddery old passengers who always got into a tizzy over the ties, whistles and lights. Then everyone had to hang around uncertainly while one of the officers roused any slackers who'd failed to turn up, to get their life jackets and join the others. Captain Browning was a stickler for the safety aspect of his ship and only when all were assembled did he begin to address the eighteen hundred passengers and seven hundred and fifty crew members on board.

'This is Captain Browning speaking,' he intoned from the bridge. 'I'd just like to inform all passengers that these safety procedures are an important part of maritime law and must be carried through as a matter of course on every voyage undertaken by the *Jannina*.

When you hear the warning signal of seven short blasts and one long one on the ship's siren, you should proceed to your boat station, carrying your life jacket, which you will find in the wardrobe of your cabin. Staff and crew will be on hand to assist you and direct you to your lifeboat, should that be necessary. Remember, no one should ever jump overboard. In the unlikely event of an order to abandon ship, you will be escorted to your lifeboats and these will be launched by the crew, who will be seeing to your comfort and safety at all times. Please make sure that your life jacket is fastened correctly. Members of staff are all here to help you. Check in the top right-hand pocket for your whistle and make sure that the torch comes on when you give the cord a tug. I need hardly add that any missing equipment should be reported immediately to a member of the crew. I'd just like to end by reminding everyone of the Captain's reception party on Thursday evening when I'll have a chance to introduce you to some more of the *Jannina* officers and crew. For those on first-sitting dinner, the party is in the Santorini lounge at six p.m. and for second sitting dinner at eight p.m. Thank you for your kind attention, ladies and gentlemen.'

The Captain finished speaking and some people sought the help of the staff with their life jackets. One very elderly couple were in such a tangle, it took Laura a good five minutes to sort them out. The little old lady was pleased and grateful.

'We're on our first cruise, dear,' she confided. 'We've been married sixty-three years, you know. He's eighty-nine and I'm eighty-seven and it's the first time we've ever been to sea. These things take a bit of getting used to, don't they? Thank you, dear. That's very kind of you.'

The old man wasn't nearly so gracious. 'So far we've had no bloody peace at all,' he grumbled. 'It's either people knocking at our cabin door to see if we want anything, or announcements on the loudspeakers about meals and line dancing. Now this. We were told we were going to have a peaceful and relaxing time if we came on a cruise. So far we haven't been allowed to relax for a minute and we've not had a bit of peace since we left Southampton. It's been all go.'

'Oh, don't be so miserable, Harold,' his wife said, and then, 'Thank you, dear,' she said again to Laura, who smiled and turned away.

There in front of her was Mr Camcorder, grinning and leering in a most offensive fashion. 'I can't manage the tapes on my life jacket,' he said, smiling broadly. 'Can you help me, Miss Barnes?'

It was an obvious try-on, but Laura decided not to let it get to her. 'Certainly, sir,' she said evenly.

She crossed the tapes and fastened them rapidly. 'There you go,' she said, and turned quickly to a young mother with two small children.

'Can I help you?' she asked, and bent to gently remove the whistle from the little boy's mouth before Bob Evans had time to engage her attention any longer. But still he was persisting, hanging round waiting to pester her again with some other sort of inanity. Laura began to feel the first signs of irritation and annoyance at his intrusive presence, and was thoroughly regretting her spontaneous bout of teasing behaviour on deck when they'd left the harbour, but just at that moment a very good-looking officer smoothly intercepted.

'Here, let me help you, sir,' he said, stepping towards him firmly, and he went through all the checks of Bob Evans's life jacket tapes, whistle and torch, again, in the most courteous way imaginable, but with a no-nonsense attitude that left no opportunity for any further stupidity from Evans.

Laura was half admiring, half resentful. She'd never seen this particular officer before and what struck her most about him was his amazing likeness to Steve. The same colouring, slightly taller maybe and perhaps a shade more tanned, but the same sort of strong features and firm chin. Laura was unable to take her eyes off him. The similarity was so uncanny, it was almost spooky. He caught her staring at him and gave her a friendly smile, saluted and moved off. Bob Evans, her aromatherapy client, also seemed to have disappeared and now the cruise photographer was circulating, taking shots of the passengers who struck comic poses in their life jacket gear. Moving swiftly for such a heavy man, Evans suddenly leaped up to Laura again and put his arm round her shoulders, squeezing her hard and posing for the photographer with his leering grin, just as she thought she'd got rid of him. She felt the unpleasant moistness and warmth of his skin as he pulled her towards him, grinning at the camera. Oh no, she thought. What have I done to deserve this damned nuisance? Her heart sank at the thought of having to tactfully put the boring old mess off.

Then Evans saw the young officer moving purposefully towards them again, and quickly melted away. Like snow in summer, she thought. Laura had been going to make her way back to the cabin but, seeing the dishy young guy approach, she hesitated. It really was strange, his likeness to Steve. She was tempted to linger a little bit longer and although she got out of her life jacket quickly and folded up the ties, ready to go, she still didn't move away.

He was right up to her now and removed his cap as he said, 'Everything all right?'

'Oh, yes, thanks,' Laura said lamely. 'Everything's fine, thanks.'

'Making himself a bit of a nuisance, was he, that wally?'

His voice was attractive too, she thought. Deep but not gravelly.

'Yes. He was, but ... er ... nothing I can't handle ... Thanks,' she said again.

His crisply curling hair shone in the bright sunlight almost as if it had been polished. He had dark lashes and sparkling brown eyes. His skin was tanned, his teeth beautifully white and even. He was almost too good looking to be real, Laura thought cynically. Judging from his uniform, he was an engineering officer, she decided. He looked about thirty, but it was difficult to tell with a man in uniform. They always looked so attractive. His shoulders were broad, his hips slim. She found him so desirable that she felt a definite tingle at the thought of unbuttoning that pristine white tunic and caressing his shapely body or running her fingers through that luxuriant dark hair.

As he came closer still, she could smell the faint lemon balm scent of his skin. Armani, she thought to herself, or perhaps Calvin Klein. She lowered her gaze and glanced at his hands. Long tapering fingers, well-kept nails, the backs of his hands beautifully tanned to a soft golden brown. All these observations passed swiftly through her mind, before he stood squarely in front of her again and gave her his wide white smile.

'Well, if you're sure. Some of these old guys can be such a pain when they start pestering,' he said sympathetically.

'No. Really. I'm quite all right. He just got a bit carried away, that's all.'

'You work in the beauty spa, don't you?'

'Yes, that's right,' Laura said. 'And you? I've not seen you before. You must be new to this cruise ship.'

'Got it in one.' He smiled. 'I'm the second engineer. I've not been doing much travelling for the last three years. Before that I was with Corniche Lines on the *Duchess of Malfi* and the *Jannina* seems so much bigger and much harder work. But how do *you* find it? Your boss seems an absolute cow from what I hear. I mean the divine Elinor, of course. She has a reputation on this ship as a bit of a slave driver. In fact, the general consensus is that she needs a good seeing-to.'

Laura shifted her life jacket on to the other arm. She felt rather uncomfortable at the idea of such open disloyalty to her manageress, even though she privately agreed with everything he'd said.

So she just laughed and said, 'And do you think you're the one to do it then?'

Again he gave her his brilliant smile, so like Steve's and yet, in an indefinable way, so different. More confident and relaxed, more poised than Steve was, she thought.

He seemed so much less tense and driven than Steve could ever be. She continued to observe him closely with her woman's questioning eyes as she watched his reaction to her joke about Elinor. And she wasn't disappointed. He threw back his head in a very youthful burst of laughter.

'Thanks, but no thanks.' He grinned. 'It would be like putting it up the cold water tap. But, if ever you need any assistance with old nuisance punters, I'm your man. Always ready to help out.'

She laughed again. 'Thanks,' she said. 'I'll remember that.'

And now she really did depart. 'Cheers,' she said somewhat reluctantly and went back to the cabin, thinking of his smile, his hair, his whole aura of wholesome male sexuality. After all this time, it was so unexpected and unusual to meet someone new who really turned her on, she reflected. But I'd better be careful, she thought. He's the second new sexy bloke I've met in the last twelve hours. I'm all right where I am and I've no reason to play away. Even so, her shapely lips curved into a smile of pleasure at the very thought of him.

After tackling Fiona about her unusual job interview, as recounted by Stanley, Laura now felt unaccountably diffident about the whole thing and they merely had some shallow chat about the day's happenings. Fiona never mentioned anything about Elinor either and Laura wondered if there was an innocent explanation for the bizarre spectacle of Fiona and her boss being naked together in the jacuzzi. If there was, she decided, now was definitely not the time to bang on about it. Instead, she tried to get Fiona to chill out a little by giving her descriptions of the old couple and the offensive camcorder man, until both girls were lying back in bed, giggling. Even then, for some reason, she didn't mention her encounter with the new crew member.

Later still, as she thought some more about the handsome young engineering officer, Laura was mad with herself for not following up any of his obvious leads. I didn't even ask his name, she thought ruefully. Still, the officer class were all either snobs or gay in Laura's opinion. Most of them either up themselves and not interested in salon bims like her, or already fixed up with expensive socialite beauty queens in every port. In any case, she consoled herself, she had Madeira to look forward to tomorrow. Steve was off before her and they would each make it to the Three Crowns in their own time. She'd put everything else completely out of her mind.

Tomorrow, it would be Steve's smooth young skin that she would be caressing, Laura thought. His lips she'd be kissing and his body that would be pleasuring hers with all the sweet familiarity of their youthful passion. She couldn't wait.

The *Jannina* berthed dead on the dot of 8 a.m. and at 8.30 all staff and crew, even the catering and kitchen staff, had to attend a lifeboat safety exercise.

Two areas of deck were cordoned off so that passengers couldn't accidentally get in the way of the crew, who had to check the lifeboats and demonstrate their ability to lower them safely and efficiently as part of the emergency life-saving procedures. Life rafts were to be checked and inflated and gas cylinders put on board each boat with its full complement of flares and water supplies, to show the competence of all the crew in dealing with emergencies at sea.

It all went as smoothly as always, except that as one of the lifeboats was being winched down a fender came adrift and dropped on to the deck below. This wasn't in itself a big problem, but unfortunately it caught Laura's handsome new acquaintance a glancing blow on his forearm and this was enough to numb the nerves from his wrists to his shoulders and necessitated a visit to the MO. After a painkiller injection, it was recommended that the second engineer should have remedial massage treatment for his injuries and an appointment was made for him to see Laura Barnes at the Shangri-la Beauty Spa.

Laura herself knew nothing of this. Both she and Fiona were kept busy all the morning, first with the safety drill and then with last-minute clients, until at last she was free to go ashore and walked down the gangway, showing her pass and carrying her leather vanity case with various little essentials for her romantic rendezvous with Steve on the island of Madeira, while Fiona went to see Elinor.

* * *

'It was horrible,' Fiona sobbed, crying on to Elinor's shoulder and letting her hot tears drip on to Elinor's naked breasts. She'd run in panic to Elinor's cabin and found her just coming out of the shower.

'Why, what did she say?' Elinor said calmly, pulling her on to the bed. She slipped her hand under the prim white uniform and ran it up and down Fiona's firm and slender thighs, finding the soft mousey fur of her mound and stroking her gently.

'She said that we'd been seen at my interview, in the nude.' Fiona sniffed miserably and tried to raise her head from Elinor's comforting embrace.

Elinor tightened her grip on the young girl's body, drawing her back on to the pillows, and said soothingly, 'Don't cry, baby. There's nothing to get so worried about.'

Elinor was revelling in the feel of Fiona's hot tears trickling down her neck and her nipples began to harden as the warm liquid dripped on to her voluptuous breasts.

'Don't cry, my little darling,' she said again to the distraught girl. She kissed Fiona's soft young cheek and touched the sensitive quivering lips, tracing each curve gently with one finger. Strong emotion made Fiona so sexy and Elinor longed to strip the girl naked and make love to her, to kiss away her hot tears and suck off the juices between her warm thighs.

Instead, she kissed her gently on her neck, on her wet eyelids and, finally, on her soft open mouth, her own mouth cool against Fiona's hot young lips.

'I can't believe that someone could be so sneaky as to report it to Laura,' Fiona said miserably.

Elinor didn't answer. She took hold of Fiona's chin and turned her mouth back to her own. Fiona stopped talking as their lips met again and her anxiety seemed to dissolve as Elinor began to unbutton the prim white overall, letting it fall open to reveal Fiona's small lacy bra.

She kissed her passionately, on the mouth and throat, on her soft young cheeks, lapping up the salty tears and moving down to kiss between her small firm breasts, pulling up the tiny scrap of a bra to expose the tight little nipples. Her hands were everywhere, pushing up the overall until it was bunched around Fiona's waist, exposing the modest little briefs and white lacy suspenders. Elinor put both thumbs in the little triangle of Fiona's panties and began to rotate them on the soft swell of her belly. She was intent on teasing and exploring the supple young body, taking the small pink nipples into her mouth, one at a time, sucking and nibbling hard until the young girl flexed her legs and began to whimper softly. Although small, Fiona's breasts were very sensitive and Elinor spent time teasing her nipples, licking, biting and sucking them to make them grow into hard red berries, then she rolled her tongue round each thrusting pert little end until Fiona cried out with pleasure and involuntarily opened her legs, inviting her lover into the sticky warmth of her slit.

Elinor kissed her mouth again and brushed her fingers against Fiona's mound, feeling the damp heat of the girl's arousal. Fiona opened herself further, eager to feel Elinor's fingers toying with her sensitive tip. She thrust herself upwards so that her lover's finger went deeper into her slit and she began to gasp for breath. Her hands had reached up and were stroking Elinor's full breasts, playing with the older woman's huge dark nipples while she rubbed herself against the fingers stroking her swollen clit. All the while, they kept kissing deeply, parting each other's lips to roll a tongue inside the mouth and to pause briefly for breath before starting again. Elinor dipped two fingers deep into Fiona's cunt and brought them out shining with love juice. She smeared a little of the glistening liquid on to her young friend's lips before enjoying the delicious pussy cream herself. The taste of it made her greedy for more and she pushed Fiona back on to the bed and began to unroll the glossy nude stockings until they were round her ankles and she could reach the white briefs and lacy suspenders. She eased them down gently and tossed them on to the floor.

She parted Fiona's legs so that her thighs were spread wide and then she eased up the starchy uniform still further to expose Fiona's pale and vulnerable naked belly. Now she could kiss the bare flesh, right down to the toes. She moved her mouth up Fiona's ankles, knees and thighs until she found the opening of her sex, pouting, wet and pink between the mousey pubes and the damp curls of fine hair. She used her fingers to open her up, pulling her sex lips wide apart to see the swollen clit red and shining with desire.

She bent over Fiona, lapping at her open pussy, her tongue lingering slowly up and down her slit until Fiona moaned and shivered, her body responding to every blissful sensation as Elinor toyed playfully with her erect love button. Fiona's whimpers and cries encouraged Elinor to go down further on her and suck it hard between her lips, biting and licking until the younger girl began to roll her head from side to side and lift herself up against Elinor's mouth. Her juices gushed out, wetting Elinor's face as she climaxed, shuddering and moaning with ecstasy.

Elinor sat back on her haunches, licking her lips and gazing greedily at the slowly flowing love juice as it ran between Fiona's legs and down the channel between her buttocks.

'Turn over on to your tum, darling,' she said avidly. 'It seems ages since we made love like this.'

Fiona obediently rolled over on to her front. Her delicate, narrow back and slim waist developed into the most beautiful muscular bottom and strong thighs. She lay with her arse tilted slightly upwards so that, from the back, her firm young cheeks and deep cleft revealed the soft fur of her pussy.

Elinor began to palm her backside gently, parting her cheeks and brushing her crack lightly with her fingertips, soothing rather than stimulating her. She leaned forward and planted a kiss behind Fiona's ear and the younger girl turned eagerly.

'Your lips are full of pussy juice,' she said dreamily, and she proceeded to lick away every last smear from Elinor's lips.

'Lift your bum up, sweetheart,' Elinor commanded, and she slipped a hand under Fiona's belly and started to massage her bottom very gently, gradually opening it up so that she could see the wetness from Fiona's sex trickling down between her cheeks. She opened them a little wider to expose the tight bud of Fiona's puckered anus.

'Oh, that feels lovely,' Fiona breathed.

'It'll feel even lovelier soon, angel,' Elinor said, and she bent over and used her tongue to spread Fiona's juice into her arsehole. Fiona shivered and pressed herself back trying to rub herself against Elinor's roving tongue. Elinor held her up higher so that her bottom was raised up even further and began to kiss her bumhole. She moistened her tongue well and then pressed it right into the tight muscles of Fiona's arse. The younger girl raised herself towards Elinor's long hard kiss, offering herself willingly, and Elinor began to rub herself against

Fiona's short muscular calves, smearing the back of her legs as she continued to suck and tickle the young girl's behind. They moved together now, Fiona's leg absolutely saturated with Elinor's sex cream and Fiona arching her back and trying to make Elinor suck more deeply into her hole. Elinor was delighted with this; she'd always loved this deliciously tight little arsehole and her lips were glued to Fiona's rear as she slurped and lapped at her young friend. Suddenly Fiona let out a loud cry, torn from her by a massive orgasm, which triggered Elinor's own climax and the two collapsed together in an intense sensation of utter bliss.

'How do you feel now?' Elinor whispered a little later. 'All better now?'

'Yes,' Fiona said happily, and she wriggled closer to press her face against Elinor's voluptuous breasts, content to shut out her worries and shelter against Elinor's strength.

Now it was Fiona's turn to take the lead. 'Lie on your side, Elinor,' she whispered.

'Why? Do you want more?' Elinor said indulgently, and obediently turned on her side. Fiona positioned herself behind her, pressing herself against Elinor's back and encircling her lover with both arms.

'Yes I do,' she answered. 'I want more and more until I can't take it any longer.'

She massaged the twin globes of Elinor's full breasts, closing her eyes and pinching Elinor's nipples mercilessly. She loved to play with Elinor's breasts. She knew how to excite the older woman beyond endurance, tweaking and pulling at her nipples until Elinor's pussy was almost unbearably hot and wet. Fiona floated languidly in a sensual dream-world. She wrapped one of her legs around Elinor and began to rub herself against Elinor's bottom.

'You're so beautiful, Elinor,' she said dreamily, and she moved her hands down to her smooth belly, stroking and caressing it until she found her pussy mound. Elinor threw her head back and half turned towards her, but Fiona pushed her back again.

'No,' she said assertively. 'I want to play with your lovely bumhole.'

Elinor obediently turned back to the wall, bending over a little to thrust out her rounded sexy backside. Fiona kneeled over her now and began to massage Elinor's bottom, moulding her small hands round the full globes, her fingers pressing deeply into Elinor's flesh. She bent closer still and was able to make out the deep-reddish hair which guarded the entrance to Elinor's pussy.

Sighing with pleasure, Fiona said, 'Push your bottom out a bit more,' and Elinor obeyed immediately, her eyes closed in utter bliss as she enjoyed the feel of Fiona's fingers and mouth. Fiona used her thumbs to carefully pull the buttocks apart and expose Elinor's tight bum-hole and parted pussy lips.

'You know I can't resist this,' Fiona said, and she bent down and planted a long slow kiss between Elinor's parted cheeks.

Elinor groaned and reached back to grasp her own buttocks and open them even further so that Fiona could tease her wide-open pussy lips and kiss her rear hole.

Fiona reached to the side of the bed and picked up two small vibrators, one of which she slipped a little way into Elinor's bumhole, while she used the other to go up and down the soft flesh of Elinor's inner thighs and then round and round her wide open sex and finally, when Elinor seemed about to explode, she pushed it firmly into her friend's pussy. Now Elinor really did explode. She came long and hard, throwing back her head in ecstasy and crying out loudly.

4

There were plenty of taxis on the concrete harbour area, all the drivers extremely polite and keen to take passengers and crew to any part of the beautiful island.

Laura sank gratefully into the first car and, leaning back in her seat, requested Rua dos Ferreiros. The Three Crowns was away from the harbour and up the steep main road past the municipal park, which was curiously British with its wrought-iron benches and bandstand set amid neat green lawns. But, unlike British parks, it blazed with tropical flowers in the most vivid colours. Poinsettias, strelitzias and huge begonias in bright paintbox hues filled every flower bed and even the ice cream parlour was surrounded by planters full of gorgeous bedding plants, familiar in appearance but gigantic in size.

Laura gazed out of the taxi window, enjoying the view and admiring the street stalls which were also filled with exotic plants and blooms, spilling in glorious profusion all over the pavements. To reach the top of the hill would have been a good twenty minutes' walk but by car it only took three minutes and they pulled up in front of the Three Crowns hotel with its distinctive gilded signboard. She got out and paid the driver before quickly mounting the steps to the front door. The smiling porter directed her to room seven and she climbed the stairs with eager anticipation.

She tapped gently at the door and went in. The room was dim, the venetian blinds being drawn down and only stray shafts of bright sunlight seeping in from between some of the slats. Steve was lying on the big double bed, his eyes closed and the duvet cast on to the floor. He only had the white cotton sheet covering him and his dark hair showed up in stark contrast against the plain white pillow. She noted that at each side of the bed he'd arranged glasses of orange juice with an iced lolly in each glass to keep it cool. Just like him to be so considerate, she thought tenderly. She unloaded a couple of items from her vanity case and placed them on the bedside table before turning to the figure on the bed.

He was playing one of their favourite games, when one of them would pretend to be asleep while the other one had all kinds of sexual liberties before the seemingly unconscious victim was at last fully awake and active.

Laura smiled to herself as she slipped out of her sundress, wriggling it down over the curve of her hips and revealing his favourite black lacy bra and satin thong. Then she slid out of her sandals and stretched her long tanned legs before laying her clothes neatly on the chair. All the while she kept a close eye on Steve, who was still feigning sleep with the utmost realism. She knew that he'd heard her come in and the soft rustle of her clothes as she undressed, but still he gave no sign. Very gently and carefully she rolled back the crisp white sheet away from his body, slowly easing it down the bed to expose his firm tanned torso and narrow hips. He was wearing boxer shorts in some very soft light-grey material, which enhanced the golden brown of his skin. The waistband fitted snugly around his slim body and there was a row of little white buttons neatly fastening the flies. Laura gazed at him approvingly and then mounted the bed and straddled him, being careful to avoid bodily contact. She slid her hands down his face, smoothing his eyebrows and gently pinching his ear lobes, then lightly caressing his bare shoulders. She let her hands run down each side of his body and then up again, sliding them down each of his arms in turn to the very ends of his fingertips. Still he didn't stir.

She leaned forward, thrusting out her rounded buttocks and letting the voluptuous mounds of her breasts almost, but not quite, dangle in his face. She enjoyed contemplating him in his pretend sleep: the clear lightly tanned complexion, the almost aristocratic bone structure, the clean-cut jaw. She'd longed for this moment for the last three days, as a thirsty traveller longs for water, yet still she didn't give him any clue as to what she would do with him. She knew the delicious uncertainty and anticipation that he was feeling as she leaned closer still, placing her hands on either side of the pillows to support herself and breathing gently on his firmly closed lips with the lightness of an angel's breath. His eyelids fluttered slightly, but that was all. Then Laura found his mouth with her own and kissed him lingeringly and thoroughly, savouring the smell of his freshly shaved male skin, the taste of his lips and the warmth of his body. He opened up to her and she kissed him slowly, again and again, letting her tongue explore the inside of his mouth with the slow lasciviousness of one who has all the time in the world. But still she didn't press herself against him or let him feel any contact with her body. She delighted in testing him and seeing how long he could hold out against his own sexual desire.

As she tongued him with practised sensuality, she became aware of the first faint stirrings inside his shorts and sat back on her haunches, the better to observe his strong wide chest and the perfect ripples of his ribs.

His upper body was almost devoid of hair, with just a faint down surrounding his hard male nipples and a line of fine hair from his belly button down to his pubes. Laura massaged his neck and shoulders, letting her hands slide down to the waistband of his shorts, teasing him into thinking that she was going inside, then pinching and flicking his nipples with her thumbs before leaning over him and kissing him again. She knew exactly how to torment and stimulate him until he was mad for her. Still he feigned sleep, even though his shorts were now obviously bulging with the beginnings of a very promising erection.

She gently raised his arms above his head and held them there with one hand while she put her other hand on his thigh, carefully avoiding touching his cock, at the same time leaning forward to flick at his nipples with her tongue, making them hard and dark. But still Steve played the game and refused to open his eyes. The hair on his legs was dark and fine, the tips golden. It was not in any way coarse or scratchy, but soft and downy. She moved her hand firmly up the legs of his boxers, still without touching his balls, and then slid both hands under his buttocks, kneading and squeezing them, parting both sides, stretching and pinching them until he gave an involuntary soft growl of pleasure. He lay perfectly still as she gently undid every single little fly button and put her hand through the opening. She allowed her fingers to entwine in his soft pubic hair, teasing him unmercifully, before finally grasping his cock and allowing it to spring free. What she saw made her gasp with pleasure. Steve's erection was already as hard as an iron bar and big enough to satisfy the most exacting woman. A little dewdrop sparkled at its very tip and wobbled as his cock thrust through the opening of his shorts. A most gratifying development, Laura thought. She let go of it immediately, not wanting to hold it in her hands yet, preferring to tease him a little longer.

Instead, she bent over him to breathe in his male scent and body heat. His cock was engorged with an enormous purple head, like some sort of exotic flower on the end of a thick stem growing from the bush of his fine dark hairs. His ballsac looked a little dry and wrinkled and Laura reached across to the bedside table for the gel. She filled her fingertips from the opened tube and smeared his balls tenderly and lightly, still being careful not to touch his swollen cock. She paused deliberately and looked intently at his closed eyes, but Steve didn't stir even though she knew he was now fully aroused. Grasping his shaft firmly, she drew back the foreskin and let her mouth hover over his exposed tip. She knew that he could now feel the moist warmth of her breath and was waiting, desperately, to be sucked off. He rolled his head to one side and gave a slight groan as she finally took him into her mouth.

Still holding the base of his cock in her fingers, she slowly moved him in and out of her lips, closing her mouth round him in long smooth movements up and down his shaft. He was now making no pretence of being asleep but was groaning out loud with anticipation. Laura teasingly rolled her tongue around his tip, again and again, tasting once more the saltiness of that first drop of leaked pre-come and pushing under his foreskin, making him thrash about on the bed. Now she leaned over him, curving her shoulders to enable her breasts to swell over their lacy cups, her hands behind her, still rubbing his swollen cock.

Steve was now fully awake, begging her to take him in her mouth again.

'No,' she said, pretending severity. 'Not until I'm ready.'

She unhooked the black satin bra, allowing her full firm breasts to be unleashed from their lacy wired cups. She dangled them in his face, tossing the bra on to the floor. She teased him by thrusting first one nipple, then the other, into his open mouth, leaning backwards on her haunches in between time so that she could continue to stroke him and then forwards again so that she could push her breasts into his eager mouth to be nibbled and sucked once more until her nipples were like swollen red bee stings.

Now he was desperate, begging to be inside her, but Laura just laughed. She eased the boxers down to his ankles and took his cock in her mouth once more, squeezing it between her lips and taking in the whole length of his shaft until he was absolutely beside himself with lust.

'Oh please,' he begged helplessly.

'Not until you tell me who is being made a mess of.' Laura laughed.

'Oh, I am,' Steve groaned.

'And who is making a mess of you?'

'You are. You know you are.'

'Just as long as we know,' Laura said with mock severity. 'And what are you going to do if I let you inside me?'

'Anything you want,' he promised eagerly.

'Are you going to make me a happy and satisfied woman?'

'Yes. Oh yes,' Steve said.

'Very well then.'

Kneeling in front of him, wearing only the brief black thong, Laura reached up to his ready lips.

Steve pulled her head down to his and kissed her hungrily, his hands caressing her thrusting buttocks, fully exposed by the brief thong. The most delicious feelings coursed through Laura's body. Every nerve ending was tingling with arousal; her nipples were tight and aching; the narrow cleft of the thong dug into her wet willing flesh and she longed for him to enter her, but Steve sat up suddenly and pressed her gently on to her back.

'My turn now,' he said, and very smoothly he raised Laura's arms on to the pillow, so that she felt the same delicious helplessness that she'd inflicted on him.

But Laura made no pretence of being asleep as he leaned over her, kissing her deeply and pinching her nipples, his glossy cock huge and dangling over her, tormenting her with its promise. He held each breast in turn and his lips sucked and nibbled strongly and steadily on her nipples. At the same time, his free hand found her wide-open legs and he pushed aside the flimsy little satin thong and began to rub her gently and rhythmically, thrusting inside her wet opening, moistening her sensitive clit with her own juices until she was aching for him. Just as Laura thought she could take no more, he pulled the thong completely off her and opened her legs wider still, burying his mouth in her warm sensitive mound, licking her pussy and searching for her little hard pearl which gave her the most intense pleasure. He began to stimulate it with his tongue, at first gently and then more firmly until Laura began to cry out with delight.

'Oh God, Steve. That's lovely. Oh don't stop. I want to come now,' she gasped. He didn't answer, but his probing agile tongue continued to lick and lap at her throbbing clit with sure firm strokes until Laura almost fainted with her excitement and need. Finally, blessedly, her body was at last engulfed in a convulsive orgasm which radiated from her toes, tingling and spreading to the very centre of her sex.

Steve paused now as she lay relaxed and satisfied, recovering from the waves of pleasure which had washed over her so intensely that it had been almost unbearable. He was breathing heavily.

'I want to be inside you,' he muttered thickly. 'Say you want it as well, Laura.'

'Yes. I want it. I want you,' she panted.

She closed her eyes and guided him inside her, letting his huge cock thrust into her slowly and rhythmically, so that he pushed deep inside her and then almost came out before he thrust himself into her again and again. He grasped her bottom, lifting her hips off the bed and pulling her towards him, so that he could push even more strongly, the base of his shaft rubbing against her greeedy clit.

'Oh God, Laura,' he groaned. 'You feel so tight when you've come first. I want to fill you right up and make you come again.'

Now he really let go and went into her even more rapidly and powerfully and Laura once more abandoned herself to the pleasure of her body, clinging to him and moaning with the exquisite enjoyment of his magnificent cock.

As for Steve, when he felt his own climax begin to overtake him, he held her more tightly still and she squealed with the pain of his strongly grasping fingers digging into her soft flesh. He was now completely carried away and shouted out loudly with the ecstasy of his orgasm as he rode and pulsed inside her. They held each other closer still as the last echoing waves of sensation gradually began to die away and, little by little, their breathing became quieter.

Laura rolled over and lay on her side, totally replete, still holding him as they each murmured words of contentment and love, speaking slowly now in the long aftermath of their passion, content to sink on to the pillows and doze dreamily for a while. She awoke some time later, not suddenly but gradually, stretching and flexing her legs with enjoyment and reaching out instinctively to feel for Steve's reassuring presence at the side of her. He lay a little apart from her now, no longer pretending but really asleep this time, his breathing gentle and regular. Laura propped herself up on one elbow and looked at him. His face was handsome and relaxed, his lips still slightly swollen with all that kissing; his eyelashes formed dark fans on each of his cheeks. He really was a dish, Laura thought.

As though aware of her gaze, he opened his eyes wide and looked at her, at first uncomprehending and muzzy with sleep, but then, almost immediately, he gave her a joyful hug of recognition and rained light swift kisses on to her face and neck. They lay entwined and at peace with each other for many minutes until Laura gently disengaged herself and went into the tiny en suite bathroom to run the shower while Steve watched her, taking pleasure in her graceful naked beauty. She coiled her long blonde hair into the plastic shower cap and stepped inside the bijou shower cubicle, letting the welcome cascade run over her body, refreshing her spirit and energising her mind.

Steve needed no persuading and joined her immediately, both of them luxuriating in the fast-flowing life-giving water. She soaped his shoulders and chest, letting her hands slide down to his firm taut belly and then massaged the dark hair round his cock, slipping one hand under his balls to hold and support them as she rinsed the soap off her hand before rubbing his quiescent penis.

'You're just like a little boy now,' she teased him. 'You're so small and soft. I don't think you can manage another hard-on, can you?'

'Try me.' He grinned and placed his hands on her shoulders, gently massaging the soapsuds further and further down to encompass her firm smooth breasts and glowing nipples.

He lingered over each one in turn, soaping and caressing them over and over again until she squirmed and thrust her hips forward, flirting with his fingertips, trying to encourage them to go lower and lower and push between her pussy lips. Obediently, he moved his hand down her belly and stroked her, casually pulling at her blonde wet hairs with his fingers, tugging them gently and then rubbing her round and round until she began to ache madly for him to enter her again. Meanwhile, he nuzzled her breasts, the warm clear water pouring over his dark head and running down his face, streaming over both of them and rushing down their legs.

Steve turned off the shower, reached out and grabbed the big soft bath towel and wrapped it around her as she stepped from the cubicle. Laura now felt only warm contented bliss as he gently blotted her wet body and cuddled and snuggled her until she was thoroughly dry. Then he towelled himself vigorously and stood naked in front of her, panting slightly as he pulled off her shower cap and towel and tossed them on to the floor.

Laura shook out her hair and he pulled her towards the bed, laying her back on the pillows as he felt on the bedside table for the aromatherapy oil. Starting at her neck and shoulders, he softly and sensuously began to oil her body, smoothing the herbal rub on to her warm skin with smooth firm strokes, moving over her breasts and rib cage until he reached her hips and had to pause to replenish the oil.

Laura was enjoying the blissful laid-back feeling of utter relaxation. Her eyes were closed and her legs slightly apart as she lay absolutely still while Steve began to stroke her further down, making her skin feel as rich and silky as cream. He worked on the inside of her thighs, gradually going higher and higher so that soft sensation of overwhelming pleasure reached her and she shifted voluptuously on the bed. Sensing that she was ready for it, he reached on to the bedside table for the vibrator that Laura had brought with her and began to stroke the smooth elegant lines of the pink love toy between his fingers. He moistened the end of it with a little of the gel and turned it on. He touched the tip of it against each of her sore nipples in turn, making them pucker and respond. He circled each one again and again until Laura was floating on soft waves of exquisite sensation. Ever so slowly, he moved the dancing dildo down to her groin, letting it play in the soft hairs for a few seconds and then just inside her thighs, tormenting her and moving it away, until Laura groaned with the frustration and longing to have it inside her. She instinctively opened her legs wider, revealing her eager clit, once again swollen and red with desire, and the opening, wet and ready to be pleasured again.

Steve now stroked the vibrator up and down over every fold and crease of her sex, giving her such a thorough going over that Laura began to breathe in short ragged gasps as her ultra-sensitive flesh responded to its inexorable pulsating throb. At last, he mercifully inserted it into her for a few seconds, making her almost numb with sensation. Then, with the utmost delicacy and finesse, he withdrew it and let it touch her tip very,

very lightly and gently, only two or three times, but it was enough to send Laura into the most panting and violent climax, fighting for breath, her breasts shaking and her thighs twitching uncontrollably at the agonisingly intense sensation.

Steve let her enjoy her pleasure for several minutes before firmly pulling her on top of him, his muscular arms flexed as he lay back on the pillows and guided her on to his cock. This time their lovemaking was long and slow. Laura's body was still gleaming with the massage oil and she was already exhausted by her intense sexual responses. He seemed not to register her natural weakness and lassitude after their previous lovemaking, but grasped her glistening buttocks strongly, pulling her on to him and thrusting into her as far as he could go and then releasing her, only to impale her again, smoothly and powerfully as though it were the first session of the afternoon.

Laura, supporting herself on both hands, felt her knees begin to tremble and her arms begin to ache as his iron hard cock slowly thrust into her yet again, but then, gradually, she felt a resurgence of the sexual fire burning inside her and began to move with his rhythm. She squeezed her innermost muscles to make him come more quickly and surprised herself with the strength of her feelings as they both finished together and she finally relaxed on top of him, emotionally and physically drained.

Laura did attempt to broach the subject of the encounter with the blond guy, but every time she attempted to say something, it never seemed the right moment – or seemed as though it would open a Pandora's box of problems. For now, everything was fine, and Steve hadn't mentioned a thing about the event, so she contented herself with saying nothing about it.

They lay in each other's arms for some time, the afternoon sun filtering through the blinds and highlighting the sheen of his dark hair and turning Laura's blonde locks into a pile of molten gold. This time they didn't sleep or use the shower and it was another hour before they remembered the orange drinks. Needless to say, the iced lollies had long since melted.

5

Next morning, Fiona had already gone to work before Laura even surfaced and had left a note hoping that they could meet at lunchtime. Laura showered quickly and came out of the bathroom in a towelling robe just as Stanley came in with her breakfast. 'I did knock, Laura,' he said softly, and turned away from her to put the tray on the bedside table.

As he bent over the little table, Laura noticed afresh his graceful sinuous hips and tight little bum in the close-fitting black trousers of his steward's uniform. The short white jacket came just below his slim waist and ended in two points, which emphasised his slinky hips even more.

Since her afternoon with Steve, Laura was more relaxed and at ease with herself than she'd been for a long time. She didn't speak a word as she deliberately waited for the cabin steward to turn round and meet her eyes. When he did, she took a short step towards him and, on a whim, loosened the tie-belt of her towelling robe, letting it hang loose, baring her breasts.

'Good morning, Stanley,' she said, and smiled happily when she saw his fine dark eyes widen, his pupils dilating involuntarily as he gazed admiringly at her firm pink-tipped tits, exposed tormentingly, brazenly for him and poking cheekily through the opened robe.

'The coffee smells good this morning,' she said, and thrust her pelvis forward a little, causing the robe to fall provocatively even further open.

His big startled eyes swivelled to her face and he swallowed audibly as Laura laughed softly. 'I'll just have a sip, see if it tastes as good as it smells. Mmm, lovely. Hot, black and strong, just as I like my men.' She knew she was being very mischievous, but she turned away from him and replaced the cup on the saucer, deliberately treating him to a good view of her shapely arse.

'Yes,' he stammered. 'It's very good. Fiona left for work early,' he finished rather lamely.

She glanced at him, noticing the beginnings of a very promising hard-on through the tight trousers and she covered her breasts with her hands, squeezing the nipples suggestively, making them long and red. 'So I've got the cabin to myself for a while, have I, Stanley?'

'Yes, Laura,' he muttered shyly, still unable to tear his eyes away from her body.

She took another step towards him, invading his personal space and feeling very horny. 'So, we'll have to take advantage of it, won't we?' she whispered, and watched the bulge in his pants grow even bigger.

He gave a soft little groan and slipped the robe from her shoulders, letting it fall to the floor so that she was now completely nude and then he leaned backwards a little so that he could appreciate her nakedness more thoroughly. His liquid brown eyes roved avidly up and down her body, lingering on her smooth tanned legs and the triangle of fine gold hair between her thighs, then up higher to linger on her hard rosy nipples. Laura gazed back at him, smiling challengingly, her own eyes hot with lust. Stanley locked the door quickly and started to remove his own clothes, throwing them across the chair, until they were facing each other once more, both naked, both equally beautiful in their different ways. His body was smooth, supple, with wide shoulders and snakey hips; surprisingly, for one so dark, he had very little body hair, just a circle of fine hairs round his maroon-coloured nipples and a pattern of silky pubes which reached up to a point on his flat belly.

Laura sighed with pleasure as she looked at the long stiff cock with the eye of an expert and he took hold of her breasts, firmly pressing his mouth to hers, his tongue between her teeth. As he palmed and tweaked her lovely breasts, Laura's pussy began to gush with love juice, throbbing and tingling with excitement. She felt joyful, elated at his supple beauty and couldn't help giving a gasp of pleasure as she took his magnificent prick in her hand.

There's a particular and special feel to the texture of a long stiff prick, newly released from the confines of boxers and pants. Stanley's was like an iron bar, its stiff hardness contrasting beautifully with the silky skin pulled tightly over its firmness. Laura rubbed gently over his smooth, circumcised tip, teasing it and pressing the skin back even further, encouraging his prick to stand ever more proudly. She could feel the strong regular throb of it like a steady pulse, in tune with her own heartbeat.

They kissed again and he slipped a hand between her legs, palming her gentle mound and the hot wetness of her slit. Laura raised one leg and wrapped it round his hip, opening herself and making it easier for him to rub between her pussy lips, doubling the amount of moisture flowing down the inside of her thighs. She pressed herself harder against him, rubbing her swollen nipples against his smooth hard chest and pressing his cock against her belly while he sucked at her lips again.

'Say what you want,' she whispered hotly. 'Do you want me to suck you off?'

'No, I want to be inside you,' he said. He looked at her with his huge brown eyes and said very seriously, 'If that's what *you'd* like, Laura. He lifted her leg even higher until she almost overbalanced and then he eased her gently on to the bed. She was somewhat disappointed that she hadn't got his lovely cock in her mouth. She wanted to feel it deep into her throat, her tongue playing with his tip, sucking and swallowing the first dew drop of his come.

He lifted her legs higher and put them round his neck so that her pussy was wide open and ready for fucking, then he slid his hands under her bottom, lifting her even higher, his cock resting at the slippery hot opening of her pussy lips, but still without entering her. He rubbed the end of his cock round her opening, again and again, pleasuring himself against her, still without penetrating, teasing and maddening her with the promise of satisfaction, building up the sexual tension without any fulfilment.

Although Laura was enjoying what she was getting, she was surprised at his lack of urgency. His movements were so relaxed and fluid, almost indolent. She wondered fleetingly if anyone would notice how long he'd been in cabin 327 and whether he'd be missed, as he moved his hands gently, to part her cheeks, opening her up still more. He began to play with her arsehole, pressing his finger ever so gently into her bum and all the while covering her lips with his own, so that her little moans and sobs of pleasure were lost in his deep kisses. Laura couldn't believe the intensity of pleasure that he was giving her with just this gentle finger-fucking up her bum.

'Say what you want, Laura,' he said wickedly, parodying her own words. 'Do you want me to stop?'

'No! Don't stop! Don't stop, please!' Laura panted desperately. 'It feels lovely, Stanley. Don't stop.' She kissed him more passionately on the mouth, wanting him to go on forever, fingering her arsehole and rubbing his hard cock against her soaking wet pussy. She began to experience that delicious plateau of sensation which always comes before a climax and began unconsciously to rub herself against him in a rhythm which matched his own. When he finally pushed his cock into her properly and fucked her thoroughly, she almost passed out with the intensity of her orgasm.

She lay back on the pillows, fighting for breath, and he sat back on his haunches, holding his glistening cock in one hand and regarding her with mock seriousness. 'How was that, Miss Laura, ma'am?' he asked mockingly. and Laura just gasped and smiled, trying to catch her breath.

'Magnificent, Stanley,' she said, and looked up at the swollen cock dangling in front of her and felt horny all over again.

'Let me have it in my mouth. Please, oh please!' she pleaded.

He leaned over her and she took his huge dick between her lips and licked off all the traces of her own pussy juice, swallowing the essence of her own wetness and licking him along the whole length of his shaft, holding his prick at the base and running her tongue under his tip, teasing him and wanking him with her fingers until she could feel the tension of his approaching orgasm. He suddenly withdrew from her mouth and turned her on to her front, parting her thighs and pushing one of the pillows under her belly. He held her firmly by the waist and drove his magnificent length into her still-tight pussy, fucking her strongly and passionately until she shook with the tremors of her intense pleasure. Only then did Stanley increase the speed and fierceness of his thrusts until his huge cock pumped its load of come into her and he gave a satisfied sigh as his thick cream filled her up and mingled with Laura's own juices.

She leaned back and closed her eyes and, very tenderly and quietly, Stanley reached to the side of the bed for some tissues and began to clean through her bush of wet hair, his eyes wide in admiration of her wide-open sex, still red and sensitive from his skilful fucking.

Laura kissed him languidly. 'That was lovely, Stanley,' she whispered.

'Glad to be of service,' he whispered back. He dressed silently and quickly and then he was gone.

Laura must have dozed because she opened her eyes to find that it was the mid-morning break and Fiona was bent over her, gently touching her shoulder and laughingly offering a cup of coffee.

'Laura,' she said teasingly. 'Still in bed and a whole new world before you in the Beauty Spa? Have you forgotten, Cinders, that tonight is the ball? We'll have all on today to cope with the ugly ducklings wanting to be swans for the Captain's cocktail party.'

Laura groaned and covered her eyes, lying back in the pose of Michelangelo's dying slave.

'What time is it?' she mumbled and peered at the bedside clock, finally noticing the tray of coffee at the side of her.

'Time you were up and at it.' Fiona grinned. 'You were already asleep when I came in last night. You must have had a good twelve hours by now. I take it the Madeira visit was successful?'

'Oh yes.' Laura smiled. She stretched luxuriously with her hands behind her head, observing the suddenly cheery disposition that had overtaken her room-mate. 'Very successful, thanks.' And so was this morning's session with Stanley, she thought wickedly, smiling at the memory. 'And how was your day?' She reached out for the coffee that Fiona had poured for her and looked across at her companion.

'Oh, OK,' Fiona said and smiled back at her. She seemed much less tense and much more upbeat since yesterday, Laura noticed.

'I went to the Golden Sands Pizza Place for lunch and saw Elinor. We shared a table. Then we took a taxi to the botanical gardens and had an hour or two wandering round in the sunshine.'

Laura was quite struck by this revelation, privately thinking that if the sour Elinor were the last person on earth, she wouldn't want to dine with her. That would really put me off my cornflakes, she thought with a wry grin. Even so, if Stanley were to be believed, she figured that Fiona and Elinor had gone much further than lunch. Still thinking of Stanley's recent visit, she smiled again, very smugly this time.

'What are you smiling at?' Fiona asked, handing her biscuit.

'Oh, I just thought of something,' Laura said airily. 'Well, if you've finished your coffee I'll go and have a shower.'

The Shangri-la was frantic all day as the staff attempted to cope with the huge number of appointments. All the hair and beauty treatments were in aid of the Captain's cocktail party, of course, and everyone wanted that extra special something that meant pulling out all the stops, whatever the cost. Needless to say, Eileen Grimshaw arrived punctually for her manicure and facial, but Laura was well prepared, as always, and she laid out a soft white salon towel on the table in front of her, so that she could inspect her nails.

'Gardener's nails, I'm afraid,' Eileen said apologetically. 'My husband finds it very hard to let go since he's retired, so I've tried to create the perfect relaxation garden for him and, of course, we have a man in for grass-cutting and so on. I've been putting in some aromatic plants to help Reggie unwind but since he had the op. he seems to find it impossible to get rid of his tensions and be the person he was before. To be honest with you, things aren't the same between us, if you know what I mean.'

Laura said nothing but kept her eyes lowered, inspecting Eileen's hands. Then she filled her little plastic soaking bowl and began to shape Eileen's nails with an emery board.

'How did you want them?' she asked. 'Oval, gently rounded or straight across?' Laura's own nails were straight across; they were polished a soft shell pink and the tips whitened. Momentarily diverted from her problems with Reggie, Eileen glanced down, taking in Laura's long, elegant and beautifully varnished fingers.

She said quickly, 'Oh, straight across, like yours, dear.'

Laura began to shape her nails and even them up, and then she gently put Eileen's right hand into the soaking bowl. The nail tips had to be left for a minute or two, so Laura busied herself arranging a selection of pearly nail varnishes on a small tray and wrapping an orange stick in cotton wool.

This seemed to be the pause that Eileen was waiting for and she said in a rush, 'What am I going to do, Laura? Reggie seems to have lost all interest in that side of our marriage. Life's not the same any more. I feel so let down, somehow. There's no contact between us. I'm only fifty-one, after all.'

Laura looked up at her in some surprise. It wasn't

often that a woman of Eileen's mature years spoke quite so frankly about intimate relationships.

She tried murmuring something comforting like, 'Oh, I'm sure it'll all come right, Mrs Grimshaw,' and then she took Eileen's hand out of the bowl and substituted the left one. But Eileen was not going to be so easily placated.

'If only I knew of something to make things better,' she moaned softly. 'So that we could be like we were before, you know, close, sharing everything in bed. And do call me Eileen,' she added.

Laura was now working gently on Eileen's cuticles, pressing them back with the orange stick and then treating them with a moisturiser. But still she was moved by the other woman's obvious distress and said soothingly, 'Well, let's finish your manicure first and then do the facial. It'll be a new you and I expect he'll fall in love with you all over again.'

Afterwards, she felt vaguely ashamed of the facile and shallow way that she'd responded to this cry for help and wished she'd said something more constructive to try to help the older woman's distress. But an hour later, Eileen certainly looked and felt a whole lot better. Laura asked about her evening gown and prompted her tactfully to describe what she was going to wear for the cocktail party.

'It sounds wonderful and you'll look really lovely,' she said encouragingly as she showed Eileen the effect of the makeover in her silver-backed hand-mirror.

'I'm sure you'll enjoy it this evening. All the staff will be there and I'll be looking out for you.'

'I do hope that Reggie likes it,' Eileen said. She looked far more hopeful when she saw herself in the mirror and left the salon seemingly very pleased with her changed appearance.

Laura went to the desk to check on her next client and was surprised to see the name Andrew Gibson, a name she didn't recognise and one which was rather unusual, being male, especially on the day when all the customers were women seeking glamour for the evening party.

She hesitated in the doorway of the reception area and caught her lower lip speculatively between her teeth as her eyes sought her next client. There was only one man among the three or four middle-aged women who were waiting and he was flicking through a copy of *Ships and Shipping* magazine, his free hand resting inertly on his knee. Laura drew a deep breath as though to calm herself and went up to him. He was none other than the second engineer.

'Mr Gibson?' she asked uncertainly.

He jumped up immediately, discarding his magazine, and once more she was gazing into those sparkling dark eyes. His short-sleeved white tunic showed off his tanned muscular arms and athletic shoulders. Both his forearms were marred by ugly purple bruises and it was obvious that his right shoulder was still painfully stiff but he gave her his well-remembered white smile and said, 'Yes, that's me.'

Laura found him very sexy.

'This way, Mr Gibson.'

'Andrew, please,' he said in his attractive deep voice.

'Come this way then ... Andrew,' she said and led the way into the salon.

He stood close to her as he explained. 'We're meeting again sooner than I expected, but there was an accident with one of the fenders during the safety exercise and the quack said I should report here for remedial treatment.'

He handed Laura one of the standard medical notes

from the MO which merely said, 'Therapeutic aroma-therapy massage recommended to shoulders and arms and treatment for localised bruising, as often as necessary.'

'I feel a bit of a fraud.' He grinned. 'It's not actually taken me off duty, you know, but it is painful and my finger ends feel quite numb.'

Laura smiled at him, then she hesitated. 'Is the pain keeping you awake at night?' she asked.

'Well, not the pain exactly,' he said, and he looked at her with such open admiration that she felt the hairs on the back of her neck stand on end.

Just give me the chance, I'd soon know how to make you sleep, she thought. One session with me and you'd forget your aches and pains and sleep like a baby.

Aloud, she said, 'Well, if you could just undress down to the waist and lie on the couch, I can begin the massage.'

She turned away tactfully while he stripped off his white shirt and lay on the treatment bed. When she moved towards him, she had the oils mixed and ready.

'I'm going to start on your shoulders first with some pine needle oil, which should help to ease the pain,' she explained softly.

Andrew looked up at her as she filled her palms with the massage oil. She was leaning over him ready to begin, the V-neck of her overall opening slightly to reveal a tantalising glimpse of her deep full cleavage. She wasn't wearing a bra and she could see that Andrew was fully aware of her warm voluptuous body next to his as she placed her hands on his sore shoulders. His lips were parted with the anxiety and expectation that it would be painful and he moistened them with a pointed glistening tongue. Glancing down, Laura briefly imagined kissing those lips and rubbing that tongue with her own, opening up to him and pressing herself against his wonderful sexy body. Then she began the firm but gentle stroking of his shoulders, starting deep in the hollows of his neck. They were both silent as her strong competent hands moved in long careful movements, working gradually down his shoulder blades to the curve of his lower spine. She was amazed at the silky even texture of his skin as she pushed her fingers into the deeper muscles of his back. Almost as if he'd been painted, she thought, as she continued to soothe away the discomfort of his injuries. She finished off by massaging his spine, just above his shapely buttocks, with no pressure at all, just a rubbing in of the aromatic oils across the smooth hollow of his hips. She could already feel a renewed tingling between her legs and dared not let her hands go lower round that tight and shapely male bum of his.

'There, that's done,' she said at last, helping him to rise. 'Sit on the chair now please and let me look at your hands.'

He obediently sat facing her on the canvas salon chair and she placed his hands gently on the folded towel as though he were going to have a manicure. From the front, he was even more devastatingly attractive, she thought. He sat straight upright with his typical easy good posture and with his bruised arms laid out before him.

'I'll start with your fingers,' Laura said, and she experienced a little frisson as she moistened her own fingers with the massage oil and took one of his hands in hers. She massaged each of his fingers firmly and steadily from base to tip and then rotated each thumb gently before moving on to his strong slim wrists. She now stroked him from wrist to fingertips, first on the palms and then on the backs of his hands, feeling the relaxation in tension as he realised that she was not going to aggravate the pain of his bruises or cause him more hurt.

'You seem to be a real little Florence Nightingale,' he joked. 'Has anyone ever told you you've got a wonderful touch?'

Laura just smiled into his wonderful brown eyes and said seriously, 'I don't intend to do any deep muscular massage on these bruised areas of your arms. I'll just rub some witch hazel in very lightly and see how it goes.'

'Feels wonderful to me,' he said. 'I even feel able to cope with Captain Browning's cocktail bash now, thanks to you, Laura. I hope you'll be there as well.'

'Yes I will, and I'll look out for you,' she promised.

'Right you are then,' he said. 'And perhaps I could stand you a drink afterwards?'

He said this with the utmost respect and friendliness, not in any way trying to milk the situation or appearing to take advantage.

'Perhaps,' she said. 'We'll see.'

Privately, Laura thought it would be unlikely that there would be time, but she couldn't help an extra feeling of excitement at the evening to come and was determined to look her best. Steve would be busy behind the bar and no doubt she would have to hold Fiona's hand a bit as it would be her first time at a *Jannina* evening do, but still ... and she smiled at the thought of yet another encounter with the handsome Andrew Gibson.

'What are you smiling at?' He turned suddenly, as she was helping him into his shirt, his arms still stiff and his fingers clumsy.

Laura looked up into those bright sexy brown eyes once again and said mysteriously, 'Just passing thoughts, that's all, Mr Gibson.'

'Call me Andrew, please,' he begged. 'Well, I won't ask

you what they are, or offer you a penny for them. Perhaps it's better for me not to know,' he said with a laugh. 'Thanks again, anyway. I'll see you later.'

And he was gone, leaving Laura still with the feel of his smooth male skin under her hands and his gorgeous white smile. She was buoyed up for the rest of her very busy day by this encounter with the sexy Andrew Gibson and every time she thought about him, she wondered what it was that attracted her so strongly. After all, she and Steve had been an item for two years now and were hoping to move on together to the new cruise ship, the *Borealis*. There was no reason for her to consider another guy. It's not as though I'm on the look-out, she thought as she finished off yet another manicure, this time with dazzling imitation gemstones and diamanté stuck on the surface of the customer's trendy green nails. Well pleased, the woman left a handsome tip and Laura went to greet her next client, who wanted the inch-reducing body-wrap treatment with mineral-rich mud from the Sea of Marmara. This meant she was busy for the next hour, trowelling on the mud and wrapping the woman in plastic, taking measurements of her vital statistics before and after the treatment, to prove significant inch loss.

But even the busiest day is finally over and she eventually met up with Fiona as both girls got back to the cabin in time for a shower and a change into their evening clothes.

Fiona threw herself on to her bed and groaned aloud. 'Oh, Laura, what a day. I don't know about Captain Browning's party. Just at this moment, I could do with an early night, never mind a social evening. Everyone wanted a special hairdo today. It's murder trying to please everybody.'

'I know what you mean,' Laura said sympathetically.

'I'll make some tea while you're getting ready and you'll soon feel better. What are you going to wear tonight?'

'I thought my lilac-coloured dress with the sequin embroidery and the matching glittery sandals,' Fiona said shyly. 'Elinor suggested it. After all, most of the women will be in black. We'll have to wear something different to stand out from the crowd.'

'That's true,' Laura said, getting out her own evening dress, which was a slender scarlet sheath.

As she rummaged in the bottom of the wardrobe for her shoes, a sudden thought struck her and she said lightly, 'I didn't know you were that pally with Elinor, Fiona. What brought that on? Did you know our Borstal Betty before you came on the ship? I can't imagine the iron maiden ever having a girlie discussion about what to wear with the likes of you and me.'

Fiona blushed up to the roots of her hair. 'As a matter of fact, we met in London, when I was doing my training. And it was just a casual conversation,' she said. 'You know, at break time. I asked her what she thought. She's not all that bad when you get to know her,' she finished defiantly, and disappeared into the bathroom suddenly, as though to cut short the discussion.

Laura gazed after her speculatively. There was definitely something more than met the eye, she thought, but Fiona was evidently not prepared to confide in her. Whatever the relationship, it was Fiona's private business and Laura shrugged and got on with her make-up.

The crowds of passengers on first-sitting dinner were already thronging the corridor as the two girls made their way to the Santorini lounge. One of the bands, a trio with vocalist, was beginning to tune up on the stage and the Filipino waitresses were collecting their serving trays, ready to circulate with drinks. Neither the Captain nor any of the officers had yet appeared, but one of the photographers had set up his station outside the lounge and the air was heavy with the smell of the various expensive perfumes and different brands of aftershave as the very well-dressed and well-heeled cruisers mustered in the finery of their evening dresses and dinner suits to meet Captain Browning and his officers.

Laura and Fiona stood rather stiffly with some of the other salon staff on the small polished-wood dance floor in front of the stage, waiting for the reception to begin. She noticed Stanley, looking tall and elegant in a short black jacket and white trousers, and he gave her a brilliant smile as they exchanged glances. He was busy circulating with a silver tray of canapés.

'Remember, we've got to do all this again for the second sitting at eight,' Laura said, as the band struck up with 'Just One of Those Things', and Fiona shrugged, laughing as another contingent of stewards arrived with trays of drinks and more savoury nibbles, compliments of the chef.

Now all the staff and officers were very much in evidence and the photographer was posing the first few couples against the artificial backdrop of a New York skyline with stars and skyscrapers. Laura could see Steve, busy behind the bar, organising glasses and cocktail shakers and giving her an occasional wave and a rather harassed grin. Then the overhead lights were switched on and the revolving globes sent out multi-coloured shafts of light to add to the atmosphere of glamour and sophistication. Captain Browning and the most senior officers were now in place and the first couples were announced by the cruise director, and then photographed as they were introduced and shook hands with the Captain. Laura and Fiona were kept busy greeting people and showing different groups to available seats and tables, then tactfully directing the Filipino bar staff to replenish drinks or refreshments where they might be needed. Laura noticed Elinor looking very relaxed for once and almost feminine in a smart green cocktail dress, which perfectly complemented her auburn hair.

'There's Elinor,' she muttered to Fiona. 'She's looking very cool tonight. I wonder who's got *her* ready? That outfit must have set her back a bit. Nice to be some people, eh?'

'I think she looks very smart,' Fiona said stiffly. 'And she's got a wonderful colour sense. Those Roland Cartier sandals are exactly the right shade of green to go with her dress.'

Feeling a little snubbed, Laura said no more, but at that moment, Andrew Gibson came up to them and said, 'Everything seems to be going well for the Captain's little do, doesn't it? He certainly seems to know how to create the right atmosphere among the passengers.'

Once she'd introduced him to Fiona, there seemed to be a bit of a silence and after a few moments Fiona drifted away to help with the drinks and they were left alone. Andrew stood in front of her with his attractive smile, the skin round his eyes crinkling appealingly as they made small talk and chattered about nothing. He was gazing at her admiringly and Laura was glad that she'd decided to wear her plain red evening dress which made the most of her slim figure. The dress was sleeveless and skimmed her body, revealing her perfect contours without clinging. It had a plain unfussy neckline, very youthful in its elegant simplicity. Most of the women present were in long dresses, but very few had the figure or complexion to wear a dress like hers.

Except Eileen Grimshaw, that is. Laura noticed her entering the Santorini lounge on the arm of a tall distinguished-looking man, who she guessed must be Reggie, and she looked absolutely stunning, Laura thought. Her dress was long and elegant in a deep-blue brocade and, being with such a tall partner, Eileen was able to wear very high heels, which enhanced the dress. It was obvious to Laura that Eileen was more than delighted with the results of her various make-up and beauty treatments. Just the way she stood up so proudly, Laura thought, and the tilt of her head as she looked about her, proclaimed the fact that Eileen was utterly confident that she was looking her very best.

As they sat down at a small table near the dance floor, Eileen gave her a brilliant smile and then said something to her partner. Laura guessed she was pointing her out to Reggie, but she had no opportunity to greet them because they were joined by other members of their table and were soon being served drinks and nibbles, as Captain Browning arrived in front of the band to say a few words of welcome and Andrew, smiling, moved away from her to join his fellow officers.

Laura just gave a little wave of acknowledgement to Eileen and then stood silent and respectful while the Captain made his speech of introduction. It was, she reflected, very well polished by now and would be repeated later at the reception for the second-sitting passengers. She had heard it, with slight variations, on several occasions already, but his audience never failed to respond to their Captain's bluff delivery and gentle jokes. They all laughed and applauded politely and, as for Laura, she looked across at Andrew Gibson and drifted off into a pleasant reverie of her own. He'd made another appointment for his massage tomorrow. She couldn't wait. As she gazed across the room to where he was standing with some of the other crew, she wondered if she could extend his treatment for a few extra sessions. It was so pleasurable to run her hands over that strong young frame, to feel the powerful muscles beneath the golden skin of his long back and to be close enough to absorb the warmth of his body and the masculine scent of him. He seemed to have driven all thoughts of Steve from her mind for the time being.

She returned to reality with some difficulty and smiled politely at various women whom she recognised as clients from the salon. By now Captain Browning was introducing his senior officers, who each joined him on the polished-wood floor in front of the stage and, at last, it was all over. People began to drift away, the staff collected up empty glasses and tidied up chairs and tables for the second-sitting guests and the voice on the ship's loud-speaker system announced that first-sitting dinner was now being served in the Patmos dining room.

Elinor seemed to have disappeared, so she and Fiona were able to take a tray of glasses to the bar and have a quick drink with Steve before the next session of the Captain's cocktail party started.

Laura never knew how the row started. It seemed to come from nowhere and appeared to be generated entirely by Steve. Afterwards, looking back on it, she wondered if some word or gesture of her own had started the disagreement between them or whether that menage à trois with the hunk had been festering in the jealous part of his brain. Whatever the cause, nothing had prepared her for the storm that followed.

The two girls had placed the tray of empties on to the counter and she introduced Fiona and ordered a couple of slimline tonics with ice. As she smiled at Steve and Fiona murmured something about it being a busy evening, he slammed down the tab violently in front of Laura and suddenly burst out with a criticism of the *Jannina*'s officers in general and then Andrew Gibson in particular.

'And what's that poncey idiot been sent to *you* for?'

he demanded belligerently. 'That's what I'd like to know. What's so special about him that he has to go to the beauty parlour for therapy? A raving poofter is what *he* is with his bad arm and his salon treatment.'

Fiona, sat on her bar stool, was transfixed with embarrassment and Laura tried to make a joke of it and get Steve to lighten up.

'Perhaps the MO's recognised it then,' she said lightly. 'And he must be coming to the right place, among all those glamorous grannies.'

Steve didn't return her smile and suddenly, unaccountably, Laura also became quite annoyed. Why should she have to laugh him out of it every time he decided to indulge in schoolboy behaviour? She usually had to turn the tide for him when he became depressed or bolshie and, up to now, she'd never questioned her role as the peacemaker. Uncharacteristically for her, she decided not to let his stupid remarks pass and said quietly, 'Anyway, I don't know what you mean.'

'I mean, I don't want my bird mixed up with the likes of him.'

Fiona got off her stool and took a few paces backwards, as if she intended to disappear altogether. Her small young face registered both disbelief and anxiety at the thought of Laura's boyfriend behaving so badly.

But Laura was made of sterner stuff than this.

'Your bird?' she said cuttingly. 'Since when have you been using rubbish expressions like *your bird*? Pardon me, but I'm not your bird. I'm not *anybody's* bird. I'm my own person, thank you very much, and it's none of your business who comes into the salon for treatment. I don't question which of the cruising bimbos you're chatting up at the bar. I don't own you and you don't own me!'

With that, she banged down her glass and walked away, closely followed by the dismayed Fiona, while

Steve stood for a few moments looking absolutely stunned. Fiona said nothing as they took up the threads of the evening again and applied themselves to their duties, in preparation for the second-sitting passengers. Laura now felt a little ashamed and embarrassed at the scene which had been played out in front of her young friend and was glad there had been no one else present at the bar, but she had no regrets. It was a matter of principle with her. Steve was free to do what he wanted and have what he wanted, both professionally and personally, but equally, these freedoms must be accorded to her as well. No probs, she thought. Fair dues, equal partnership. If they were to progress to the *Borealis* together and make a future for themselves, he must be prepared to accept her and trust her as she was, she decided soberly. She knew that he'd be sorry for the anger that he'd played out in front of Fiona. That was the down side of Steve's character, she thought, as she carried another tray up to the bar and studiously avoided looking at him. His ungovernable passions of jealousy and temper were another aspect of his capacity for tempestuous love and devotion.

'But I'm not going to stand for it,' she muttered to the sympathetic Fiona. Fiona made little noises of commiseration and concern.

'If Steve wants to continue with me, he's got to stop these stupid laddish outbursts. This isn't the first time he's shown me up in front of someone, but it had better be the last.'

6

Within half an hour, the empty Santorini lounge was ready for the next group of passengers. One of the maids appeared swiftly and ran a carpet sweeper very efficiently over the floor, while another polished each coffee table in turn. The ship's officers disappeared to the officers' mess for half an hour and the photographer returned and began setting up again. The negatives from the first-sitting passengers were already being processed by the time Laura and Fiona were back on parade for seven thirty. The same format applied the second time around, the same introductions, the same speech and jokes from Captain Browning, and the same drinks and nibbles to keep the passengers happy. But the staff were very good humoured about everything and things were soon going well. Laura exchanged a sympathetic grin with Fiona as Elinor went up to the younger girl for a brief word while the guests chattered and sipped their drinks.

One of the shoulder straps on Fiona's dress had slipped a little down her slim shoulder and she actually observed the cold Elinor reach tenderly across and adjust it for her. Now there's a turn-up, Laura thought rather cynically, still feeling raw at Steve's unexpected attack on her. The ice maiden was behaving suddenly like a fussy mum at the school concert, she thought, but she had no time to speculate because the room was now beginning to fill up. All the passengers were very interchangeable, Laura decided. This lot were very like the first. Quite a number of grey heads and black frocks, with small exquisite evening bags in velvet or sequins and all wearing expensive jewellery. There was a goodly number of baldies and Brillo soap pad hairdos, with just the occasional distinguished elderly beauty or handsome escort to add interest to the crowd. Laura saw the blond hunk again, still with the same partner, and he caught her eye and smiled. People queued up, chatting rather stiffly before the official photograph, waiting patiently to be introduced to the Captain and to have a photographic record of it.

Most passengers entered quietly and sipped their drinks very decorously during the reception. It was all pretty much the same as usual, Laura thought, waiting around while the Captain and first officer greeted the guests. She wondered how Eileen Grimshaw was getting on. They'd be on to the second course by now, she thought. She just hoped everything was going well and that Reggie really was falling in love with his wife all over again. Eileen had certainly looked the business this evening and had definitely outshone the other women at their table. And it was all my doing, Laura thought proudly. Amazing what a bit of moisturiser and some good-quality make-up can do to improve a woman's morale. Looking round at the gradually increasing crowd of guests, Laura noticed several women who could be improved by a visit to the Shangri-la. The men in their penguin outfits were all practically indistiguishable from each other and there was only Andrew among the officers who looked particularly special. She seemed to have lost sight of him for the moment, which was rather disappointing, so she figured she'd better get on with the job in hand.

The only person destined to stand out from the crowd on that particular evening was Bob Evans, who literally staggered into the room after his photograph with the Captain. He was correctly and impeccably turned out in the evening suit and bow tie, his thin hair plastered greasily against his head, but his usually pallid face was bright red and he was sweating copiously. Laura saw the two young barmaids exchange meaningful glances and no one moved towards him with a drink or any words of welcome. It was fairly obvious that he'd had plenty already as he weaved his way across the carpet towards a steward who was standing by a whole tableful of drinks. He grabbed a glass of red wine and gave a big gulp, downing half of it in one go. Then he turned, as though to get his bearings, before swallowing the rest. To her horror, Laura saw that he'd spotted her and was now lurching purposefully towards her. She hastily picked up a plastic bar tray and, pretending not to see him, busied herself putting empties on it, as though to defend herself. But it was useless.

He stood very close to her, grinning foolishly and speaking rather too loudly.

'Why hello, Miss Barnes, Laura, I should say, now that you've rubbed my body with oil and we've got to know each other. May I say, Laura, you're looking very swish and shexy this evening in that lovely dresh? That massage you gave me, sensual, wasn't it? Well it certainly turned me on. I'm yours any time you want me. How about it?'

He leaned closer still and she could smell the stink of whisky on his breath as he tried to take her hand. But Laura was quite an experienced operator as far as inebriated gentlemen were concerned. She smiled politely and looked round. Then she stepped backwards smartly, while continuing to hold the tray before her in exactly the same position, with the result that he reached into thin air, overbalanced and knocked several glasses off one of the coffee tables. Two of the bar staff came up immediately to pick up the pieces and wipe up the mess, while Laura stood where she was, looking at him calmly and dismissively without saying anything. Andrew Gibson now appeared from nowhere and with a gentle hand on Bob Evans's elbow, he guided him to a seat and reassured him soothingly that everything was fine but that they must give the staff time to clear up.

'Miss Barnes is on duty at the moment, sir,' he said smoothly, 'but one of the waitresses will serve you with some canapés and macadamia nuts. Perhaps a soft drink, sir?' Andrew suggested. 'It's nearly time for dinner and I'm sure you'll be served a choice of wines at your table.'

Bob Evans had the grace to look abashed and sat down very meekly, but still with a defiant glance around, trying to seek Laura's glance and smile ingratiatingly at her, but Laura wasn't heeding him. She had eyes only for Andrew, who had already gone up even higher in her estimation after this uncomfortable little episode.

Most of the passengers were too busy talking among themselves to notice Bob Evans's fall from grace and those who did notice him made a point of tactfully looking away and pretending not to see. Captain Browning and most of the senior officers departed at this point and Laura smiled gratefully at Andrew, who returned her smile with a conspiratorial wink as he left the room. She was very aware that Steve had observed this whole scenario and, even from a distance, she could see the scowl of displeasure on his face. Poor Steve, she thought. He just hated the idea of one of the punters entertaining unprofessional ideas in her direction, but he was obliged to stay where he was, unable to come to her rescue or help in any way and, at the same time, he had to witness the handsome second engineer intervening so successfully on her behalf. No wonder he wasn't a very happy little bunny, Laura thought. She tried to look reassuringly towards him, but felt it wasn't convincing. Steve was obviously angry and frustrated that the bar was so busy and he couldn't come across and speak to her and that she didn't need him anyway.

She was pleased when the ship's entertainments manager finally announced dancing in the Crow's Nest bar and the voice on the ship's loudspeaker system informed the guests that second-sitting dinner was now ready. Leaving Bob Evans still slumped on his deeply upholstered lounge chair, Laura helped the young stewards to pile glasses and surplus food on to the trays and clear them away before going in search of some food herself. She had now given up on Steve. Not only was he still obviously in a filthy humour but, judging by the way the crowd was still heaving at the bar, he wouldn't be free at any time this evening. Laura decided she'd have a quiet meal in the mess bar, as even Fiona seemed to have vanished. Tonight, the menu in the staff canteen included lamb cutlets and Laura suddenly realised she was very hungry. There was now no sign of Andrew Gibson and she could no longer see Steve, so she drifted off and made her way down to the mess room on her own. She walked along the corridor on C deck, dragging her feet slightly, feeling all at once unaccountably tired and rather weary.

One of the utility room doors was open slightly and as she was about to walk past it, it was opened even wider and Steve leaped out, seizing her and dragging her into the little room, where ironing boards and cleaning materials were kept. Suddenly, unexpectedly, he was standing at the back of her, ever so near and in a very confined and claustrophobic space. He kicked the door to behind her and she was aware of his heavy breathing as he ran a finger down her neck and the bare back exposed by her sexy evening dress. Laura felt the effect of his touch as though it were an electric shock shooting down her spine.

'Your back feels very tense, sweetheart,' he whispered. 'You need an aromatherapy massage, don't you?'

She could hear the sarcasm in his voice and, in spite of his quiet tone and gentle stroking of her skin, she shivered as he hissed, 'That bastard! Who the hell was he? What did he mean by massaging his body and getting to know each other? How many more are you seeing to in the bloody Shangri-la? *Shagri-la*, more like.'

Laura felt suddenly helpless and unable to respond adequately. Unusually for her, the emotional turmoil of the last couple of hours had wearied her and the last thing she wanted was a confrontation with the man she loved in this cramped store room, jammed as it was with window leathers and mop buckets. His breath was fanning the back of her neck as he made an ineffectual effort to control himself and when she didn't reply, he spun her round roughly, so that they were facing each other.

Laura stared at him silently. After all the time they'd spent together, she'd seen all Steve's different personality facets, his playfulness and humour, his tender sexuality, the seriousness of his ambition as well as the immense strength of his love for her and she'd thought she knew him well. At this moment, she wasn't sure that she knew him at all. She looked up at him with a question in her eyes. He looked so handsome with his familiar, slightly untidy dark hair and the glint of passion in his hazel eyes.

'Steve,' she finally managed to gasp. 'Where did you spring from? I thought you wouldn't be able to leave the bar all evening.'

To say that she was surprised at his sudden appearance was an understatement, especially after the scene in the Santorini and Laura didn't know whether to be flattered or annoyed.

'Got Jason to cover for me for half an hour,' he muttered briefly. 'I had to see you, Laura. Had to have you. Had to make sure you're really mine, even if it is only for a few minutes. I can't stand the idea of you touching old creeps like that drunk fellow and that frigging Gibson.'

'I haven't –' Laura started to say, and she got no further because he gave her no chance to reply, but crushed her into his arms with an almost frantic urgency. Throughout their relationship, Steve had always been considerate as well as passionate and Laura wasn't used to this sort of frenetic kissing. Steve's belief in 'ladies first' had always been a controlling factor in their sex life, but this kiss had nothing to do with principle – it was based on pure lust. There was neither the time nor inclination for unhurried, considered lovemaking. He brought his lips down savagely against hers, pressing them so powerfully that they felt crushed and painful. Laura began to tremble as he forced her lips open to take in his probing thrusting tongue.

He raised his head from the kiss for a brief moment and said thickly, 'Say you love me. Say you want me as well. Oh God, Laura, say you want me as much as I want you. Say you can't stand that piss artist either.'

'No of course not,' she faltered. 'I've given him no encouragement. You can't believe that of me, surely? But Bob Evans and Andrew are clients. You know I have to do my job.'

'I know, I know,' he gasped out shamefacedly. 'It's just that since ... since that bloke and us did ... well, you know ... I feel like I'm a spare part in your life.'

She put one hand on his neck to try to comfort him, very much as a mother comforts a small child, and he bent his lips to hers again, murmuring endearments and taking in her well-remembered perfume and then burying his face into her shoulder, the better to breathe in her scent, heavy with the sensuality typical of the Dior perfume. His whole posture seemed to be registering shame at his earlier outburst, but Laura could feel his heart thudding against her with a strength and power which seemed to express all the excessive energy of his male sexuality.

His excitement gradually infected her too and she began to forget her resentment and tiredness as she responded to the urgency of his need. He found her lips again and when they paused for breath, Laura tipped her head back, exposing her long neck and bare, deep cleavage, which he began to cover with passionate kisses, so that she tingled and shuddered all over with the desire to be fucked.

His hands moved down either side of her slim body and then up again to find her breasts, cupping them through the thin fabric of her evening gown and kneading them with his fingers until Laura was alight with these delicious caresses, her hunger entirely forgotten.

'Tell me you love me,' he muttered thickly. 'Tell me you want me now.'

He didn't give her a chance to reply but reached behind her and pulled down the long zip of her evening dress, slipping it off her shoulders to reveal her voluptuous bosom. She wasn't wearing a bra and as the cloth brushed past her nipples, they stuck out proudly, all stiff and pert from the contact with the silky material of the dress. He tossed the scarlet sheath carelessly over one of the metal clothes horses and then ran his hands down her body to find the elastic waistband of her tiny panties, then dragged them down over her hips until she was completely naked. Laura shivered with the sudden coolness of the room after the warmth of the Santorini lounge and pressed herself closer to his warmth. Steve's body was tense with the unease of the evening's events, his barman's dark trousers and turquoise tunic stiff and unyielding.

In spite of the limited space, she began to undo his tunic buttons and trouser zip. This seemed to excite him uncontrollably and he threw off the tunic himself and kicked off his trousers and pants violently, eager to be even closer to her. Now they were both naked and her breasts were crushed hard against him as they tongued each other's mouths, pressing and releasing each other and then intertwining tongues yet again.

Steve was now so stiff, his cock reared up on to her belly, hard with desire as he pressed and squeezed her breasts, cupping them and sucking at her swollen nipples as though he literally meant to devour her. All the while he was pressing her further and further backwards until finally she folded, reclining awkwardly on the floor and then there was nowhere else to move to. In the very restricted floor space of what was virtually a broom cupboard, it was impossible for them to lie side by side and Steve heaved her feet up on to the white sink, opening her legs wide and crouching between them so that he could still hold on to her magnificent tits. Laura's hands were caressing his body, trying to soothe him, urging him on and offering herself for his pleasure, all at the same time, until Steve could wait no longer.

With no preliminaries, he thrust himself into her unprepared body. Her pussy was unbelievably tight and Laura had to raise her legs even higher against the cold porcelain to accommodate the strength of his onslaught. Gradually, she began to envelop him in their usual rhythm, moving forward to meet him as he pushed himself into her, then pulling back before he pounded even harder. Now he grasped her even closer, squeezing her unbearably tightly as he pulled her towards him to bury his cock deep inside her yet again.

Laura pressed her face into his neck so that her gasps of pleasure were muffled, desperate that no one should hear them from the corridor, and she dug her nails into the flesh on his shoulders, clawing him with the urgency of her desire for him, which made him grind her even more savagely.

They both forgot their surroundings, the dismal cramped space, the smell of cleaning fluid and spray polish, even the icy cold of the porcelain sink, as their movements built up to an almost impossible intensity of pleasure. They were so close, it seemed impossible to get a piece of tissue paper between them, yet somehow she managed to push her hand down and find her crotch, pressing her clit and rubbing it gently in time to his thrusts. Her climax came suddenly from nowhere and she threw back her head in ecstasy. Moments later, Steve gave a great shout of satisfaction as he throbbed and exploded inside her. For a few seconds they both shook and trembled together, still tense with the need to be silent, and then they lay still, listening to each other's breathing and the thumping of their heartbeats. They held one another tightly, eyes closed, as their pulses gradually settled down and they became calm again, absolutely satisfied.

It was Laura who came to her senses first. Aware of the noise that Steve had made and the discomfort of something digging into her back, she raised herself slowly and painfully from the hard floor. She eased him gently away from her and reached for some paper towels to wipe herself.

She felt the fatigue which often follows sex as she picked up the red dress slowly and rolled up her discarded panties into a small ball. She turned towards him and was surprised to see the shaken expression on his face and the almost dazed way that he searched for his clothes on the tiled floor and pulled them on.

They should now be lying in each other's arms, she thought, giving each other time to cool down from the heat of their passion, time to calm the storminess of their emotions, the hurrying heartbeats of their shared excitement. Instead, they had to concentrate on getting decently dressed before leaving the scene of their hot and unexpected burst of sexuality. It certainly couldn't be called lovemaking, she thought. Not this hurried quick scuttle in a broom cupboard. She did up her dress and watched as he smoothed down his uniform and mechanically ran a small comb through his hair.

'I've got to go, Laura,' he gasped, holding her to him closely for one last kiss. 'I'll see you tomorrow. Say you love me,' he said again, suddenly pushing her away so that he could look into her eyes.

'Of course I do,' Laura said rather unsteadily, but truth to tell, for the first time in their relationship, she didn't feel convinced about her own feelings. Perhaps it was just emotional reaction to his outburst of anger or the speed of their passionate encounter. Maybe even his possessiveness when he recognised that she fancied the handsome Andrew Gibson, but whatever it was, there was a small voice of calm within her which told her that her feelings towards him had changed, perhaps for ever.

In spite of her lack of conviction, Laura smiled at him and kissed him on the lips before he left her and hurried back to the Santorini bar. She already knew in her heart that it was all over between them.

7

There seemed to be such a coolness between them after their tempestuous session in the utility room and, thinking about it, Laura was quite ashamed of the way they'd acted. Suppose someone had come in and caught them at it, she thought to herself with a shudder. The blond stranger, for instance. It didn't bear thinking about. There were no phone calls or messages from Steve and she wondered if he too was a little bit regretful at giving way like that.

At coffee time, she saw the blond hunk again. He was strolling outside the salon as usual and, as Laura passed him, he gave her a friendly smile. 'Hello again,' he said, and stopped in front of her.

He must be at least six foot four, Laura thought as she smiled back at him rather uncertainly. She felt uncharacteristically shy. 'Hi,' was all she good manage, but he wasn't to be put off.

'Fancy a coffee?' he said.

'Yes. Er . . . I was just going to the coffee shop in the leisure centre.'

'Sounds like a good idea. Mind if I join you?'

'No, not at all,' Laura answered, suddenly very intrigued.

'I'm Tom Walton, by the way. You're Laura Barnes, aren't you? I asked at the desk.'

They ordered coffee and sat down at one of the little bistro tables, facing each other. Gazing into his bright blue eyes, Laura said on an impulse, 'There seems to be a lot more younger and trendier people on board this trip. I don't know why. The usual golden oldies are still queuing up for the beauty treatments, as usual, but we've had a number of women in their twenties and thirties. Some men too.'

He nodded and said, 'To be honest, I wasn't turned on by the idea of a cruise, but my wife wanted it, so I agreed to give it a whirl. I'm glad I did.' Once more, he gave his slightly mocking smile. 'We're only just picking up the pieces again after we were nearly divorced.'

So he was married. How smug of him to casually throw that into the conversation! Still, what did she expect from an egomaniac like that? He'd pulled a number on her in that cabin, and now he was rubbing her face in it. He must be in his thirties and Alpha males like him were always snapped up quickly. Aloud, she said, 'That must be tough, facing a divorce, I mean. What do you do?'

'I'm a solicitor, and my wife's an area manager for a swimwear firm. Works away from home quite a lot. That was one of the problems, I suppose. We'd been married for nine years and had no children. Other people's babies seemed enough for Emma and I was working all hours, trying to get further with my career. Emma worked in the evenings sometimes, because the swimwear is custom-made and clients aren't always available in office hours. I never realised how far apart we'd grown, until ... until one night, I came home and found I'd a very successful career but a failed marriage. I caught my wife in bed with someone else – another woman as it happens. They never heard me come in. When I opened the door, Emma was lying on the bed naked except for black glossy stockings with a pair of black patent leather shoes and tight black suspenders that pulled at the flesh of her thighs. Her legs were hooked over her lover's shoulders, the stiletto heels digging into his bare back. I say "his", because he was kneeling over her stark naked and could have passed for a man anywhere. It was hard to take in at first. With close-cropped hair, no breasts to speak of and a pink dildo strapped around her, she was, in effect, a man. Emma was obviously very excited and I could hear her moaning with pleasure, the dirty bitch.'

'So, what did you do?' Laura asked, trying to suppress a giggle. That explained a lot. Also, in her line of business she was well used to men whose wives didn't understand them, but she was intrigued with his story, all the same.

Tom's sparkling eyes changed to icy blue chips. 'I just said, "Good evening, Emma," and the result was electric. They both sat up in bed and pulled the dildo out, all pink and glistening with Emma's juices, and then there was the mother and father of a row.'

Laura took a sip of her coffee. 'It must have been a terrible shock to all three of you,' she murmured, laughing to herself at the expression she could imagine him making.

'It certainly was,' Tom said. 'I won't bore you with all the details, but we didn't get divorced. After all the dust had settled, I decided what was sauce for the goose would suit me as well. We discussed it calmly and neither of us was keen to end the marriage with all its plus points. We agreed that we could use Emma's relationship as a starting point. Sex is terribly important to both of us. We both need it and we both want it. We started to place discreet adverts in contact magazines, for willing female partners who could satisfy me *or* Emma, while the other one watched. So far, it's been very successful. We both still love each other, but we like a varied sex life. It's not possible to make those sort of contacts on board a ship. Too risky for one thing and there isn't time to set it up. Except,' he said, rather less confidently now, 'that after the other night, I had the idea *you* might be a kindred spirit. I've told Emma about you. She's longing to meet you.'

He stopped for a moment and took a drink of his coffee, looking at her quizzically over the rim of his cup. Laura felt a familiar excitement, a stirring between her legs at the whole idea, but said cautiously, 'I suppose there's no harm in meeting your wife.'

'Exactly.' He smiled. 'You can see what the set-up is and you don't need to do anything you don't want to. After all, we're adults. How about coming to our cabin for a drink? Tonight? Tomorrow? Cabin 36, B deck.'

'OK. Yes. I'd like that,' Laura said bravely, wondering how the hell she was actually going to play this one. 'But I've got to get back to work now. I'll get in touch a bit later.'

He stood up politely, his blue eyes gleaming like glass, as she drained her coffee cup and hurried back to the Shangri-La.

When Eileen Grimshaw came for her facial, Laura was still thinking about the conversation with the solicitor. She was also thinking about Steve – and what she was going to do. For the moment, she was very pleased that he'd not contacted her. She was confused about her change of heart, if indeed it was a change of heart and not just a passing phase. Could she be falling out of love with him? It seemed unlikely. After all, they were so ideally suited. Both had the same desires and ambitions. Sex with Steve was so great and always had been. They were used to each other, but didn't take each other for granted. What was the problem then? She shook her head and decided not to think about it. She fancied the idea of a threesome with no strings attached. Despite her nervousness at the thought of a threesome – and with a woman as well – she'd definitely make an effort to contact the high-flying solicitor, Tom, and his wife, she decided.

She cleansed and soothed the older woman's face with aromatherapy oils and gentle massage, but she was doing it quite mechanically and not giving her usual close attention to her client. Eileen too seemed a bit quiet.

In an effort to make conversation, Laura finally asked, 'And how did you enjoy the Captain's reception party? You looked really lovely last night and I thought Mr Grimshaw was so handsome. I hope everything's OK now and that you're enjoying life. Your dress was absolutely gorgeous, Mrs Grimshaw. That colour really suits you, you know.'

Eileen appeared not to be listening to this gentle chat, but suddenly burst out with, 'But things are no better, Laura. It doesn't seem to matter what I do, I can't get through to him. I've tried my very best, but he still doesn't want me – in that way, I mean. It seems that side of our marriage is over. He's shut up shop, for ever. I don't know what on earth to do.'

Laura watched helplessly as tears the size of peas rolled down Eileen's cheeks. She felt somewhat inadequate in the face of the older woman's obvious distress and couldn't think of a single thing to say, so she contented herself with murmuring comforting little noises while she wiped the tears away with a tissue and hastily applied Eileen's face pack.

Finally, when she produced the mirror to show Eileen the effect of the facial, she squeezed her hand and whispered, 'Try not to worry. We'll work something out, you'll see.'

But what it was that she could work out, Laura didn't

know. It seemed an impossible situation and she couldn't for the life of her think of any way of resolving it and making things right between Eileen and Reg. As always, Eileen left a large tip for her, but her whole body language as she left the salon was one of dejection. What on earth could she do to help a relationship like this? Laura wondered. Yet one thing was certain, she really did want to do something. She liked Eileen, even though she was so much older than herself. She admired the other woman's quiet elegance and her generosity of spirit. If only she could do something to help her marriage. But what? She looked at the appointments book and noticed that Eileen had booked an algae body-wrap treatment for Friday afternoon. Perhaps she'd have thought of something by that time. She glanced further down the page and was very relieved to notice that Bob Evans wasn't on her list of appointments for today and that her next client was in fact Andrew Gibson. At least he'd take her mind off Eileen's problems, she thought as she greeted him with a friendly smile. He was looking as handsome as ever as he strode into the Shangri-la and Laura's heart gave a small but significant lurch as he removed his shirt and made himself comfortable on the couch. Today, he was booked in for a back treatment as well as the massage on his hand.

She slid her oiled hands on to his warm smooth back. She could feel the strong beat of his heart and the well-defined muscles beneath his tanned skin and longed to experience the power of his strong young body. Having him lying there, helpless, with his head down, she was able to observe him more closely. He was well over six feet tall and not at all skinny. His limbs were long and straight, she guessed they were quite strong. Laura found it very pleasurable to stroke his lithe manly body and gave herself up to the sheer sensual pleasure of massaging his shoulders and back. Starting in the centre of his spine, she let her hands press outwards and radiate towards his neck, sliding her thumbs down his vertebrae and starting the movement again a little lower. She could feel the gradual reduction of the tension in his muscles and the audible release of his breath as he submitted to her touch.

'Mmm,' he said dreamily. 'That feels good. Really good, Laura. You seem able to hit the exact spot as far as my pulled muscle goes.'

And I know what other sort of spot I'd like to hit, Laura thought, tingling slightly as she imagined stroking him more intimately, but that would be most unprofessional, she chided herself. If I were a doctor, I'd be struck off for that.

Out loud she said, 'How have your arms and hand been? Are you still getting any pain? Cramp? Pins and needles?'

'A bit of tingling,' he said. 'But only when I'm lying in bed.'

He raised his head suddenly and turned to look at her over his shoulder, with a most wickedly sexy grin. 'When I'm lying on my own, I should add!'

His mouth was suddenly on a level with Laura's right breast and she drew back hastily, but not before she had brushed against his lips with the gentlest of friction between them.

'No, seriously.' He smiled, lowering his head again. 'Everything's so much improved, all due to your healing touch, I expect the quack'll have me doing press-ups in a few days and I won't be able to come to the Shangri-la any more. But I'll miss you ministering unto me, Laura. It's so relaxing and therapeutic, what you do. I thought I'd never use my right hand again, I can tell you, after that pratt dropped the fender on me.'

Laura realised then how much she liked him and how much she looked forward to their little sessions. She didn't want them to end. She was aware of a sudden increase in her heartbeat and a quickening in her breathing. All sorts of ideas to delay the speed of his recovery flashed through her mind as she continued to stroke him and enjoy feeling the rippling muscles of his strong sinuous back. None of her schemes had any credibility and Laura smiled to herself at her foolish daydreams. They were both silent while she continued the massage. Many clients went to sleep at this point and he was so quiet, she wondered if Andrew had, in fact, dozed off. But he obviously hadn't.

'Tell me something about yourself, Laura,' he demanded suddenly. 'Where are you from and where do you hope to be going?'

'Well,' Laura stumbled. 'I'm twenty-four and I've been on the *Jannina* for nearly six years. I love the work and I've applied for a more senior job on the *Borealis*. I've not heard anything so far though. How about you?'

'Oh,' he said slowly. 'I'm not very interesting. I'm twenty-nine. I studied engineering at university, but I've always fancied a life at sea and did a course at naval college before I got my first job on one of the old P&O liners. This is my first experience as an engineering officer.'

Judging by his accent, he'd probably been to public school, she guessed. Laura imagined him in an all boys' school, being very physical and playing rugger. Covered in mud and sweating with exertion, he'd go with the others for a communal shower, she thought, his lovely young body wallowing in the warmth and comfort of the water. She almost had to cross her legs to smother her desire at the image of Andrew naked and ready for it.

'Get a grip, Laura,' she told herself. He's probably fixed up already with a girl in every port. Aloud she said, 'Can you sit up for me now, Andrew? I've finished the massage on your back, so I'll look at your arm and hand.'

She put a folded towel on the trolley and he obediently placed himself in the chair opposite her and put both hands out for her inspection.

He was still naked to the waist and Laura couldn't help noticing anew his strong muscle structure and the taut healthy flesh of his torso. She dipped her fingers into the aromatherapy oil and taking his right hand in hers began to stroke it from wrist to tip with long firm movements. For some unaccountable reason she felt shy about looking him in the face, but was very much aware that he was gazing intently at her.

'I'm serious,' he said softly. 'I really don't want my treatment to end. The sessions with you have become so precious. I'll do anything to prolong our time together.'

At this point, Laura did raise her eyes to his and, with a wicked sparkle, he said, 'I'd even think it was worth it to have a fender dropped on my other hand.'

She was obliged to laugh, but then she lowered her gaze and began to run her hands up his smooth muscular arms, gently kneading the tense muscles, all the while very conscious of his nearness.

'I mean it, Laura,' he said quietly. 'Can't we get together, you and I? We reach Tenerife at midday. Don't you have any time off? How about lunch with me?'

'Well ... I ... Yes. Of course I have time off,' she stammered, feeling almost embarrassed at his intensity.

'Will you have lunch with me today then?' he asked promptly. 'An old friend of mine has a super little bistro in Santa Cruz. The Abona. The food's simple, but absolutely marvellous. Fresh fish, salads, fruit, that sort of thing. How about it? I know you'll enjoy it.'

Laura had always liked Tenerife, an island of such luscious contrasts that she felt she'd never be able to take in all its many varieties of landscape. It was such a complex place, she thought, with its range of tourist facilities and, at the same time, its long history right from the time of the Spanish conquest. And she was tempted. It would make a nice change to go ashore and be wined and dined by such a personable young man. Fiona was working in the salon all afternoon. Steve was on duty in the Santorini bar until ten o'clock this evening. What harm could it do? After all, they sailed for Lanzarote at midnight and she'd be working in the Shangri-la tomorrow.

'Well, yes, all right.' She smiled. 'Where shall I meet you?'

'The gangway'll be set up on deck two,' he said. 'They'll be ready to check people off from about twelve fifteen. I'll see you there with your boarding card at twelve thirty.'

The arm massage was over. He stood up and she helped him on with his shirt. He turned, giving her another brilliant smile. 'It's a date then,' he said, looking deep into her eyes and holding her gaze.

'Yes. See you at twelve thirty,' she promised, feeling rather weak at the knees as he strode out of the salon with a friendly wave.

She glanced at her watch. It was already eleven o'clock. Thank goodness no one else was booked in for this morning. Most of the passengers would be going ashore anyway.

Fiona was startled when Laura appeared suddenly in the hairdressing salon and whispered rather breathlessly, 'I'm going ashore, Fiona. Unexpected lunch date. I'll see you this evening.'

Fiona carried on rolling the client's hair on to the foam rollers and looked at her questioningly.

'I'm going out for lunch with Andrew Gibson,' she explained.

For some reason she continued to whisper as though it were a secret. Which I suppose it is, she thought. She saw that Fiona's client was straining to hear what was being said and hastily left the salon, saying, 'Bye then. See you later.'

'Yes, of course. Have a nice time,' Fiona said mechanically and stared after her, totally bemused by this turn of events as Laura tore down to the cabin to get showered and changed.

By eleven thirty, the *Jannina* had docked and the port officials had completed all the necessary formalities. The gangway was in place and passengers were advised that they must have boarding passes if they wished to go ashore.

Laura, wearing a beautifully cool cream linen dress, was on time for her date and was extremely gratified to see the smile of pleasure in Andrew's dark eyes as he looked her up and down. She was also aware of the admiring glances of the crew on duty as she and Andrew showed their boarding cards and started to descend the gangway to the dockside. She was pleased she'd splashed out more than a week's wages on this designer dress, even though it had seemed horrendously expensive at the time and she'd wondered if she'd ever have the occasion to wear it. Now, she decided, it was well worth the money to look and feel so good on her first date with Andrew.

He took her elbow and opened the door of one of the yellow taxis. 'Abona Bistro,' he said, and they were whisked away almost up to the highest level of the town, to a cool, whitewashed building with stone floors and stunningly simple gardens of wooden trellising covered with bougainvillea and hibiscus. All along the steps leading up to the bar were ceramic pots of bright red geraniums. The air was fragrant with flowers.

They were met in the cool interior by Andrew's friend, Tim McGregor, and after the introductions, Laura was able to look round more carefully. There were a few people in the bar, some on the high stools, mostly English, but at a circular table under the open window there was a group of Spanish people. No one was using the tables outside, in spite of the umbrellas and awnings. It was just the wrong time of the day to sit in the sun, Laura thought. Tim brought a bottle of chilled wine and some glasses to their table and he gave Laura a friendly smile.

'And what's your job on the *Jannina*, Laura? What role do you fulfil on the luxury cruise scene?'

Tim was a huge man. He'd once been handsome, but now his belly was enormous and even his mahogany tan couldn't disguise the years of overeating and drinking which had taken their toll on his face and figure. Nevertheless, he had a good head of dark hair and bright blue eyes and seemed a most happy and contented man, at peace with himself. He had such an open and friendly smile, Laura decided she liked him.

'I work in the beauty spa,' she said. 'I do facials mostly, but remedial massage and aromatherapy treatments as well.'

Tim glanced at Andrew. 'Well, I'll tell you what,' he said with a grin, 'your young lady can massage me any time she wants.'

They all laughed at this and Laura felt completely at ease with both of them. How different his approach was from the creepy Bob Evans, she thought. Then Andrew said, 'How about a spot of lunch, Tim? What's on the menu, mate?'

The bar was beginning to fill up now and Tim led them to a side room and presented the menus with a flourish. 'The specials today are fresh grilled sardines, locally produced chicken with prawn sauce and wild tarragon, or giant crevettes with a spicy salsa and rice. Just sip your wine until you're ready to order.'

They sat opposite each other, each studying the menu. 'The crevettes sound good,' he said. 'Tim usually serves things with some warm fresh-baked bread from the bakery down the hill. What do you fancy, Laura?'

Laura was still looking at the menu and didn't answer straight away. She could feel Andrew staring at her.

She became self-conscious and said quickly, 'I'm sorry. I can't decide whether to have the sardines or the chicken. They both sound so good. What do you fancy?'

'Oh, I can think of a few things I'd fancy,' he said in a very sexy voice. 'But I'll tell you what they are when I get to know you a bit better.'

Still holding Laura's eyes with his, he smiled, silently inviting her to share his little joke. Their hands touched as they both reached out for their wine at the same moment and she drew back as though she'd touched a hot plate. Panic-stricken at the sudden strength of her feelings for him, Laura hastily decided on the chicken and made a great play of arranging her napkin as the waiter took their order.

For some reason, she felt so nervous, so unable to relax and be natural with him. She stole an anxious glance in his direction, but he continued to pour the wine and chat to her about nothing in particular until their meal was served. He sent for another bottle and Laura gradually began to relax. During the dessert of macerated strawberries with a lemon sorbet, she unwound enough to tell him about Eileen Grimshaw and her problems with Reggie. It was some time before she realised that it was not something one automatically thought of to discuss on a first date with a new man, but he was so positive, so responsive and helpful, that Laura felt as if she'd known him all her life. Finally, as the coffees were brought in, she became aware of how much Eileen's marital problems had dominated their conversation.

'So you see,' she ended rather lamely, 'I've been rather drawn in to it, but quite honestly, I don't know what to suggest to her.'

He took a dark chocolate from the glass dish and bit into it with his white teeth. 'How about a blue movie?' he said seriously.

'Well ... I ... don't know ... what ...?'

'Think about it. The old guy needs a bit of inspiration. Eileen's still game if he is. One of the chaps in the mess always travels with a bit of the Danish blue-type material. I could fix it up. No problem.'

He reached out and took her hand. 'Whatever you decide,' he said, 'is all right with me. I'll arrange it if you want.' He took a deep breath and then said, 'I'll do anything you want me to, Laura, and that's a promise.'

Good Lord, the man's incorrigible, she thought. Fancy thinking of a porn video.

But then, as she finished the last morsel of her strawberries and cream, she began to see the possibilities in the idea. She scraped the very last spoonful from her dish and, much to his amusement, licked her spoon with a delicate tongue, in the most unladylike fashion.

'Mmm, that might be an idea,' she conceded slowly.

'But where could they go to see it and who could put the idea forward to them?'

'Well, you could,' he said gently. 'You're well in with Eileen and you could leave it to her to suggest it to Reggie, couldn't you? We could set it up in my cabin, Saturday night after dinner.'

She frowned. 'Do you always have the answers to such difficult problems?' she asked coolly.

'Only when I feel thoroughly involved in the problems,' he answered smoothly.

'Perhaps you're too easily involved then,' she said, trying to stand back a little, but it was useless; she really fancied him.

'Yes, perhaps,' he said and stroked her warm cheek with two fingers.

'Perhaps I'm surprised at myself. Wanting to be involved, I mean.'

He took both her hands in his. 'If you've finished your coffee,' he said, 'let's go back to the ship and find out what video's available. Then we can take it from there.'

Looking into his eyes, Laura was forced to believe that he meant every word he said and that his offer of help was genuine.

'All right,' she said and smiled at him. He let go of her hands while he paid the bill and they went to say their farewells to Tim.

He held her hand again as they waited for the taxi. It was still only five o'clock when they were deposited at the quayside and, as they boarded, he once more took her hand and guided her this time to the lift and up to his cabin.

Laura was impressed when he opened the door and she stepped inside. It was just as big as the one she was sharing with Fiona, but had only one occupant – Andrew. It was, she noticed, very neat. No clothes kicking around, no clutter beside the single bed. Just the usual shelf with TV and video recorder and a pile of cassettes neatly stacked at the side. She looked around her appreciatively as he dialled an internal number on the bedside phone and spoke to the 'Aussie chap in the mess' who had access to the porno movie.

'So, that's settled,' he said after a brief conversation, and turned to smile at her. 'What do you think then, Laura?'

'Well, I think you're very organised, for a man.' Laura smiled back at him.

'That's rather sexist and indefensible,' he said, and lifted a hand to brush her hair back from the softness of her downy cheek. The fresh air and the wine had conspired to heat her beautiful complexion to a soft pink flush. Andrew had a sudden longing to put his lips against her skin and taste this healthy peachy glow as if it were a fresh fruit.

He smiled again as she gave him her mock disapproving look and then he leaned even closer to her until his mouth hesitated only a few inches from her own.

'What a lovely face, Laura Barnes,' he murmured. 'And have you got a lovely nature to match it?'

Although his tone was light hearted, Laura took him seriously and said in her most authentic north Manchester voice, 'What you see is what you get, kiddo. I'm the original wysiwyg and I can't be any other way.'

He leaned closer still and she tensed up as she sensed what was going to happen. She didn't move away but her eyelids were unaccountably heavier and she licked her lips nervously with the pointed tip of her tongue.

His eyes were now so close to hers that she could see the light golden glints among the dark brown of his irises, and then he slipped his arm around her waist and pulled her gently towards him. Laura didn't resist, but relaxed against him, as he brushed her lips with his own, first tentatively, and then more firmly as he became aware of her positive response. Laura's smooth full lips parted softly under his and she felt his arm tightening round her as he drew her even closer still and kissed her deeply.

'Wow,' he said softly as he drew back. It was obvious that he was somewhat shaken by the intensity of his feelings. 'How did you learn to kiss like that?'

'I suppose the same way you did,' Laura answered evenly enough, but she was aware of feeling slightly breathless.

He prepared to repeat the kiss and was just about to do exactly what he'd been wanting to since he'd first seen her when they were rudely interrupted by a buzzing at the door of his cabin.

'There's someone at the door,' Laura whispered warningly.

'I know. Damn!'

She looked away as he stepped to open it, frantically trying to smooth down her hair and appear normal. But even a blind man with both eyes closed could observe that she had the flushed, soft-lipped look of a woman who's just been thoroughly kissed.

'Hi. How you doin', Andy mate?'

It was the friend with the video, which was in a white padded envelope and was simply called *The Babysitter*. He held it out to Andrew and gazed somewhat curiously at Laura, as Andrew invited him in and, of course, had to introduce them.

'Thanks, Barry,' Andrew said. 'We thought maybe we'd show it tomorrow evening after dinner, so I'll get it back to you Sunday.'

There was a somewhat constrained silence and then, muttering, 'Well, cheerio. See you around then, mate.' Barry departed.

'I should go as well,' she started to say, but whatever excuse she was going to use was lost when he seized her again and covered her lips with his.

She clung to his shoulders to prevent herself from falling beneath the force of his kiss. She didn't even try to resist him. It was the most wonderfully hot kiss she'd ever had and she realised it was what she'd been longing for since their lunch date at the Abona. She reached up and stroked the back of his neck with her fingers and he slid his hands round her waist to pull her tightly against him.

'Laura,' he murmured in a voice that was almost a groan.

And she didn't disappoint him. She responded eagerly to his kiss, pressing herself against him as though she'd waited for this moment for ever. She felt so right for him. So perfect. He could feel the warmth of her body through the linen dress, smell the perfume of her healthy young skin and fragrant hair. He hardened immediately as he got absolutely carried away by the strength of his desire to have her naked and to possess her completely.

Once more, they were interrupted. This time it was a cabin steward with Andrew's freshly laundered white trousers.

As soon as the man had gone, Andrew began to stroke her face very gently and place soft kisses on her neck. He was so excited at this sudden turn of events. It wasn't exactly what he'd been expecting when she'd agreed to have lunch with him this morning. Nevertheless, it had been the most powerful turn-on of his life. He'd had numerous girlfriends, in more than one port of call, and yet this girl was so unexpected, so exceptionally marvellous in every way, he was sure she was the one for him and this realisation shook him up completely. At the crucial moment, his mobile phone started to bleep. He was wanted immediately in the officers' mess.

He put up a hand to touch her lips and said slowly and reluctantly, 'I'd better be heading off. The Captain wants us, like immediately.'

Equally reluctant-sounding, she said, 'I don't want you to go. Don't want it to be over.'

Again, he brushed her hair back from her face, letting his fingers twine into the thick blonde mass, and she raised her face to him again, willing him not to leave her and bring their encounter to an end.

'I must go,' he said again, and she sighed as he released her.

It must be nearly dinner time already. Heaven knows what interpretation Fiona's putting on my absence, Laura thought. As for Steve, well it was obvious she wasn't going to be able to see him until after ten this evening. So be it. For the second time today, Laura contemplated a life without Steve. Maybe it's fate, she thought as she opened the door, promising to speak to Eileen about *The Babysitter* video. Maybe it's for the best, her brain continued as she pressed her lips against his, thanking him for the lunch.

Promising to get in touch soon, she made a hasty exit.

Almost the first person she met as she approached the lift was Eileen herself, who was alone and looking quite tanned and relaxed.

'Hi, Laura. Had a nice day?'

'Yes, thanks,' Laura said without going into details. 'How about you?'

'We went on a coach tour of the island,' Eileen said. 'Now Reggie's gone for a lie down in the cabin before dinner and I'm just going to look at the photographs from the other night.'

Laura walked along with her to the studio where all the pictures for sale were displayed on large screens. She quickly spotted the obnoxious Evans, with his arm round her waist and leering at the camera. Then the old couple at the safety drill. Finally, not looking too bad considering his drunken state, Evans shaking hands with Captain Browning. Eileen had meanwhile quickly found the pictures of her and Reg at the cocktail party and was obviously pleased with them.

'Well, for once, neither of us is pulling a face and I've not got my eyes closed.' She smiled. 'We're not looking bad for a pair of golden oldies, are we?'

'You look lovely,' Laura said, and meant it. 'And your husband is very handsome, Eileen.'

A faint shadow passed over Eileen's face, momentarily cancelling out her smile of pleasure at the photos, and Laura said tentatively, 'How are things, anyway?'

'No better,' Eileen said tersely and sighed. 'Maybe I'm just being a fool, Laura. 'We've been married twenty-eight years and perhaps this is what happens to everyone. Events just overtake you and relationships change, but I'm only fifty-one, you know. I feel as if it's too young to give up on sex. I still want what we had in our marriage before. Before his op. I mean. He's always been such a stud in that department.'

She broke off and looked away in some embarrassment at her outburst and Laura put a comforting hand on her arm and cleared her throat.

'Umm ... Have you ever considered a ... a way of rekindling things with some sort of ... some sort of ... you know ... adult entertainment?'

'Sex toys, you mean?' Eileen looked dubious.

'No ... Not exactly ... But one of the chaps in the officers' mess has a porn movie, which might help things along a bit.'

Laura gazed at the photographic display as she let this sink in. When she glanced back at Eileen, the other woman was looking extremely thoughtful. At least she hasn't rejected it out of hand, Laura told herself.

'Well, why not?' Eileen said slowly. 'Why not? It could do some good and I don't suppose it'd do any harm. I've never seen a porn movie before. It'd be an experience for both of us.'

'Yes. Quite a learning curve, in fact.' Laura smiled. 'One of the officers could arrange to set it up for us. He's said that he's prepared to fix it up in his cabin, privately, you understand. But you'd have to ask Reg – your husband, that is – if he's up for it as well, before I tell him that you're interested.'

'I will,' Eileen said determinedly. 'And I *am* interested. I'll have to sound Reggie out first. In fact, I'll go now. I'm pretty sure he'll be up for it.'

She strode off purposefully, leaving Laura wondering what she'd let herself in for, but meanwhile, still feeling horny after leaving Andrew, she boldly decided to pay a visit to Emma and Tom on B deck. She tapped at the door of number 36 and waited. She could hear sounds of movement inside but it was a few seconds before anyone answered her knock. Then the door was opened by the small brunette she'd seen with Tom.

Laura's heart was beating fast but she managed a smile and said, 'Hi. I'm Laura Barnes. I've met your husband and ... and ... he thought we should meet.'

The questioning expression which had been on Emma's face when she opened the door remained for a second and then changed to a smile of welcome. 'Why, yes. Of course. Come in. It's Laura, isn't it? Pleased to meet you, Laura. Tom's just popped out to get some wine. He'll not be a moment. Please sit down, Laura.'

She looked admiringly at Laura's expensive cream dress. 'You look lovely, darling. Almost too posh to stay on board. Have you been ashore?'

'Yes, I went out for lunch,' Laura said without going into any details, and she returned Emma's scrutiny, taking in the other girl's flawless appearance. Emma's rather round face was beautifully made up, the grey eyes enhanced by the softest pink eye shadow and her full lips coloured with a pearly lip colour in a deeper shade of pink. She was wearing a white sundress and high-heeled yellow sandals. Her shining dark hair was fastened up in a pony tail.

She seems very warm and welcoming, Laura thought, and she looked around her appreciatively. Cabin 36 was, in fact, one of the luxury suites on the *Jannina*. It had a reception room, luxurious bedroom with en suite, complete with bath, and even had its own private balcony with sun loungers and a drinks trolley.

'I hope you don't mind me coming round like this,' she said, 'only Tom – your husband – said . . .'

'I don't mind at all. In fact, that's what we both wanted. An informal visit. Just a chat and a glass of wine. Then no one gets offended. See if you like us. See if we like *you*. Well, I know Tom likes you already. He told me.'

Laura blushed. I guess that's not all he's told her, she thought, thinking of their early tryst. Aloud, she said, 'Good. I'd like that, Emma.'

They sat in the reception area of the suite, on two identical small settees with a glass-topped coffee table between them. After the close confinement of her shared cabin, this was luxury indeed, Laura thought. The décor and the curtains were of the highest quality, the brocade of the seating picked out the palest cream of the patterned curtains. The carpet was a deeper biscuit shade. The pictures on the walls were original limited edition prints by modern artists and, although chosen to blend in with the colour scheme, were interesting abstracts. Very tasteful. I could live with this, Laura thought, and the idea came to her that one of these days she'd be cruising as a paying passenger and not just as a beautician.

As though reading her thoughts, Emma said, 'You're a beautician, aren't you?'

'Yes, I work in the Shangri-la Health and Beauty Spa.'

'I thought so. Your skin's so lovely. You're a good advert for the beauty parlour, Laura.'

'Thanks,' Laura said.

They both looked up as the door opened and Tom came in with two bottles of wine. 'Hello again, Laura,' he said, and went to get three glasses from the drinks cabinet.

'Would you like some wine, Laura?' Emma asked her. 'Or would you rather have something else?'

'No, wine is OK, thanks,' Laura said, and Tom opened a bottle and poured some out for the three of them.

Tom and Emma seemed very much at ease, which Laura supposed was because they'd been in this situation many times before. Tom looked particularly relaxed and opened the conversation with, 'I've explained things to Laura, Emma, so you can take over now. I'm sure Laura wants to find out a bit more about us before she commits herself to joining in our games.'

Emma sat back on the sofa and stretched her elegant tanned legs out in front of her. 'I expect Tom's told you that it was through me that we got involved in this,' she said. 'I'm afraid I was really out of order, inviting Janet to the house and entertaining her in our bedroom. Tom was understandably hurt but we still love each other. In a way, our little arrangement seemed like a good way to save our marriage. I get satisfaction from my partners and Tom gets pleasure in watching us and it seems to heighten his desire for me. It leaves him with this incredible urge to have me immediately afterwards. Looking back, I can see that I've always been attracted to girls and women. Even at school, I couldn't take my eyes off the other girls in my class when we had showers after the hockey match. I realise now that our games mistress was just as interested as I was. She insisted on everyone stripping off and getting in the shower, even those who'd got a note from their mum. There were no cubicles and no shower curtains. Just rows of nubile teenagers, naked as nature intended, standing under the water jets. As for me, I didn't just like looking, I loved touching and hugging my mates, but no one seemed to think anything of it.'

'Yet you got married,' Laura said.

'Yes, I got married. Tom's very handsome and we fell in love almost at first sight. I never gave other women a thought at the time.'

'What changed it?'

'We've no children and I work for a firm which manufactures made-to-measure swimwear, body-shapers and bras, that sort of thing. Don't look so surprised, Laura. There's still a big market for them, particularly among older women and those who've had surgery.'

Laura nodded. 'So, what happened then?'

'I had to go to the apartment of a very wealthy client who wanted three bespoke bathing suits. For a cruise as it happened. She was absolutely gorgeous, tall and voluptuous, with lovely auburn hair. She wasn't the usual type of customer who needs foundation garments to disguise figure faults. She was absolutely stunning. I took her measurements and she chose the colours and designs she liked and then, instead of getting dressed, she just stood there, in her panties, smiling at me and showing her beautiful big firm tits. She asked me if I'd ever slept with another woman. I didn't know what to say. It's true I *hadn't* ever been with another woman, but I was very excited and curious at the idea. Well, to cut a long story short, we ended up in her king-sized bed. She was marvellous. Gentle and sensitive and yet passionate and sexy. She did things to me in bed that I'd never dreamed of and she really gave me a taste for same-sex lovemaking.'

'And do you still see her?'

'No. She went on her cruise holiday and met the love of her life. A young doctor from Leicester. They live together in London now. It was when I'd picked Janet up in a gay bar that Tom found out and, as he's told you, he caught us in the act. Janet was no lipstick lesbian. She made a very convincing butch. Crew-cut, square jaw, muscular body. She really was the business.'

Tom and Emma both laughed at the shared memory and Laura began to feel very relaxed and at ease with them both. She took a sip of her wine and Tom said, 'Well? Are you game, Laura? We're not offended if you don't want to know, but if you're up for it, we'll give you a good time.'

Any doubts that Laura had were dispelled by the natural good humour of both of them as they sat opposite to her, smiling and relaxed. She smiled back at them. 'So what's the agenda?' she asked.

'There isn't one,' Tom said. 'If you decide to join us in

bed, you can choose one of us as a sex playmate. If you choose me, Emma's allowed to watch. If you choose Emma, *I'm* allowed to watch.'

Laura suddenly felt very excited. 'And if I choose both of you?'

'That's an added bonus.' Emma beamed. 'So far, we've only had either straight girls or gay ones. If you choose both of us, it'll be fun for all three of us. What do you say? Are we on?'

'Definitely,' Laura said.

'What about tomorrow night? Are you free, Laura?'

'How about tonight?' Laura said softly. 'I'm free now.'

'Great.' Tom beamed. He disappeared into the bedroom, leaving the two girls to undress each other. Emma kicked off her high-heeled sandals and Laura unzipped the white sundress for her and let it fall to the floor. Emma stood naked except for a minute pair of white panties cut so high that Laura could see the creases of her bikini line. Her small shapely breasts were already excited, the nipples lengthened and red. 'Here, let me help you now, Laura,' she said.

Laura obediently raised her arms and Emma peeled off the cream dress, revealing Laura's tight white satin body and the glossy flesh-coloured hold-ups with the white lacy tops.

'Wow,' she said, 'Tom'll love these. And I do too,' she added admiringly. 'Let's go and join him.'

He was standing naked in the bedroom, his body just as sexy as she remembered it from the other night.

'Bring that magnificent pair over here,' he invited her and patted a space at the side of the bed.

Laura just laughed and said, 'No, Tom. Ladies first, if you don't mind,' and she took Emma's hand and led her to the other side of the big bed, leaving Tom to sit on the small bedroom chair, sipping his wine good humouredly and watching the two of them. As for Laura and Emma, they were in a world of their own, like two beautiful concubines disporting themselves in the harem. They weren't quite naked yet though. Emma was still in her tiny little panties and Laura was still in the tight body and her stockings. The body was cut very low and barely contained her full breasts, which swelled tantalisingly above the decorative white lace.

'You look lovely, darling,' Emma breathed. 'I wish I had a pair of tits like yours.'

She stroked the soft satin material and slid her hand up to cup Laura's left breast, squeezing the soft flesh and finding the hard bead of the nipple, while she put her other hand behind Laura's neck, pulling her closer. She pressed Laura's mouth with her own and plunged her tongue between her lips, gently massaging the other girl's tongue. Now they were both sensually tonguing each other. Laura already knew that sex with a woman was always going to be different from sex with a man, but she was struck again at how different it was. The tender sensitivity of Emma's touch, the yielding softness of Emma's body pressed against her own added so much to the sexual equation. She loved the other girl's experienced caresses, and yet she still wanted Andrew's hard cock in her vagina. She felt the familiar tingling excitement as Emma pinched her nipple really hard and the sensation travelled unerringly down to her sex. Laura gasped with the pleasurable wanting of it and, without breaking the kiss, Emma immediately slid her hand down to the crotch of Emma's teddy, stroking between her legs until Laura thrust her pelvis upwards, begging silently for Emma to undo the fasteners and touch her naked pussy.

Emma pulled her mouth away from Laura's and whispered, 'Slow down, darling. Be patient. I haven't finished with the magnificents yet.'

She moved her mouth to Laura's shoulder and began to give swift little pinching kisses as she eased down the narrow shoulder straps of the body and then released Laura's arms. She lay back against the pillows while Emma kissed every inch of the soft skin of her neck. Laura's eyes were half closed and her body shuddered as she revelled in the sensual feel of Emma's skilled mouth. Unconsciously, she thrust her breasts towards Emma's lapping tongue, but the other girl had her own pace and wasn't to be hurried. Only when she'd covered every inch of Laura's neck and shoulders with these nibbling kisses did she move her hands to the front of the body. Then she began to ease the lacy top down slowly, so slowly that Laura wanted to scream with the slowness of it. She bucked and thrust again, but Emma was not to be hurried. Silently, she carried on pulling down the top, continuing with her swift pinching kisses until, finally, Laura's beautiful breasts were fully bared.

'Wonderful. Gorgeous,' she said softly. 'They really *are* magnificent, Laura. I wish I had a pair like these.'

She leaned forward and began to kiss them all over, paying particular attention to the ends, until Laura's nipples were twice their usual size, like red juicy loganberries and her crotch was soaking wet. Her clit was now throbbing uncontrollably and she moaned helplessly as Emma smoothly and inexorably rolled the white satin past her waist, nibbling and licking every inch of Laura's responsive flesh. She kissed Laura's flat belly and then slid her hand between her legs to get at the fastenings, holding the satin with her thumbs while she slowly prised the press studs apart. Laura writhed and bucked again as Emma rolled the body further down her thighs and pulled it over her ankles and feet so that she was naked except for her glossy hold-ups. She opened Laura's stockinged legs wide and began to kiss her golden mound, holding her hips steady with both hands and using her tongue to part the blonde hairs between Laura's legs, so that nothing was hidden.

Now she held Laura's pussy lips wide open with her fingers and pressed her mouth greedily on to her, moving her tongue against Laura's clit and licking strongly and regularly, touching every sensitised nerve ending. Laura gasped for breath and her body arched with the ecstasy of her long awaited climax.

She lay still, unable to move a muscle, and felt Emma move her mouth away and lie down at the side of her. She sensed that Tom had come close to the bed and when she'd recovered somewhat and opened her eyes, saw that he was looking down at them both, holding his huge erection in his hands.

'Can anyone join?' he said jokily, and looked longingly at his wife's naked body. Emma smiled and sat up.

'Invitation only,' she said, and straddled Laura's body, her breasts dangling in Laura's face, inviting her to suck them. Laura reached up eagerly and grasped one in each hand, squeezing them both together and kissing the cleft between them, then she took the nipples into her mouth in turn and bit them until Emma gasped with pleasure.

Tom came closer and kneeled behind his wife. Her small round arse was cocked up provocatively and he stripped the little panties off her, parting her cheeks so that he could see her juicy sex lips. Laura heard Emma's grunt of satisfaction as Tom took hold of her hips and thrust his cock hard between her legs. He began to shaft into her, strongly and steadily, each stroke thrusting her breast further into Laura's mouth. Laura kept her mouth and teeth firmly on the nipple, so that each withdrawal pulled Emma's breast into the shape of a cone. Emma was beginning to whimper with pleasure as Laura moved to the other breast and slipped her hand between Emma's legs. It seemed a most exciting sensation to Laura, feeling the strong rhythm of Tom's cock pounding powerfully into his wife's sex and Emma's breast moving against her mouth in the same rhythm. She felt this was only one stage removed from having sex with Tom herself. She could feel every movement and tremor of both of them as he slammed into Emma. Laura felt her own body was on fire with their passion. She began to stroke Emma's pussy lips, which had been pushed wide open by the force of Tom's huge cock, and found her clit. Very gently and delicately, Laura brushed it with the tips of her fingers, until Emma twitched and shouted with exquisite pleasure. She felt Emma's juices suddenly pulsing and gushing against her fingers as Tom thrust strongly into his wife, one last time and they both climaxed together.

'That was so good,' Emma said to her later as Laura prepared to leave. 'When Tom described you to me, he said that you were gorgeous and sexy, but I'd no idea you'd be quite so beautiful. I'd only seen you from a distance.'

'Did he tell you how we met?' Laura asked diffidently.

'Yes,' Emma said, 'he did. He said that he'd invited you for a coffee and you'd got chatting. He didn't enlarge on it, except to say how lovely you were. We have an open marriage. No secrets and nothing hidden. It's very liberating.'

She turned to her husband and smiled. 'I bet you're glad I persuaded you to come on the cruise now, aren't you?' she teased.

'Yes.' He grinned. 'We'd never have met Laura otherwise. It's been great, Laura. Let's hope it'll continue.'

Laura murmured something noncommital, but neither of them saw it as a negative answer. They both smiled and kissed her when she was ready to go and hoped they'd meet her again.

Laura wasn't so sure. In spite of the very pleasurable experiences she'd had with them, she was acutely aware of the risks if anyone found out. Elinor, for instance, would dismiss her immediately. If she got the sack from the *Jannina*, she might never see Andrew again. Still, she'd thoroughly enjoyed being with Emma and Tom. She'd revelled in the sensual delight of Emma's subtlety and sexual experience, her soft lips and sure touch. Emma knew exactly how to pleasure another woman's body. She didn't need to be told what a woman wanted – after all, she was a woman herself. At the same time, Laura wanted a man and a man's hard, even slightly rough approach to lovemaking. Her mum would call this 'playing both sides to the middle' and Laura knew exactly what she meant. She smiled at the thought of her mum in Manchester. What did mums know about sex? Perhaps I need the best of both worlds, she thought to herself as she walked quickly to the cabin.

8

Stanley had left a couple of messages on the notepad for her. One was from Fiona to say that she'd see Laura in the mess room at eight o'clock. One was from Steve to say he'd see her in the mess room a little after ten. So that's my evening taken care of, Laura thought and hurried to get out of the posh cream frock and into her casual trousers and T-shirt, before she went in search of Fiona.

She was absolutely stunned to see her young cabin-mate having a drink with the formidable Elinor. They were sitting quite close together and Elinor pointedly moved away a little as Laura approached them, although she greeted her affably enough. It was Fiona who seemed rather embarrassed and, to cover it, she offered to buy the other two a drink.

'Not for me, thanks,' Elinor said politely. 'I want to change my book before the ship's library closes and I'm eating out later. We sail at eleven thirty, but I'll make jolly sure I'm back by then.'

Laura accepted the offer of a drink though and Elinor rose to depart, actually smiling and promising to ring Fiona when she got back. Laura was surprised at this different, more pleasant side to Elinor, which she'd never even glimpsed before in all the six years they'd known each other. She was still intrigued by this unlikely friendship between the young innocent Fiona and the hard-bitten older woman, but made no comment. Fiona came back from the bar with a slimline tonic for her and they chatted about the day's happenings in the hair-dressing salon.

Then Fiona said shyly, 'And how did your lunch date go, Laura? He's very good looking, isn't he?'

'Oh it was all right,' Laura said airily. 'Yes, I suppose he is good looking, and he's good company.'

She decided not to mention anything about the porno movie or going to Andrew's cabin, let alone her steamy session with Tom and Emma. Instead, she talked calmly about the damage to his hand. 'I expect he felt he owed me lunch, because I've improved his hand so much,' she said by way of explanation. 'And I was planning to go ashore anyway on my half-day.'

Fiona nodded understandingly. 'You don't think Steve minded then?'

'I haven't told him yet. Shan't be seeing him till later tonight,' Laura said shortly. She couldn't explain why she felt she must keep her meeting with Andrew private, but her instinct told her it was better not to talk about him at all, and certainly not Emma and Tom. After all, Steve had such a short fuse where other men were concerned and it was no business of anyone else's, she told herself. If she married him, there'd be no such open arrangement as Tom and Emma had; no secrets, nothing hidden certainly wouldn't be a feature of life with Steve. She remained silent and Fiona sensitively chose not to pursue the topic, but changed the subject, imitating some of the priceless characters who'd been in the salon that day. Her gentle mimicry and soft voice belied quite a feisty sense of humour and she soon had Laura laughing and giggling at her accurate observations of the customers. Then, out of the blue, she suddenly drained her glass and stood up.

'I'm off now, Laura. I'll see you later. I'm expecting a call from Elinor, so I'm going to the cabin.'

Laura looked up in some surprise at this hasty departure, but all she said was, 'OK, Fiona. See you.'

Behind Fiona's back, she could see Steve approaching and he didn't look very pleased. The nearer he got to her, the deeper his scowl became. She could see his fists clenching and unclenching by his sides as he strode towards her, his whole body language expressing extreme anger and irritation.

She decided not to respond to this display of aggression and stood up to kiss him as though she'd noticed nothing wrong, saying, 'Hi, Steve. Fancy a drink?'

He stood rigid beneath her embrace, not offering to smile or return her kiss, and just muttered tersely, 'Budweiser, thanks.'

She made her way to the bar, the distance between them giving her a bit of a respite from his glowering looks. She knew he must have found out about her lunch date with Andrew and while she stood at the bar, waiting to sign for the beer, she tried to order her thoughts into some reasonable way of dealing with Steve's jealous rage.

Definitely not another quick scuttle to give him the male reassurance that he craved, she thought. Certainly no lies or prevarication. After all, nothing had happened with Andrew and she'd definitely been a willing party to what happened in suite 36B. Anyway, she told herself defiantly as she walked slowly back to the table with the drinks, he doesn't own me. We're not married – yet, at any rate. She put the drinks down carefully and gave him her most open, charming smile. This did nothing to alleviate his scowl and, in fact, he immediately broke into resentful angry recrimination.

'What do you mean by going ashore with that smarmy engineer?' he demanded hotly. 'What did you think you were up to, swanning about while I was tied up in the bar, going behind my back to join another guy for lunch? And a bit of the other, I shouldn't wonder,' he added bitterly.

'It wasn't like that,' Laura started placatingly. 'It was just that –' But she didn't get a chance to finish.

'It was just that you fancied a bit on the side and I was busy in the bar,' he interrupted her savagely. 'So where did you go with this fancy man of yours? Up to one of those knocking shops in Playa de Las Americas?'

'No,' she said quietly, becoming increasingly tired of his old-fashioned attitude. 'I've told you. It wasn't like that. He invited me to lunch at his friend's bistro. I was going ashore anyway. There was nothing –'

'I'll bet there wasn't,' he snarled angrily. 'Pull the other one, darling. A chap like that doesn't invite a girl like you out on a date unless he's interested in one thing. And I'm not having it, Laura. I don't want time-wasters like him muscling in on my patch.'

In spite of all her good resolutions not to row with Steve, Laura was again stung by this kind of language.

'I'm not "your patch", as you call it,' she said coldly. 'It's not up to you to tell me who I can or can't have lunch with. I'm not married to you.'

'No, and you're not likely to be,' he ground out savagely. 'I'm not interested in slags.'

With that, he pushed away his unfinished drink and stalked out of the mess, leaving her alone, feeling humiliated and utterly demoralised. She sat for a few more moments, trying to gather herself together. Steve was very volatile, but she'd never known him to be as bad as this. She knew he'd been doing quite a lot of overtime lately, partly to impress his boss, partly to get together enough money to enable him to take a full three weeks leave before joining the *Borealis*, if he got the job that is. She sighed. He was certainly a Jekyll and Hyde. One side of him was so gentle, so humorous and supportive and sexy, and yet the reverse side was so impatient, so angry and aggressive. His irritability was worse when he was stressed or tired, she supposed. He often came round fairly quickly and in no time at all was her own lovely fella again, as though nothing had happened. But this time, something had changed, she thought.

Somehow, there was a little sneaking, secret, steely resentment inside her, which made her feel more than a little defiant. If that's how he felt, he could push off, she told herself. There was more to life than making concessions to his macho mood swings. She'd no intentions of smoothing him over and getting him back on her side again. He'd gone one step too far this time and she decided he could fall into the pit he'd dug for himself and, as far as she was concerned, disappear forever.

The bar was closing now and she supposed that Fiona had already had her promised phone call from Elinor. Once more, she thought speculatively about her enigmatic boss, then she dragged herself to her feet and made her way to the cabin. To her surprise, as she slipped her swipe card into the slot on the door, she could hear Fiona almost cooing down the phone and then, as she heard Laura enter, the hasty 'I'll have to go. See you tomorrow'-type farewell.

'Sorry, Fiona. Hope I didn't interrupt you,' Laura said.

Fiona was sitting up in bed with the phone at her ear. 'No. That's OK. Elinor was just rearranging some of my appointments for tomorrow, to fit in with the Beauty in the Sun Demonstration tomorrow afternoon. She's demonstrating five-minute skin analysis and I'm doing the hair restyle makeover.'

She placed the phone firmly back in its cradle and turned away.

'Goodnight, Laura. I'm absolutely bushed,' she said, and switched off her bedside light with some finality.

Laura got ready for bed quickly and lay for some time thinking over the events of the day. My God, everything seemed to be happening on the *Jannina*, she thought. First, her lunch with Andrew, frustrating as it was when they were interrupted. Then the gorgeous sexy three-some with Tom and Emma. Tomorrow, Eileen Grimshaw would be coming for her body-wrap treatment and no doubt would be able to say yes or no to the video. Whether she and Steve made up their disagreement or not, she wasn't going to tell *him* about any of it, or make any moves in that direction. As far as she was concerned, he could take a running jump. And anyway, she figured, video or no video, she was looking forward to being with Andrew again. As she turned off her light and snuggled down into her pillow, his was the face she saw in her mind's eye and she gave a little wriggle of pleasure at the thought of his kisses that afternoon.

Next morning, as always, Eileen was on time for her beauty treatment and was very positive about the idea of the video in Andrew's cabin.

'Reggie's prepared to give it a go,' she said enthusi-astically. 'As for me, I'm open-minded about it. After all, it might do some good and it can't do any harm, can it?'

She was lying on a large sheet of plastic on the treatment couch, wearing only a pair of disposable paper knickers, and Laura was intent on applying the mineral-rich algae with a wooden spatula over the whole of Eileen's body. Eileen was stretched out almost sacrifi-cially on the treatment couch and she was obviously enjoying the feeling of Laura's touch on her breasts and belly. Laura spread the green paste slowly and methodically, carefully avoiding the suddenly lengthening nipples. Oh-oh, she thought as she saw the tell-tale goose pimples on Eileen's skin, Eileen's finding this a turn-on. As she finished each breast, she used the edge of the spatula to scrape each nipple, as though accidentally, and saw Eileen flush slightly.

She was only half attending when Eileen said, 'We'll be with you and Andrew at eight thirty, after dinner. I hope it's all right, but Reggie's invited one of the stressed-out execs to come along with us. Is that OK, Laura?'

Laura nodded. 'I'm sure it is,' she said, not taking in the implications of this, or asking who the exec in question might be.

She moved her spatula down to Eileen's waistline and belly and began to stroke the algae across it in long slow strokes until Eileen's skin was completely covered. She made a point of opening the paper knickers slightly, so that she could run the spatula a little nearer to Eileen's mound. And Eileen twitched with pleasure, so Laura did the same for Eileen's thighs. She applied the algae from the knees upwards and opened the knicker legs slightly, to stroke a little higher up.

'Can you turn over for me?' she said, and she started on the backs of Eileen's thighs, going as high as she could, opening the knicker legs a little and going higher than was necessary to the crease of her buttocks. Then down her back, opening the waistband and smoothing the loaded spatula across Eileen's behind, before wrapping her up in the large plastic sheet.

She left her lying on the couch for the required twenty minutes while she went to look at the appointments book. Andrew didn't have a session today but there was no shortage of clients and the time passed very swiftly.

This was a day at sea and there was no contact with Steve. She felt almost relieved at that and, once more, Fiona went to have lunch with Elinor and she was left on her own.

9

Laura arrived at Andrew's cabin at eight thirty, and so did the Grimshaws. The stressed out exec unfortunately turned out to be not one of the handsome hunks, but bloody Bob Evans! Laura decided to ignore this and merely nodded to him, after brushing her cheek against Andrew's mouth with just the merest trace of an airy social kiss.

Eileen and Reggie had brought some wine and plastic glasses and as soon as they were all gathered together in the cabin, sitting on the bed and the couple of chairs, they poured everyone a drink while Andrew slipped the video cassette into the recorder and then glanced round at the audience. Eileen and Reg were holding hands, Bob Evans was nursing his wine, gazing straight ahead, and Laura was sitting quietly, hands clasped around her own wine glass and her eyes turned to the screen. There was an atmosphere of excited anticipation.

'*The Babysitter*,' Andrew announced with mock solemnity. 'If you're all sitting comfortably, then I'll begin.'

They all smiled to cover their embarrassment and Bob Evans said loudly, 'All right, Jackanory, get on with it,' and Andrew flicked the remote.

The image of a nubile young woman dressed in the sober uniform of an old-fashioned Kensington nanny filled the small TV screen. Incongruously, she was carrying a black leather shoulder bag and wearing high-heeled open-toed court shoes. She teetered across the suburban road to a Victorian terrace, which had steps leading up to the front door, and rang the bell. The dark-haired man who opened it led her immediately up the stairs to the nursery and gestured to her to take off her navy blue coat and soft felt hat and hang them up.

But this was no ordinary nursery. For a start, there was no baby, only the dark-haired man, who now stripped himself naked and put on a lemon-coloured sleepsuit in stretch terry towelling. It had built-in feet and fastened all the way down the front with press stud poppers, for all the world like a giant baby-gro. They all watched with interest as he donned a giant baby's bonnet and popped a big toffee dummy into his mouth. He leaped into the huge crib, lying at full stretch and reaching out his arms to the young dark-haired woman, but, for the moment, she chose to ignore him.

Underneath her coat, she was wearing the uniform of a professional nanny, complete with blue frock and white apron, albeit the frock was a mini and her shapely legs were encased in black glossy stockings. Her make-up was heavily applied, her eyes thick with eyeliner, quite whorish in fact. Her thick dark hair was back-combed into a 60s-style beehive; her mouth was a red gash. She walked slowly and purposefully around the room and began to pick up his discarded clothes, still pretending to ignore the giant baby lying on the plump pillows of his crib, with the covers folded back neatly and precisely. Her scent had obviously begun to pervade the bedroom and the one in the crib was definitely breathing in her perfume, very appreciatively, his head thrown back on the pillow, sucking suggestively on the toffee dummy, with his eyes taking in her every move.

As the nanny bent down to pick up the socks and underpants from the floor, the complete absence of any panties beneath the mini-skirted uniform became all too apparent. The lower curves of her rounded bottom came into full view, giving a tantalising glimpse of the twin orbs of her shapely buttocks. When she crouched to tidy up the shoes and place them neatly under the crib, the perky half globes of her generous arse now stuck out proudly, as the starchy dress rode ever higher up her thighs, revealing the tops of her hold-up stockings and displaying even more of her pale voluptuous flesh.

They could all now see the light sprinkling of pubic hairs round her back passage and the juicy lips, small and pink, as she remained poised on the floor near the crib on all fours with her knees apart. Then, slowly and deliberately, she went over to the chair. Every single nuance of her movements was done with the utmost calculation. Every glimpse, every inch of flesh revealed was carefully judged for maximum titillation. She bent only slightly this time, arranging the discarded clothing with exaggerated care before turning towards her huge baby.

Slowly, she began to unpin her white apron, letting it fall down in front of her as, deliberately tantalising, she slowly began to undo the small buttons of her prim dress. The camera lingered over her outfit which, when she pulled it open, revealed her naked breasts and hard nipples, coloured with dark red blusher and hugely pointed. She leaned towards the adult baby and pulled the dummy out of his mouth. Then she stroked a big firm breast across his sticky lips, allowing him to suck and chew on it while she slid her hand down the sleep suit to find his long thin cock.

Lightly and sensually, she caressed him through the stretch material until he began to swell and harden beneath her hand. Then, teasing him, she shifted position and stretched one leg over the low rail of the bed as she dangled the other breast into his eager mouth. He reached out trembling eager fingers to slip between the nanny's voluptuous thighs, but this was not allowed. She brushed away his hand brusquely and began to slowly undo the poppers of his sleepsuit one by one. Each time he tried to reach for her or assist in the process, she slapped him firmly away, until he was mad for her.

The sleepsuit was now open to the waist and she slipped it down over his shoulders until he was half naked. Starting just below his neck, she began a systematic nipping of his skin, using only her lips, not her teeth. She hardened her lips deliberately and worked across his body, from armpit to chest, until his skin looked red and heated. Gradually moving lower, she now stimulated the other side of his chest and nipples in the same slow, deliberate way, until he was writhing with the desire for more and tried to push her mouth lower.

Once again, she slapped his hands away and pulled the yellow baby-gro even further down, so that she could now work across his belly with her hard biting lips.

By this time he was gasping and heaving with the desire to have her mouthing him more intimately, but she merely dragged the sleepsuit down to his feet, letting his cock spring free, nipping the soft flesh of his inner thighs with her lips, first one side then the other, while he opened his legs obediently to let her have her way with him.

There was a gasp from the audience in the cabin as she finally leaned over to take his hugely erect cock between those hard biting lips, making him writhe and squirm even more helplessly. This was a silent film, without even music or sound effects, and was all the more powerful for that.

Laura took a surreptitious look round and saw that Eileen was clasping her breasts and her mouth had fallen slightly open as she gazed on the actor's massive development. Evans was openly fingering his crotch and had even forgotten about his wine for the moment. Reggie too was obviously very affected and slowly wiped his gleaming forehead on an immaculate white handkerchief. Andrew's eyes met Laura's briefly in a mockingly sympathetic glance and he raised his eyebrows and widened his eyes slightly at the effect the video was having on the other three.

A few moments later, the nanny climbed into the crib and, parting her stockinged legs, she straddled him, her bare pussy only inches from the big baby's face. Now, at last, she allowed his trembling fingers to slip between her thighs and then tilted her big behind higher still so that everyone in the cabin was treated to a close view of her moist full lips with the bright red clit protruding between them. She arched her back, pushing her naked pelvis towards his probing fingers and he explored the moist folds between her legs, thrusting gently into her willing pussy, so that her twitching, yearning clit was fully revealed. Laura heard Eileen draw a deep breath at this point and even Bob Evans left off touching himself and took an audible gulp of his wine.

Now the nanny had firmly removed his hand and was bearing down on his eager mouth, letting him lick her and lap at her with his tongue, forcing him to eat her pussy until he was almost gagging. Her big rounded buttocks were still tilted upwards, her stretched legs wide open as the camera revealed her red juicy sex and tight, closed anus, while her eager clit disappeared fully into his mouth.

Laura noted the rapt expression on Reggie's face while they all watched the magnified close-up of the nanny's steady rhythmic movements as she pleasured herself against this probing tongue. He obediently covered every nook and cranny inside and out, while she urged him on, using her fingers to open her swollen lips even further to the thoroughness of his ministrations. Then she came in a triumphant, twitching orgasm and lay still.

For a few moments she remained spreadeagled across the adult baby, panting slightly and slowly recovering. As the camera remained trained on his face, he meanwhile turned his head on the pillow, eyes closed in ecstasy, mouth wet and glistening, drenched in her copious love juices. He licked his lips slowly with obvious enjoyment and the scene gradually faded out.

Laura took a sip of her own wine and once more looked about her. Reggie and Eileen were obviously mesmerised. They'd never seen anything like this before. Bob Evans was almost slobbering. Andrew was looking at her, rather questioningly, she thought. She wondered if he expected her to say something. Faintly embarrassed, she looked back at the film.

The scene had now changed to the bathroom. Nanny was still in charge and the adult baby was soaking in the warm bath. She was completely naked and bent over the bath, soaping the baby gently from top to toe. Her big pale buttocks were fully exposed as she bobbed up and down, concentrating on the task in hand. She swung her breasts over him and he tongued them thoroughly and seductively again as she slid her soapy hands over his body, stroking and massaging his flushed shoulders and abdomen until they glistened. Once more, the huge pillar of his erection rose up from the bubbly water. It was red and throbbing and she didn't touch it, but began her usual tormenting stimulation of him.

Very efficiently, she turned him on to his side and soaped her fingers purposefully. She slid one soapy finger along his crack. The camera focused on the puckered opening of his arse as, ever so gently, she soaped her finger yet again and slid the tip into his tight opening, carefully easing it in as far as the first knuckle and then to the second, while still letting him suck at her swollen nipples.

He began to writhe and thrust himself forward and upwards, importuning with every movement for his own satisfaction, but her movements remained slow and unhurried. She now bent even further over the side of the bath to suck him off, while she let her fully inserted finger stay inside him, without moving it. Slowly and calmly, she began to lick the tip of his swollen knob, running her lips round the end of his shaft with sensual enjoyment, pressing his foreskin back gently with her rigid tongue and then taking him fully into her mouth and sucking firmly and smoothly.

He rolled about helplessly in the water, absolutely overcome with the desire to finish. He was now so obviously on the verge of orgasm that he couldn't delay it any longer, but still he had the presence of mind to grasp the back of her neck, holding her and making certain that she stayed in position with her mouth grasping him until he came fully and spectacularly into her mouth.

The nanny spluttered and coughed as he spilled his copious come down her throat and then he lay back replete, with his head resting on the end of the bath, still trembling very obviously and breathing heavily.

After a few moments she helped him up and dried him off with a large towel. She led him to the bed and covered him up, tucking him in with exaggerated care and even giving him a goodnight kiss as the scene gradually faded out.

It opened up again with the huge baby misbehaving. He was throwing his toys and picture books on to the floor and, finally, the big toffee dummy, causing the nanny to bustle in looking very displeased. She was dressed once more in her nanny's uniform and carried a short leather strap, which she tapped ominously against her thigh as she walked purposefully towards the bed.

Without ceremony, she tore the bedclothes back, revealing the still naked baby, who was pretending to cower in fear before his nanny's anger. The nanny turned him roughly on to his stomach and proceeded to crack the strap across one side of his bare bottom, again and again, until his skin was flushed and bright red. He lay quietly and passively, his face pressed into the pillows, obviously enjoying it as the first cheek became red, then bright red and, finally, scarlet under her vigorous ministrations. The flesh of his other buttock quivered and contracted briefly with anticipation as she turned her attention to the other side, slapping him with the strap even more energetically, until his flesh shook with each hard stroke of the leather.

The white skin of both his cheeks had now taken on a deep flushed colouring and looked hot and glowing and it was obvious he was beginning to harden again. He shifted upwards a little, easing his body to accommodate his obvious erection and she naturally took this as a signal to beat him even harder. She began to crack the strap straight across the crack of his behind, beating both buttocks at once until he began to wriggle and struggle against the stinging pain.

At last, mercifully, she threw the punishing strip of leather on to the floor and allowed him to turn over. The big naughty baby now had his dander up yet again and turned to get his own back on the strict nanny. Not waiting for her to take off her clothes, he pulled her into the crib and urged her on to her back. He removed the skimpy uniform, swiftly and carelessly, laying her naked on the bedsheet, except for her glossy black stockings, that is. She lay passively, just as though preparing for an afternoon nap, her legs slightly parted, her arms above her head. Only her rapid breathing and the sharply rouged points of her large nipples revealed her sexual excitement to the watchful audience. She closed her eyes and lay there obediently as he began to caress her body, his probing fingertips exploring the delicate outlines of her full breasts and gliding lower to trace light circles on her belly and the pale flesh of her upper thighs which was exposed above the stockings. Now he began to concentrate on the sleek black mound which lay beneath the nanny's rounded belly. The pubic hairs were shaved and combed into a stylised pattern, oiled and shiny, as black as her stockings. The camera lingered lovingly on this and the watchers in the cabin began to show keen interest as he spread her legs a little wider to reveal the swollen red clit just poking out between her lips.

Taking care not to touch the excited nub, he hoisted her legs further apart and raised her knees so that she was even more thoroughly exposed to the audience. The bright red slit of her pussy was now overflowing with juiciness and the shiny lubricious flow began to slowly ooze from her moist lips and down her wide-open thighs. She let her arms fall down to her sides and thrust herself towards him, ready and eager to be penetrated. He, meanwhile, was holding his huge swollen cock in one hand. There was no need for any helpful jelly to smooth things along; he merely pried her open with his fingers and spread some of her love juice along the whole length of his cock. She shivered as he opened her again and stroked the crimson flesh of her clit smoothly and firmly, over and over again, until she appeared to be beside herself with helpless lust.

Only then did he finally lower himself on to her

yearning body, guiding his massive cock expertly into her willing flesh and still rubbing her bright red clit. She wrapped her stockinged legs around his waist as he ground himself into her, urging him on to harder and swifter thrusts until he paused for a moment and pulled back a little so that he could rub her with his other hand. They both climaxed and lay still.

Once more, the scene faded out and the film ended with the usual credits and warnings of the laws of copyright.

Without looking at the audience, Andrew turned on the lights and said, 'Well, that's your lot, folks.' He began to wind the video back.

Laura was very aware of the sexually charged atmosphere in the small cabin as Bob Evans continued to openly finger his crotch. Reggie squeezed Eileen's hand more tightly before standing up and thanking Andrew for the film show and saying firmly that they really must be going to their cabin.

They said their goodbyes and repeated their thanks and departed quickly, in very good humour, Eileen promising Laura that she'd be in touch. Then, without knowing how it happened, Laura was suddenly aware that Andrew had also got rid of Bob Evans and that they were now completely on their own. She took a deep breath. The video was still whirring softly as he turned to her with his attractive brilliant smile and took both her hands in his.

'Alone at last.' He grinned, and then pulled her firmly towards him, clasping her closely before she had time to protest. 'Why are we wasting time on spectator sports like video watching, when we could be doing our own thing?'

She could smell the fresh male scent of his hair, feel the warmth of his masculine body and Laura wanted desperately to be doing her own thing with Andrew. Why think about Steve, or anyone else for that matter? He's cooled off towards me anyway, and I'll probably never see Emma and Tom again, she thought. Why not give this handsome second engineer a bit of a whirl?

He dropped his hands to her waist, his eyes still looking into hers, still questioning smilingly to see what her response would be. Laura didn't speak, but merely reached up and put her arms round his neck, smoothing down the dark glossy hair at his nape, raising her lips willingly to his. For a moment he continued to look into her eyes. It was a moment of tension, but also a moment which held the promise of something very new and powerful for both of them. Finally, he bent to kiss her, his tongue roaming against her own, flicking and darting with the strength of his passion for her.

Laura could taste the wine still on his lips as he kissed her and she stroked the soft hair at the back of his neck, over and over again, feeling the powerful muscles under her fingers. She pressed herself against him, willing him to take things further.

Instead, he pulled back, looking at her very seriously. 'Do you want this, Laura? Are you sure you want me to go ahead?'

'Yes. Oh, yes,' she breathed. 'Don't stop now ... Please ...' She gazed into his handsome face and, to prove how much she wanted him, she pushed her body even closer to his, aiming eager kisses at whichever parts of him that she could reach, trying frantically to find his mouth.

She could see that he desired her just as much, but was still in control of himself, though only just, she thought. If she wanted to back off now, she could, but she didn't want that. What she wanted desperately, urgently, was to see him naked.

'Take your clothes off for me,' she whispered to him, and stepped back a little to give him some space.

It was just then that the mobile phone on his belt began to sing and beep insistently and, with obvious reluctance, Andrew had to answer it.

'Yes, sir,' he said neutrally. 'Yes, I understand, sir. No. No problem. Right. At once. Give me three minutes. I'll be there.'

'Shit,' he said apologetically. He looked at Laura and sighed. 'Problems, I'm afraid. A small fire in the engine room. Everything's been contained and there's no danger, but I'm afraid it's all hands to the pumps at the moment. All personnel are required to report to the chief. Damn! I'm so sorry about this,' he said softly, regretfully. 'I have to go. I'm on duty for a while, but I'll be in touch soon.'

'Never mind,' she said. 'It happens. Can't be helped.' But she felt almost sick with disappointment and frustration.

He was already holding the door open for her and gave her a chaste kiss on the cheek. 'Cheers. Bye for now,' he said, and hurried off.

'Yes,' she said rather mechanically. 'See you, Andrew.'

She felt flat and let down. There were actually tears in her eyes as she slouched reluctantly back to the cabin. Perhaps she'd have an early night and read something light, she thought. When she reached the cabin, Fiona was nowhere to be seen and Laura was long since asleep before she returned.

10

'So, where were you last night, you dirty little stop-out?' Laura joked next morning.

Fiona coloured and sipped her tea without replying.

'I expect you were you on deck, charting the ship's progress to La Palma,' she persisted. 'I suppose it's all so new to you that you couldn't bear to lose a minute of the ship's schedule.'

Fiona remained silent for a few more seconds and then burst out with, 'If you must know, I was having supper with Elinor. We got talking and ... and I ...'

'Forgot the time?' Laura prompted her sympathetically.

She looked more closely at her young cabin-mate and noticed the light smudges of navy blue under her eyes, the fine, almost gaunt bone structure of her smooth face and the faint lines round her mouth. Fiona looked very strained, she thought, and Laura began to feel a little worried about her.

'Is everything all right, Fiona?' she asked. 'Are you sleeping OK? You're not homesick or anything, are you?'

'No,' said Fiona shortly. 'I just find it a bit claustrophobic at times. Everyone on top of each other and minding other people's business, that's all.'

'Sorry,' Laura said, mortified. 'I was just a bit concerned about you. Sorry,' she said again.

'Look, I'm fine,' Fiona said, appearing to make an effort to be more pleasant. 'Just a little tired, that's all. It was so hot in the night and I didn't sleep too well. I was quite relieved when we docked at La Palma.'

Both girls were silent now, each thinking her own thoughts. Laura wondered what was going on between Fiona and the formidable salon manageress to suddenly make such a pleasant girl so tetchy and defensive, but she was soon to have these speculations driven from her mind.

Bob Evans was booked in for an aromatherapy massage at eleven and came into the salon with his usual cheeky grin. Laura was a little uncomfortable with him, after the video session the previous night, and she left the cubicle curtain slightly open as he settled himself on the couch. He started as soon as Laura had oiled her hands in readiness for the massage. He lay on his stomach waiting for her to begin on his bare back but, just as she was about to start, he twisted his bullet head on its thick red neck and ogled her over his shoulder.

'Enjoy the video then, Laura?' he leered.

'Yes. It was amusing,' Laura said non-committally, trying not to be drawn in to any of his suggestive talk, but Evans was incorrigible.

'Don't you get any time off?' he asked. 'Can't I persuade you even to meet me for a drink?'

It was obvious he hadn't noticed that she'd stayed behind in Andrew's cabin after the video. Laura thought quickly. It wouldn't do to alienate a cruise customer entirely. She'd have to string him along a bit.

'Well, we do get time off,' she countered. 'But it's quite unsocial hours, you know. Split shifts this week, so I only get an hour here and there.'

He pounced on this eagerly. 'So, what about an hour there? In the Crow's Nest bar, tomorrow night. Or lunchtime?' he pressed her, when she didn't reply straight away.

'I'll think about it,' Laura said unenthusiastically. 'I'll let you know.'

He almost leaped off the couch in his enthusiasm. 'And I'll be thinking of nothing else until I hear from you,' he enthused. 'That and the video last night. A real turn-on. Let's hope it did the trick for good old Reggie. It certainly worked a treat for me.'

He began to squirm about on the couch and Laura hastily started work on his neck and shoulders, so that at least he couldn't turn and look up at her. She continued in silence, while he chattered on about the video and she was relieved when at last the session was over and he stood up to put on his shirt.

'Don't forget,' he said urgently, grasping her arm quite roughly as he prepared to leave the salon. 'Don't forget, we're on for tomorrow.'

Not if I can help it, Laura thought, but she smiled politely and remained neutral, merely waiting for him to go.

When Eileen Grimshaw came in for her facial, it was obvious that she was feeling somewhat happier and she could hardly wait for Laura to adjust the cushion under her knees and smooth her dark hair back under a protective band before bursting out with her usual marital confidences.

She needed no prompting and as soon as Laura had started to cleanse her face she said, 'Oh, Laura, that video has had such an effect on Reggie. I can't tell you how grateful I am, we both are, and to your friend for inviting us.'

'That's good,' Laura murmured soothingly, massaging the crepey skin under Eileen's chin.

'Not that ... well, you know ... not that it's worked a hundred per cent yet. But when we got back to the cabin, we tried ... you know. Reggie tried, that is, to make love again. Not a hundred per cent successful but still a try, you know. One thing he did say, Laura, was what a turn-on the water play had been in that video. The bathroom scene, you know. I reckon Reggie might respond to that kind of thing. There's only a shower unit in the cabin of course. Perhaps we could fix something up in the Shangri-la jacuzzi?'

Her voice trailed off a little uncertainly and she looked questioningly at Laura, who started to apply the toner before she answered, 'I'm not sure about that, Eileen. I'd have to check it out with my boss first.'

'Oh, would you? We'd be so pleased and grateful. And, of course, no one need know. We'd be so discreet.'

However discreet they were, few things would get past the eagle eyes of Elinor, Laura thought. Still, if they left it very late and the salon doors were safely locked, who would possibly know? She glanced into Eileen's eyes and saw that they were shining like those of a young girl.

'I'll see what I can do.' She smiled, and with that Eileen seemed content.

Laura finished the facial with the minimum of conversation and took the telephone number of Eileen's cabin, promising to let her know.

When she'd gone, Laura started to clear up the cubicle and tidy her trolley, putting lids on bottles and pots, clean disposable tissue paper on the couch, washing her manicure things, and all the while thinking of Andrew and what he'd say to Eileen's idea. She knew what Steve would say. He'd be appalled at the thought of her having anything to do with such a project.

'Too-oo risky,' he'd say, drawing out the words for effect. 'That's just the way to get your P45, Laura, and you wouldn't get a look in on the *Borealis* without good references.'

As she washed her hands and prepared for her next client, Laura thought about her relationship predicament.

She'd cooled down a bit about Steve's latest possessive outburst and was trying to be pragmatic, weighing up her options. She compared the two men in her life and wondered if it was possible to love and fancy both of them at the same time. Steve, she thought, was so focused, so down to earth; a north Manchester guy, true to his origins. He was hardworking, willing, eager to get on and, if there was any justice in the world, he was bound to succeed. So far, she'd imagined a future for them both, together. Now she wasn't so sure. There was no doubt that she and Steve had grown apart on this voyage, except for the sex, that is. Perhaps it's my fault, she told herself. After all, even passionate love can't thrive without nurture.

But she knew Steve would never co-operate in the sort of marriage that Tom and Emma enjoyed. If she married him, she'd have to stay on the straight and narrow. There'd be no room for alternative sex. In any case, Steve had seemed so distracted by the job in the bar and so obsessed at the idea of promotion aboard the *Borealis* that she'd begun to feel their relationship was a definite second in his priorities, while she was relishing her recent sexual experimentation. She had to admit that her attraction to Andrew Gibson had influenced her behaviour lately. Face it, Laura, she confessed to herself, you've made no overtures whatsoever towards your ever-faithful stud in the last few days. What's a guy to do if his regular girlfriend decides not to help things along and just takes him for granted and, on top of that, he's pulled out with hectic work and long hours while she's experimenting with alternative sex?

Steve was so solid, so honest and straightforward. He seemed to be a one-woman guy and wasn't ashamed of it; quite the reverse, in fact. He never played hard to get and was always totally open about the way he felt about her. In spite of their recent coolness, she knew that underneath he loved her with a steadiness that was like the proverbial rock. At the same time, a still small voice inside her told her that their future would be equally certain. Boringly so, in fact. Throughout their married life together, she'd have to soothe his temper tantrums, reassure him when things went wrong and never be more successful than he was himself. There would definitely be no room for experimentation. In spite of his undoubted love and passion for her, it all seemed to add up to a life of tedious banality. Since meeting Andrew, she was no longer sure she wanted that safe life.

Andrew, of course, had been handed his education, engineering degree and officer status on a plate. His confidence and self-esteem had been developed over years of privileged training and encouragement. She doubted if anything in Andrew's cushioned life could ever shake that sophisticated confidence. It was obvious that he was used to the adoration of women. They would always be attracted to his good looks and well-heeled background as well as his obvious sex-appeal. There was something else she had overlooked, because she enjoyed his company so much: he hadn't mentioned any follow-up to their last meeting. For all Laura knew, their passionate interlude in his cabin was just a one-off, a little episode for someone who was interested in filling in a bit of time on a routine and tedious voyage.

She was immediately ashamed of these thoughts. In his haste to report for duty in the engine room, he'd had no chance to take things further, or arrange another date, she told herself. And now that his treatment was finished, she wasn't even going to meet him in the salon any more. She finished her tidying up at last, but before she went to seek out her next client, Laura had decided that she must consult Andrew about Eileen's jacuzzi project. That was a valid reason for getting in touch, she thought, and smiled to herself with anticipation.

The day seemed a long one, with a steady stream of clients who were all wanting beauty treatments designed for sun-damage limitation, or a session on the toning tables to persuade themselves that they could lose the excess baggage on the tummy after ten days of five meals a day with five courses at each meal. Laura knew that an hour of passive activity on the exercise beds couldn't counteract their unhealthy lifestyles, but she smiled pleasantly and adjusted the speed of the moving couch to suit the bulk of the client. Then she measured waists and thighs to bear out the promise of inch loss. She was always so reassuring and so charming that even the grumpiest of the fatties always left the salon in a warm glow, feeling that the treatment had been effective.

But even the longest day must come to an end sooner or later and she switched off the tables, threw the towels into the linen bin and prepared to depart. It was seven o'clock and the first-sitting diners were already eating in the restaurant. The double doors of the Shangri-la were on an automatic lock, so whoever was last to leave made everything secure. As she picked up her bag and turned to go, she was surprised to see Stanley appear in his usual silent way, holding a piece of paper.

'Phone call from Mr Gibson while I was replacing the linen in the cabin, Laura,' he said. 'I'm just going off duty, but I agreed I'd take a message. He'd like to see you for a drink in the mess bar around eight, if you're free.'

Laura blushed with pleasure at this and was about to thank Stanley warmly when they heard the unmistakable sound of a key turning in the lock and Elinor entered the salon with Fiona.

Stanley and Laura both froze as Elinor let the door swing to behind her, effectively locking them all in. Laura was about to step forward and greet them when Elinor's voice came over clear and cool – a voice that Laura could hardly recognise. It was obvious that she thought she was alone with her young friend. Stanley seemed turned to stone and, thinking quickly, Laura silently drew together the small gap in the curtains of the cubicle until it was just a chink. After all, she thought, they won't be here long and it wouldn't do to let Elinor think I was spying on them – and with Stanley tagging along too. He was definitely not allowed in the salon and would be in trouble if he was discovered.

But, as it turned out, it would have been better if she'd declared herself there and then. Before Laura's horrified gaze, the formidable Elinor started to strip off and remove all her clothes, down to her bra and knickers. She stood confidently in front of Fiona for a moment or two, gazing into the younger girl's eyes and murmuring something inaudible. Then they were in each other's arms, kissing one another on the mouth. Fiona was still in her salon overall and Laura could see that underneath it her breasts were bare. Her pointed young nipples stood out proudly through the white fabric as she strained towards her companion, kissing her deeply and with passionate abandon.

Laura was so completely taken by surprise at the scene in front of her that, like Stanley, she seemed rooted to the spot. Elinor's face was unusually soft and luminous as she smiled into Fiona's eyes and placed her hands on the young girl's gently rounded buttocks. Fiona reached up again and her eager mouth sought Elinor's as their bodies pressed even closer together. Elinor held herself back, allowing Fiona to slip her small pointed tongue into her mouth, kissing and exploring her very delicately and sensually.

Then she stood quietly passive while Elinor massaged her small tight bottom very firmly and then nudged her gently towards the nearest of the toning tables. They stood swaying over the plastic-covered exercise bed for a few moments and then Elinor began to slowly run her hands down Fiona's slim body, caressing her nipples through her overall, rubbing the soft flesh of her belly through the thin fabric until Fiona appeared to almost shiver and swoon under the stimulation of those experienced capable hands.

Laura was acutely aware of Stanley's presence. He stood behind her like a statue, his face inscrutable, but she could sense his excitement, like a tethered magnificent animal, quivering and aroused by the sight of Fiona's pleasure. Elinor undid the buttons of the overall, baring Fiona's girlish breasts, and then pushed her gently on to the table.

She pulled Fiona's overall up round her waist, revealing her tiny wispy panties, and began to pull them down gently over her slim hips, revealing the fine downy hair of her mound. It glinted golden in the dim light, nestling between surprisingly well-developed thighs. Laura heard Stanley take a deep breath as Elinor stripped off the rest of her own clothes and stood for a few seconds absolutely nude with her back towards them. Elinor had the wide shoulders and narrow waist of a strong swimmer. Her back was firm and muscular and Laura could sense the power in the older woman's taut thighs. Fiona lay back like a slim willowy wand, completely at ease, and she seemed to be willing Elinor to caress her naked girlish body. She raised her hands behind her head, thrusting her delicate breasts towards Elinor, urging her to touch them.

Elinor bent towards her tenderly and whispered so softly that Laura could barely hear her. 'Oh, my little darling. How beautiful you look,' she cooed. 'What shall I do to you?'

Fiona just quivered at this and gave a little moan as she lay back on the table, ready and eager to be pleasured in any way that pleased her lover. Elinor put her hands inside Fiona's open uniform and placed a hand on each line of the girl's ribs. She began to stroke her with small gentle movements, nearer and nearer to her tight, stiff little nipples, feeling the firm flesh of her breasts, then rubbing the aroused apricot-coloured tips with her thumbs until Fiona was nearly frantic with the tension of anticipation.

Now Elinor leaned over Fiona and took her hands in her own. She lowered Fiona's arms and held them at her sides as she began to kiss the pale skin of her delicate shoulders and slim neck. Bowing her auburn head, Elinor began to flick her tongue across the girl's pale body, wetting her pointed nipples and turning them a deep coral. Fiona strained her face upwards and grasped Elinor's head in her hands, seeking the teasing tongue with her lips and sucking it into her soft mouth as though she were drinking thirstily.

Elinor returned her kisses very deliberately and forcefully. Her own rather heavy breasts were pressing against the girl's slender body as she gradually moved lower, kissing the flat belly and the narrow groin. She slipped her knee between Fiona's legs to open her up and then her deft fingers found Fiona's warm wet sex. Fiona opened her legs obediently and now Laura and Stanley were treated to a view of the crinkled flesh between her pale thighs, glistening and juicy with arousal and the pink little love bud already swollen and waiting to be rubbed.

Laura heard the normally inscrutable Stanley gasp at this point and looked at him anxiously. 'Shh, we're trapped,' she whispered. 'I'm sorry about this, but we'll just have to stick it out and hope for the best.'

She felt inadequate, to say the least, but Stanley just nodded silently and continued to observe the two women through the gap in the curtains as though he were no longer capable of looking away. Elinor stroked the sopping folds between Fiona's legs until the young girl wrapped herself round her, urging her hips forward eagerly. She raised her knees even higher and opened the lips of her swollen sex, offering herself to her lover. This unconsciously sexy movement made even Laura begin to tingle and she wondered how much more of this peep show she could take. She felt her own sex becoming wet and ready as the two women on the table continued their lovemaking in the fond belief that they were alone. She could see that Stanley found the erotic scene as stimulating as she did but she suddenly longed to be with Andrew. The aloof and inscrutable Stanley was handsome and slender, but Andrew was more on her wavelength.

Elinor was now astride her young friend and brought her more fleshy hips down on top of the slight figure lying on the exercise couch. She also opened herself with her fingers and began to grind herself against Fiona's groin, mashing their clits together and almost hiding Fiona from the voyeurs' view. Laura restrained herself with difficulty from touching herself and even joining in with the other two. She dared not even look at Stanley and could only guess at the state of his arousal by the large bulge that had appeared in the front of his trousers.

The perspiring women continued the complicated pleasuring of each other's bodies, until they were both satisfied and lay back breathless and panting. They released each other very slowly, their hands falling to their sides and leaning slightly away from one another as their breathing gradually steadied. They continued murmuring in low voices and slowly recovering for a few more minutes, before eventually sitting up and reaching towards each other for one last kiss.

Through the one-way windows of the Shangri-la, Laura could see the shadows already lengthening across the promenade deck, as they finally began to reach for their clothes. Their departure seemed almost hasty after such protracted lovemaking but finally they left quietly and Laura and Stanley were alone in the dim cubicle.

'Well,' Laura said with an embarrassed laugh. 'They've well and truly gone at last. We can come out now, Stanley.'

He attempted to hide his arousal and embarrassment with a dismissive, 'Just one of those things. I'll be off now. Don't forget your telephone call.'

He opened the door noiselessly and disappeared.

Just as if I would, thought Laura. But what a turn-up for the books this little scenario proved to be. Who'd have thought it about the starchy Elinor and the virginal Fiona?

11

Later, as the ship prepared to leave La Palma for Spain, Laura sat with Andrew in the mess bar, and was a little undecided as to what to tell him and what to leave out. Looking into his warm brown eyes, she was surprised at herself for her feelings of reluctance and wasn't even sure how to begin. She frowned slightly as she tried to marshal her thoughts and he seemed to read her expression very accurately.

'Something wrong?' He smiled at her. 'Don't you like the Chablis? I thought I'd chosen your favourite.'

He waited, his handsome dark head a little to one side, still smiling at her but observing her quite closely all the same.

'Yes, of course. It's fine,' she answered mechanically.

She was very aware of his scrutiny and took a deep breath.

'Well?' he prompted her gently. 'What is it then? Mayhem in the salon? Toning tables collapsed under the strain? Eileen and Reggie demanding his and hers leg waxing? The divine Elinor given you your cards?'

Laura was obliged to giggle, but almost immediately was serious again.

'Something like that,' she said. 'Eileen's been for her facial and she said how much she and her husband enjoyed the video. They want me to fix up a skinny-bathing session in the Shangri-la jacuzzi for them.'

She paused for effect and looked at him to try to guess what his opinion would be.

'And?'

'It was obvious from what Eileen said that she wants a foursome. She thinks it's just the sort of thing to get Reggie going and she's all in favour.'

Once more she waited, trying to assess his reaction.

'What's the problem then?' he asked, still smiling at her.

'Two problems,' Laura said soberly. 'First, it's strictly against the rules to mess about in the salon after hours, even for something legit like hair washing or using the foot spa. Second –' she paused and her eyes flicked up to meet his '– even if I do them a favour and go along with the idea, I don't know if I can find a fourth.'

Now her eyes were held by his own and she waited almost without breathing as he said quietly, 'Would I do? As the fourth, I mean.'

'Yes, of course you would,' she stammered, and actually felt herself blushing. 'But the risk, Andrew. If anyone found out, I'd lose my job.'

'So would I,' he said cheerfully. 'But I'm game if you are. I'm sure that between us we could give Eileen and Reg a few creative ideas to help their love life along and have some fun ourselves. We might even conclude the other night's unfinished business,' he said thoughtfully, and Laura felt a little thrill go through her at the thought.

'We'd have to be very careful though,' she warned. 'I'd have to make sure I was the last one left in the salon, so that I could open it up to you and the others. If Elinor found out it would be catastrophic.'

'I know,' he said with his devastating smile and, just at that moment, Laura would have been prepared to risk anything for an opportunity to have sex with him.

Sitting opposite him and looking into that handsome tanned face, she was shaken to her very foundations by

173

sudden overwhelming desire. But even as she felt her warm moist pussy begin to tighten with her longing for his body, she realised that it wasn't just straightforward lust which was driving her to fancy him. She had to acknowledge to herself that she found him utterly fascinating in every way. There was absolutely no aspect of his personality or physical appearance which she didn't consider a powerful turn-on, but in spite of the intimacy of massaging his body and seeing him practically naked, she still didn't feel she really knew him at all. It was almost painful, this sudden tightness in her chest, the irresistible urge to confess her feelings for him, to say, 'Andrew, I think I love you.'

She controlled this urge with some difficulty and, instead, said coolly, 'I'll let Eileen know then that we're on for the jacuzzi session tomorrow night.'

'Right. I'll leave it in your capable hands, dear Miss Barnes,' he said with mock solemnity. 'You'll have to coordinate the arrangements with Eileen and Reg and then keep me informed.'

'We're at sea all day tomorrow, before we arrive in Vigo,' she said thoughtfully. 'I'll get them to agree that it's best to make it tomorrow evening. After all, everyone who wants a beauty treatment will have been seen to by then and the passengers'll all be at the Gala Variety Show. The clocks have to advance one hour before we get to Spain, so it might be the safest time to use the jacuzzi.'

He took both her hands in his and kissed the palm of each one in turn while his eyes looked deeply into her own, making Laura quake like a jelly at the sexiness of his gaze.

'Till tomorrow then.' He smiled.

Then, rising to his feet, he said, 'I'm on duty now, but

I'll make sure I'm free for tomorrow night. I'll look forward to it with ill-concealed impatience.'

With another smile and a mock salute, he was gone.

Laura sat on a little longer, still mulling over all the varied events of the day. She wondered where Fiona was and what she was doing. She still hadn't completely taken in the implications of her cabin-mate's relationship with the Shangri-la manageress and wondered idly just how long the two of them had been an item. The cruise was into its second week at sea and they'd be back in Southampton in four days. Was that long enough for a relationship to have been developed to the sort of intense stage such as she and Stanley had witnessed today? She considered the idea of attempting to draw Fiona out and encouraging her to confide her feelings for Elinor. It was obvious from their body language and the loving way they'd acted that they were sexually and emotionally committed and she guessed this had started even before Fiona had taken up her job on the cruise ship.

But as it turned out, Laura was overtaken by other events. As she was sitting there, Steve appeared quite suddenly in the mess bar, holding a bundle of papers in his hand. In spite of a coolness in the atmosphere, he was impeccably polite.

'Hi, I've got an hour off, Laura,' he said as he came up to her table. 'If you agree, I thought we might fill in our application forms for the *Borealis*. You'll need to give Elinor as one of your referees, of course, and I thought we might ask the purser to be the second referee for both of us.'

Laura looked at the application form as though in a dream and nodded mechanically. The moment of decision had arrived and she was no longer keen to move to the *Borealis*. Sure, Steve would be moving with her, but Laura knew she was now reluctant to have wall-to-wall Steve, for ever and ever.

But, she'd said she would put in her application and so she would. She began to fill in the form conscientiously enough, in spite of her lack of enthusiasm. She wondered what sort of reference Elinor would give her if she were to find out about them using the Shangri-la jacuzzi after hours. That would surely mean curtains for the *Borealis*, she thought. Steve seemed to have no doubts at all and he filled out his application confidently and neatly, giving the manager of the Santorini bar as his first referee and the ship's purser as his second.

'It says here, "Are you prepared to be ready at short notice for the first voyage of the *Borealis*, which is to be to the Caribbean",' he said. 'What about you? Would your mum mind if you only had a couple of days' turnaround before we set off such a long way?'

It was clear from his expression that he himself would be prepared to go with no notice whatsoever. Laura pretended to consider it.

'I don't expect she'd mind too much,' she said slowly. 'Particularly if it means I get promotion.'

He smiled with some relief. It was obvious to Laura that he'd been on edge about the job application and her response had done much to reassure him. But it was a response she'd made without much conviction. Truth to tell, she sounded more positive than she actually felt.

There would come a time, she thought, when she'd have to disabuse him of the idea that they would be sharing a future together, either on the *Borealis*, or anywhere else. She realised with something of a pang that she'd finally outgrown her relationship with Steve. Regretfully, it no longer fulfilled her to imagine the realisation of their previous youthful dreams of living together, happily ever after. Now, looking at his expression of careful concentration as he filled out the application, she was suddenly overwhelmed by a feeling of almost maternal tenderness towards him. After all, she could never forget that he was her first serious partner. What they had shared together was their exploration of that intense experience of sex in a relationship where both of them felt comfortable and safe with each other. She would always be fond of him, she thought, but that magic had now gone and it was time to reassess her feelings.

He looked up at this moment and said seriously, 'I'm very keen on this job, Laura. I'm absolutely desperate to gain the promotion and experience that working on that ship will bring me. But I don't really want to go without you.'

'I know that,' she said quietly. 'Still, if there's no job for me, you must move on anyway, Steve. It's what we agreed and I still want it for you.'

For a moment his eyes looked bleak and sad, as though he could read everything in her heart and could recognise that this might be the parting of the ways for both of them.

'We've not been getting on quite so well lately,' he said tentatively.

'I know,' she said, and covered his free hand with her own. 'But we've had some good times, Steve, and you never know what the future might bring.'

'That's true,' he said soberly.

He looked at her for a long moment and seemed about to say something else, but instead looked at his watch and gathered the papers together in a big envelope.

'Shall I post them both together?'

'OK,' she said. 'Good luck, Steve.'

'Yes. Good luck,' he said, and he turned and left the bar.

Laura felt somewhat subdued by this encounter with Steve. She knew that it was the end of the road as far as their relationship was concerned. Her feelings were mixed – partly sadness at the thought of parting, partly optimism at the excitement of her developing friendship with Andrew Gibson and all the promise that it held out for the future. She sighed. Perhaps she'd have an early night. She left the bar slowly, still deep in thought and, as she reached the cabin, she was so preoccupied that she inserted her swipe card with no preliminary warning to her cabin-mate. She gave no knock, no discreet cough or any other signal, but pushed open the door and walked straight in, utterly unprepared for the scene before her.

Fiona was half lying, half lounging on her bunk, wearing brief blue shorts. Her little white cropped top was pulled up high to reveal her naked breasts. Having no outside window, the cabin was dependent for light on the bedside lamps, but Fiona hadn't put them on. Instead, the cabin was lit by the fluorescent glow from the half-open bathroom. She seemed agitated and was even paler than usual. She turned her head quickly as Laura came into the room.

'Fiona, I'm sorry ... I shouldn't have burst in like that,' Laura stammered. 'I thought you were out ... Are you all right? You look a bit upset.'

'Well ...' Fiona hesitated awkwardly and, rather shamefaced, she pulled down her little T-shirt. 'I ... c-can't ...'

'Just one minute,' Laura said gently, and went to lock

the cabin door and then walked over to Fiona and sat beside her on the bed. 'What is it? What's wrong, Fiona?'

It was then that she noticed a big black vibrator, shaped like a phallus, lying on top of the sheet, next to Fiona's hand. Oh-oh, she thought. I've interrupted more than a fit of the cruise blues, but aloud she said, 'What seems to be the problem?'

At first, Fiona refused to meet her eyes. She just said miserably, 'I ... I ... don't know if I can talk about it.'

Laura waited, tactfully avoiding looking at the sex toy, which seemed almost incongruous in connection with the young Fiona.

'Don't then, if you don't want to,' she said gently. 'I'll make us a coffee.'

'No. Thanks. I don't want one.'

Then, 'It's Elinor,' Fiona burst out suddenly. 'She says this cruise is ruining our relationship.'

She raised sad, hollow eyes to meet Laura's. 'You see, Laura, I've known for some time now that I'm gay. Elinor understands this and she's been very good to me. But she says we don't have enough time for togetherness and that I ought to move in with her. At the moment, she's got a double cabin to herself.'

She gave an anxious pleading look at Laura, who nodded understandingly.

'I think I guessed a while ago about you and Elinor. So what's the problem?' Laura asked again, very gently.

'Well, you're so confident and you have a lot of friends ... I've been grateful to you, you're very kind ... but I thought you might not understand things,' Fiona said inadequately.

'What things?' Laura asked softly. She leaned forward a little and took Fiona's hand in hers. As she did so, her low-necked top fell open a little to reveal her full voluptuous breasts contained in the underwired cups of her sexy bra.

'What might I not understand?' Laura persisted quietly. 'Tell me, Fiona. I can't help if I don't know what's wrong.'

Fiona gave a gulp and her little pointed red tongue shot out nervously to moisten her soft young lips, as she glanced down at Laura's beautiful deep cleavage. 'Well, I like you so much. I just can't bear the thought of letting you down.' She shook her head and a deep blush suffused her delicate features. Her lips looked dry and tense.

'I wouldn't worry about that if I were you,' Laura said reassuringly. 'If it's what you want, how about waiting till we set off for the eastern Mediterranean cruise and then just see the purser about quietly moving in with Elinor? You might as well have what you want, Fiona. After all, you have to have a lot of things you *don't* want in life, don't you?'

'But ... but what about you? You've been so good to me and you're ... you're my friend.'

'Don't worry about me, I'll be fine.' Laura smiled. 'We're losing Imogen at the end of this trip. She's finally taking the plunge with her Peter and she'll be lost to us. That'll leave Thelma on her tod. She'd be delighted to share with me and we get on well together, so no probs.'

She decided to say nothing of her application for the *Borealis*. Cross that bridge when they came to it, she thought. She had a sudden mental picture of Elinor and Fiona in the Shangri-la and she began to definitely feel a tingle herself as she recalled entering the cabin and seeing Fiona's tiny little T-shirt pulled up almost to her chin.

On an impulse, she smiled and picked up the vibrator. 'So were you about to forget your problems with this little toy?' she teased, trying to lighten Fiona's mood.

Fiona almost laughed with relief. 'Yes,' she said shyly. 'It's Elinor's really, but I sometimes use it.'

Laura drew the black shiny vibrator slowly across her hand, caressing her fingers with it.

'Can I help?' she asked encouragingly, and Fiona gave a sigh as she relaxed against her friend's shoulder.

'Oh yes, Laura,' she breathed and lay back utterly reassured and confident.

Laura grasped the vibrator with one hand as she stroked Fiona's hair and face very gently with the other. She caressed Fiona's lips lightly with one finger, but didn't kiss them. Instead, she moved her hand downwards to touch the little pointed nipples, which were already poking proudly through the white T-shirt. Carefully, she raised Fiona's cropped top to its former position and the girl closed her eyes as her naked breasts were now exposed once again. The coolness of the air conditioning in the cabin lengthened the pink rubbery tips of her breasts until they stood out even more invitingly and Laura switched on the vibrating phallus and began, ever so gently, to touch the outer edges of her areolae, working nearer and nearer to the delicate pink centres. Little tiny raised spots were now appearing on the pale surrounding circles and Fiona, aroused, arched her back and thrust herself forward eagerly to try to make the vibrating phallus touch her nipples. Laura ignored this and continued to slowly brush each of the little red spots in turn, lingering lovingly on each one and then moving the toy across to the other breast to do it all over again. Fiona's lips parted and she gripped her lower lip with her teeth, moaning softly, and then Laura moved to her aroused nipples, flicking them very lightly with the tip of the black vibrator until Fiona squirmed with lust and opened her legs, longing to have the plastic cock thrust between them.

But Laura wasn't going to be rushed. She'd learned from Emma not to rush things when making love to another woman. She knew how a woman liked to be pleasured and was enjoying this experience tremendously. For the first time, she realised how a man must feel when he has a woman on her back, writhing and squirming desperately for the pleasure of his touch. For the first time in her life Laura felt that power through the phallus in her hand, and she'd no intention of hurrying. She traced a line with the tip down to the girl's ludicrously brief shorts and opened the waistband a little to sweep it lightly from side to side across her fluttering abdomen so that Fiona raised her hips up from the bed in frantic longing for it to go lower.

Instead, Laura attended to the already sore nipples one more time before switching off the vibrator and pulling up one of the legs of Fiona's shorts. She pulled firmly so that the fabric rolled tightly into Fiona's crack, exposing the already swollen lips and the moist red clit standing erect and ready. She switched the vibrator back on and began to stroke the inside of her thighs, up and down each leg in turn before she twisted the fabric of the shorts so unbearably tight that Fiona gave a little intake of breath. Her sex was now almost cut in half and her clit was twice its usual size as Laura began to tease it with the tip of the vibrating tool. The blue shorts were soon darkened by Fiona's gushing juices and she began to roll her head helplessly from side to side, whimpering as she sensed her approaching climax, then shuddering and trying ineffectually to pull back from the unbearable stimulation on her sensitive erect clit as she came with glorious relief and gratitude.

Only then did Laura release the bunched up leg of the shorts and, while Fiona was still tight with her first orgasm, she thrust the vibrating cock unerringly into her young friend's pussy, stimulating her steadily and rhythmically until Fiona came a second time, squealing with delight.

She lay back on the pillow, her fine cropped hair wet with perspiration, her thin young limbs limp with the aftermath of sex. Her face was relaxed now and she moved her hands to cover her small breasts and to stroke them softly, languidly, as she gazed gratefully at her friend.

'Oh, Laura, that was fabulous,' she said admiringly. She was almost incoherent with gratitude. 'I didn't know you ... How did you guess what I wanted? How did you know? ... I always thought ... I thought you were straight ...'

'That's right, I am,' Laura said cheerfully. 'That doesn't mean I can't enjoy alternative pleasures. I must have been inspired by Black Johnny here.' She gave a wicked grin and handed Fiona the vibrator.

'My turn now,' she said pointedly, slipping quickly out of her clothes and lying down on the bed naked at the side of her. Unusually, Fiona, still in shorts and cropped top, got out of bed and kneeled on the floor. As Laura settled herself on the pillows, she became aware that Fiona was examining her silently, without touching and without speaking.

'What's up, Fiona?' she said rather uncomfortably. 'What are you doing down there?'

'I'm just looking,' Fiona answered her. 'I haven't been as close to you as this before, Laura. I'm just admiring your lovely golden pussy. Lie back and relax. I want to unroll your lips and look at your clit before I start with the vibes.'

Laura did as she was told and submitted with good

humour to Fiona's examination as the younger girl opened up Laura's pussy with her fingers and bent closer to breathe in the musky scent of Laura's sex.

'It's lovely, Laura,' she breathed. 'You've got a really beautiful clit, do you know that?'

Laura felt herself being fully splayed for Fiona's inspection and breathed deeply and easily as she waited for Fiona to take the initiative. She began to slowly manipulate Laura's clit with her finger and used two fingers of her other hand to tickle the slit below. Her touch was extremely delicate, but not in any way tentative. Laura's crimson opening oozed its copious sticky liquid and her wetness trickled downwards towards her bottom. Laura began to feel the usual delicious throbbing and her clit seemed to be twitching on its own, swelling and pulsating with the pleasure of Fiona's firm stroking of her.

Fiona now leaned closer towards her and used the lubrication of Laura's slit to gently open up her bumhole. She drew Laura's much enlarged clit into her mouth, sucking hard on it while she continued to stimulate her two openings, making Laura almost beside herself with her desire to come, but Fiona was still firmly in charge. Keeping one finger in Laura's anus, she reached for the black vibrator and switched it to its lowest setting before thrusting it into her.

Now she was able to concentrate on Laura's magnificent breasts, licking her large areolae and nipples until Laura groaned aloud. Laura had to concede that the quiet shy Fiona was a force to be reckoned with, sexually at least. Under Fiona's mouth, her nipples grew long and rubbery and Fiona's finger was driving her to distraction, tickling her bumhole. Her whole body felt on fire. She felt on the verge of orgasm yet, perversely, she wanted to hold it off for a little while longer. She writhed and panted under Fiona's ministrations, on a delicious plateau of longing to come, yet still fighting it off. Fiona seemed to understand this, and taking hold of the vibrator once more, she switched it to full pitch, withdrawing it a little and touching Laura's clit with it, then pushing it in again until Laura couldn't hold out any longer.

She shouted as she came and her juices pumped out of her and quiet, shy little Fiona laughed and said, 'What took you so long?'

Days at sea are always busier for the crew than days in port and the next day was no exception. Both girls were involved in a demonstration and skincare workshop in front of the Sun King bar. Being outside on the sun deck, they needed to get things ready before it became really hot, so they were up early. Fiona was still a little tremulous and guilty about enjoying her favourite sex toy without Elinor, but Laura just laughed easily and said, 'Take your pleasure where you find it, Fiona. That's all it was – pleasure – and it's done you a power of good. You're looking really relaxed and peachy this morning.'

'So are you, Laura,' Fiona said admiringly.

'What Elinor doesn't know, she won't grieve over,' Laura said, and gave a stage wink, making Fiona giggle with relief at being so easily absolved from her guilty conscience.

Laura was very aware of Bob Evans as they set up for the workshop. He was much in evidence at the edge of the bar area, lying on a sun lounger, fat red belly exposed to the bright sun, a white pork pie sunhat half-tipped over his cynically grinning face, ogling Imogen and Louise as they set out the equipment in the shade of the bar's awning. He certainly wasn't there to learn about skincare and she suspected he only hung around so he could stare at the pretty women. She hoped he wasn't going to cause any trouble and that he'd not had any hint of tonight's activities in the jacuzzi. The thought made her shudder, but at least he seemed to have stopped pestering her for the time being as he tried to flirt with the other salon girls, for which she was profoundly grateful. Fiona was helping Elinor with the free skin and scalp analysis, advising on what products to use for various skin types and how best to avoid hair damage from the sun and chlorinated water. Laura was giving the aromatherapy demo to passengers, who could receive advice on achieving a well-balanced body using special oils for the relief of stress and tension and even buy some to take home. She just hoped Bob Evans wouldn't bother to turn up for a personal consultation.

Laura was also acutely aware of Elinor's presence, not just because of the need to help each other with equipment and chairs, but a subtle, indefinable atmosphere of malevolence emanating from her boss, which had the effect of subduing both Fiona and herself. But Elinor couldn't know anything about Fiona and herself pleasuring each other in the privacy of their cabin. Surely Fiona wouldn't have told the older woman everything she'd been doing? Several times Laura glanced up as she arranged her aromatherapy oils and essences and each time Elinor was fixing her with a very speculative gaze. Nothing was said but Laura felt uneasy. They worked steadily and efficiently and by nine thirty were ready for their first clients.

Laura shrugged off the feeling of being watched, concentrating instead on the job in hand and, all in all, the day was a great success. Even Elinor's grim face cracked into a thin smile at the compliments and praise from their clients and Fiona was quite elated by all the attention she was getting. She had the radiance of a happy and satisfied woman, Laura thought smugly. Evans just contented himself with the odd flippant remark during the various demonstrations and wasn't really any trouble. His twisted grin was easily ignored.

Now all that remained was to make sure that the jacuzzi evening was a success for Eileen and Reg. Laura guessed that Elinor and Fiona would be spending the night together now that Fiona had confessed her interest. She was pleased for the kid. If that was what she wanted, well, good luck to her. She had such a soft spot for her young friend, she wished her all she wished herself. As for the passengers, they were to be treated to an evening of the Gala Variety Show, with two good vocalists and a famous theatre company. Not only that, being at sea meant the shops and boutiques on E deck would all be open for duty-free fashions, jewellery and perfumes and, at this stage of the cruise, they would have some startling reductions to tempt the cruisers. The casino would, of course, be open all night and the photographers would be assiduously snapping and developing pictures of all the events for anyone who wanted a record of the good time they were having. What could go wrong? She didn't know, but still felt an unaccountable tremor of apprehension, which she only just allowed to be overridden by her excitement and anticipation at seeing Andrew again.

She'd already put her bikini and evening sarong in her locker, so all she needed to do was dilly-dally over the job of putting her stuff away, washing out the various bowls and containers she'd used, combing her hair and freshening her make-up, while waiting for everyone to leave. It all worked like a dream. Gradually, the other beauty therapists, receptionists, hairdressers and even Fiona and Elinor packed up and wished her goodnight before they departed. The cleaners wouldn't be in till seven the next morning. She finally had the salon to herself.

It was spookily quiet now. Although it was still quite light outside, the promenade area on the other side of the one-way windows was absolutely deserted. Everyone was otherwise occupied and, at last, Laura let herself relax and look forward to what was still to come. Only another half hour before the others were due, she thought, and felt again the familiar tingle of nervous anticipation.

12

Although Laura was wearing a bikini and Reg sported a pair of modest swimming trunks, Eileen had decided to throw caution to the winds and lowered herself into the soothing warm waters of the jacuzzi, stark naked.

She wasn't in bad shape either, Laura thought as Eileen leaned backwards and spread out her arms along the tiled rim of the pool. No sign of wing wobble under Eileen's fiftysomething arms and, although her breasts and belly had spread a little, most women her age would envy her the trimness of her body. She was now a picture of relaxed sensual enjoyment. Reg had seemed a little tense at first but now contented himself with copying Eileen's pose, appearing to lie back and enjoy the soft bubbling jets of water while stretching out his feet and paddling them gently up and down. Andrew still hadn't appeared and Laura confessed to herself that she was a little disappointed.

But then he arrived, tapping softly on the door for admittance, giving her his lovely smile and mouthing 'Sorry', as he disappeared into a cubicle, to emerge a few seconds later wearing one of the Shangri-la's fluffy towels around his waist.

'Have I got the right dress code?' He grinned at them and, leaving his towel on the floor, got in the jacuzzi beside Laura.

With Andrew's arrival, the whole atmosphere now lightened considerably and Reg even made a little joke about having a foursome for bridge. As for Laura, she was utterly enchanted at the sight of Andrew completely naked at last and could hardly keep her hands off him as he stretched his tanned muscular legs, flexing his knees and wriggling his toes as he lay back and relaxed. His cock, though large, was at the moment quiescent and bobbed lazily in the water as he smiled round at his companions. She saw Reg give a startled glance at Andrew's immodest nakedness, before looking away tactfully and whispering some sweet little nothings into Eileen's ear. Laura drew in a deep breath as she gazed at him. His tanned body was absolutely superb, magnificently firm and muscled, sleek and shining with the water. His skin was smooth and tactile, except for between his legs where the crisp dark curls enfolded his wonderful penis. She continued to stare at him, awestruck, unable to look away. In no time at all, he had the biggest erection she'd ever seen and he was holding it towards her as though for her approval. And Laura did approve. She approved of its iron-hard stiffness and the impressive smooth length of it. The big tip was purple with excitement and, as she continued to stare, fascinated at so exceptional a specimen, she gulped dry mouthed with her longing for him.

Meanwhile, it seemed Andrew was wasting no time at all. Before she could say a word, he leaned over her, kissing and tonguing her mouth with the utmost dedication and thoroughness. She enjoyed the slightly salty taste of his lips on hers and the strength of him as he clasped her waist and she put her arms around his neck, returning his kisses with interest. It felt as though they were having a sword fight as first Andrew and then Laura won this duel of sensuality with their thrusting tongues. It was as if they were the only two people in the world. Both of them were entirely oblivious to anyone else as they stood in the water, welded together.

Then he slipped both his hands behind her back and removed the top two triangles of her little bikini which he tossed over the side of the spa on to the tiled floor.

Laura's legs almost gave way and she felt the same surge of sexual excitement as she'd felt when she was in his cabin as his hands moved inexorably upwards to fondle her bare breasts. Her body responded immediately to the expertise of his fingertip stroking, her swollen nipples pressing insistently and eagerly against them. His hands slipped down to her waist and he stripped off her bikini bottoms, bending his knees under the water to drag them free of her ankles, before returning his lips to hers as though he couldn't bear to be away from them.

Completely carried away, forgetting the presence of the other two, Laura slipped further down into the water in front of him and positioned herself between his legs so that she could take his cock between her breasts. She began to move up and down, squeezing and massaging him with her voluptuous tits while he lay back ecstatically, his taut eager shaft standing even harder and more erect. Gently and firmly, she increased the pressure and speed of the massage, squeezing him more tightly and signalling with her eyes that she was willing him to come.

And he did. Groaning and spurting out his thick milky come all over her breasts, shuddering, with his eyes rolling upwards as the uncontrollable spasms only gradually subsided and he lay back, sated.

Laura waited for a few moments before gently disengaging herself from his now quiescent cock. She ducked lower into the water and let it wash over her neck and breasts until all traces of his come had disappeared. She glanced up at Eileen and Reg. They were looking decidedly left out and, making a swift decision, she went over to Eileen and, smiling, whispered to her to move to the jacuzzi steps. Eileen obeyed as if in a dream and Laura reached over to the tiled shelf and put a generous dollop of the spa's rich herbal moisturiser on to two of her fingers. She began to massage the hot fiery slit between Eileen's legs with long firm strokes. The older woman responded immediately by opening wide and leaning back on the tiles, supporting herself on her elbows.

Laura now inserted her slippery fingers slowly and methodically all the way into Eileen's eager pussy. Just as slowly and carefully, she withdrew them to play for a moment or two on the older woman's frantic clit, before repeating the whole procedure again, while Eileen moaned and sighed with ecstasy and Reg was goggle eyed and transfixed at the sight of his wife's excitement.

For several minutes, Eileen revelled in the pleasure of Laura's delicately probing fingers, her clit now so hungry that it only needed the younger woman to roll back the swollen lips and pinch and tweak it with her thumb to make her cry out with the sudden pleasure of her orgasm. Laura didn't allow her to recover from this but whispered to her to turn over while she replenished the herbal moisturiser on her fingers. Eileen obediently turned over and then gasped with surprise at the repeated intrusion of Laura's fingers, this time into her anus, but she made no move to pull away. She presented her smooth bottom passively, while ever so gently and slowly, Laura eased more of the herbal mixture into her opening. The Shangri-la jacuzzi boasted a hand-held shower spray for the convenience of the cruise guests and, when Eileen began to feel excited at the sensations, Laura switched it on and directed it at her still swollen bright red clit. The insistent spray of liquid against her already stimulated sex brought on the first faint stirrings of another climax and Eileen began to moan with increasing pleasure as she tried to steady herself against the wet tiles. Laura ignored these struggles and continued to use the full force of the warm water on her ultra-sensitive tip until Eileen's body quaked with a second massive orgasm of such intensity that she collapsed fully on to edge of the jacuzzi and lay breathless and panting with ecstasy after such a prolonged and violent climax.

Laura replaced the shower head slowly and smiled charmingly at the two men. Both of them were visibly affected by what they'd seen. Reg was still lolling back on the side of the jacuzzi, but he was no longer relaxed. One hand was plucking nervously at his modest swim trunks, as though they'd suddenly become uncomfortable, and Laura could see by the bulge inside them that he had a huge hard-on. He adjusted the close-fitting leg of his trunks, and never once took his eyes off Eileen, who had now reached for a fluffy Shangri-la towel and wrapped herself up in it.

'My God, Eileen,' was all that Reg managed to say, but Eileen was beyond speech and just sat on the edge, patting herself dry and looking like the proverbial cat with the cream.

'Yes. My God! Wow, Laura,' Andrew echoed.

Laura could see that Reg was aroused at the sight of his wife being pleasured by another woman. He smiled at her and said, 'I want you to have me too.' He lay back a little further against the edge of the jacuzzi, his lips parted and dry. Laura's hand tingled and she looked down at his bulging swimming trunks. She was suddenly curious to know what he'd be like with nothing on and she leaned forward to pull them down. Being wet, the trunks were delightfully awkward and difficult to remove, but gradually she eased them down and pulled them over Reggie's ankles and feet, tossing them on to the tiled floor. His cock sprang free and Laura was delighted with what she saw. He had a neat, tight little bum, which was admirable in a man of his age and which he pressed harder against the edge of the jacuzzi, so that she'd have the full benefit of his superb erection. His cock was long and hard, the glossy purple dome at the top of his shaft already tipped with a dewdrop. Reg sighed as she began to touch him. His cock was taut and eager, the skin smooth and easy. In spite of being in the water so long, it had dried quickly and felt silky under her fingers. She caressed the soft hairy pouch of his balls, which was drawn up tight with the swelling of his cock. Reg was quite a dish in the sex department, Laura thought. She opened her mouth to taste him, but Reg caught hold of her hair and pulled her head back.

'No,' he said. 'No. Do it with your hands.'

Laura obediently curled her fingers firmly round his taut shaft and began to stroke him steadily and rhythmically along its whole length. Reg adjusted himself slightly and groaned with pleasure.

'Oh God,' he whispered. 'It's been so long. So long. No. Don't stop. Please don't stop.'

Laura's other hand went beneath his cock and once more found his balls. She tickled and squeezed them until Reg groaned again with the delicious agony of it. The inside of his thighs tautened and then hollowed under her firm stroking. Laura pulled all the way to the end of his prick and then all the way back to base, over and over again, and Reg excitedly thrust himself along the channel of her fingers. He was trying to make her go faster and let him climax. Even Eileen, watching mesmerised from the sidelines, seemed to be willing Laura to let him finish. Reggie's eyes were shut as though he were overcome with the amazement and delight at having achieved an erection and of being wanked by a lovely young woman. Laura glanced sideways and noticed that, although Andrew was lolling back, apparently relaxed and at ease, his eyes were following every movement of Laura's busy hands and his own cock was beginning to swell again. Reggie now increased the pace of Laura's wanking.

'Faster, faster,' he begged, and then he gasped, 'Oh God, it's really happening. I'm going to come. Don't stop. Oh God, please don't stop.'

He arched his back, his face transfixed with lust as he thrust himself harder into her wanking fingers. He gave a shout as his orgasm suddenly swelled and overwhelmed him and Laura felt him shudder and tremble helplessly as he came in one big spurting spray.

There was a silence after that. Eileen handed her husband a towel, smiling admiringly at him, and, after a moment, Reg sat up, smiling back at her and holding on to her hand as she helped him up from the floor. 'Christ, Eileen,' he said happily, 'I never thought I'd be able to do *that* again.'

All four of them smiled delightedly at each other, as though they'd conquered Everest. Laura looked at Andrew. She wished Reg and Eileen would disappear and leave them alone, and her wish was granted almost immediately.

Reg had now left the side of the jacuzzi and joined Eileen in one of the changing cubicles, and when they both emerged, they were fully dressed and smiling shyly like newly-weds. It was obvious that they both wished to leave her and Andrew together because they couldn't wait to go back to their cabin and be alone themselves.

'I think we'll have an early night, dear,' Reg finally managed, somewhat embarrassed, and Eileen, with a radiant smile, took his hand, wished Laura and Andrew goodnight and hurried off with him.

Andrew was looking at her, still paddling his legs lazily in the jacuzzi. 'Well, I think that's done the trick, Laura. I'm glad Reg has managed to get satisfaction tonight and I'm sure if Eileen has anything to do with it, he'll have his end away again before the night's over. But what about you? Do you want me to make you a happy and satisfied woman now we've got the place to ourselves?'

He advanced towards her, smiling, and she leaned back against the edge of the pool, her breasts thrusting and taut with unfulfilled desire.

'Yes. Oh yes,' she breathed huskily. Her legs were like jelly as she saw how big he was.

But she was destined not to accept this invitation, phrased with such a pleasant and charming expression on his part, because just at that moment they both paused at the sound of a key in the door of the Shangri-la.

Laura's eyes swivelled instinctively at the distinctive sound of the door to the salon being opened and at least she had the presence of mind to grab a towel and to hurl one in Andrew's direction before whoever it was entered the room. Only one person had the key and that was Elinor. Laura watched in frozen horror as her worst fears were realised and her boss came marching in determinedly with an extremely disagreeable expression on her face.

'So,' Elinor crowed triumphantly, 'what do you think you're doing, breaking the rules like this? You know it's entirely out of order to be disporting yourselves in the jacuzzi at this time of the night, when everything is supposed to be closed up until tomorrow.'

'I . . . We . . . We aren't doing any harm.' Laura began to stammer excuses, but she knew it was no good. Elinor was now in triumphant full flow, her normally cold expression changed to one of smiling elation. Her cheeks were flushed with pleasure at having caught them out.

'Quite apart from the breaking of the rules, there's the question of health and safety at work. If there were to be a fire on board, no one would be searching in here for anyone. Do you realise that firefighting crew would be putting their own lives at risk by wasting time looking for you? I shall have to report all this to Captain Browning.'

She gave a satisfied but bitter smile, more like a grimace and her eyes remained coldly merciless as they raked over Laura's pretty figure encased in the blue bath sheet, taking in the flushed beauty of her young face as she stood at the side of the pool. For once in her life, Laura was unsure of herself and utterly downcast and humiliated at being caught out like this. Elinor recognised her discomfiture and it gave her even more satisfaction at her victory over the younger girl.

Laura glanced at Andrew. At least he was decently covered up, she thought. Perhaps he'd be able to intercede with Elinor, use his influence, pull rank or something. But Andrew was Andrew. Just the same with Elinor as he was with Eileen and Reg. Civilised, well mannered, unflustered.

'What seems to be the problem?' he asked her mildly, and he sat on the jacuzzi steps and began to dry in between his toes with the corner of his towel, just as if he'd been legitimately using the facilities.

Elinor flushed more angrily. 'The problem,' she spat out, 'is that you and Laura have no right to be here when the spa is closed, much less entertaining cruise passengers in such ... such an inappropriate fashion.'

'And how did you know about it?' he asked her, still in the same mild tone, but Laura could see a little pulse beating constantly in his cheek as he bent once more to dry off his feet. She could only guess at his anger and chagrin.

But Elinor didn't have time to answer this because at that moment Stanley appeared silently through the half-opened door, moving as gracefully and smoothly as always.

'I know how she knows,' he said in his usual quiet way. 'One of the passengers, Bob Evans, informed her, didn't he, ma'am? I overheard Mr Evans telling you that there was going to be a gang-bang tonight and that he wasn't invited as it was to be officers only.'

Elinor flushed even more deeply. 'None of your business,' she said. 'Kindly get out of here, Stanley, you've no right to be in the spa, unless you're on duty.'

Laura had sidled into one of the cubicles and dried herself hurriedly before reappearing fully dressed, rubbing her hair with a towel and resigned to what she saw was her certain dismissal when they arrived back in Southampton. She looked at Andrew, who was now also preparing to go and get dressed, but he was arrested in his flight by what Stanley said next.

'And you, ma'am,' he said accusingly, 'you've used the facilities in this spa after hours before now, to take sexual advantage of a young trainee, who needed the job and had no one to look out for her.'

Stanley spoke these words with such dignity and disapproval that Andrew was obliged to listen.

'What do you mean?' he asked, staring hard at Elinor.

'I mean,' said Stanley, 'that the day before we sailed, Elinor invited Fiona to come on board for an induction course. While the rest of us were preparing the cabins and cleaning the public rooms, Fiona was being shown the beauty spa and, as I was distributing clean towels and linen in here, I saw Elinor undressing her, and ... well ... I'll leave the rest to your imagination.'

'Shut up, *you*, you cabin boy!' Elinor spat out vindictively. 'What do you know about anything?'

'I know what I saw,' he said proudly. 'And although you may call me a cabin boy, I am not a liar.'

'Is this true, Elinor?' Andrew asked in mock disbelief. 'Did you really take advantage of an innocent kid like Fiona?'

Elinor flushed and was now on the defensive. 'Rubbish,' she said waspishly. 'She was perfectly willing and she knew what she was doing.'

'Well, in that case,' Andrew continued almost caressingly, 'perhaps I'll have to report the incident to Captain Browning. See what he has to say about a manageress having lesbian sex with a new recruit.'

Elinor was now visibly flustered and had gone from red to deathly white as she faced her three accusers.

'Unless,' Andrew said remorselessly, 'you'd prefer to pay a forfeit?'

'A forfeit?' she faltered.

'Yes, you know, you're prepared to enact a little scene for us. Something along the lines of the boss and the young assistant, only it would be the mature lady and the cabin boy. Just for our private entertainment, of course.'

'What do you mean?' Elinor demanded.

'Well, that's up to the cabin boy, but I feel honour would be satisfied if he were allowed to have sex with you, just as you did with Fiona.'

Even Laura was a little stunned by this suggestion, but Stanley merely nodded and seemed totally unfazed by the idea. He disappeared into one of the changing cubicles.

'Well, what's it to be then, Elinor: sex with the cabin boy or total disclosure to Captain Browning?'

Elinor scowled. 'Stanley, I suppose,' she muttered angrily.

'Are you sure, Elinor?' Laura asked, somewhat anxious at the incongruous idea of the starchy Elinor with the graceful, sexy Goan.

'Yes,' Elinor said shortly. 'Come on. Get on with it. I suppose you two want to watch?' she asked Andrew, and proceeded to remove her clothes very matter of factly and wrapped herself in a towelling robe.

So far, this was extremely unsexy, Laura thought. And then Stanley emerged completely naked, his tall sensuous body glistening and golden brown, his dark eyes quite stern and unforgiving. Laura thought he looked magnificent and when he began to massage his gorgeous brown cock with the herbal oil, it grew twice its length and even Andrew looked impressed. The only person who appeared unmoved was Elinor herself. She gave him a filthy look and climbed on to one of the treatment couches, lying on her back with a look of bored resignation.

'No,' Stanley said firmly. 'I want to take her in her arse.'

There was a moment of shocked silence and then Elinor, with tight lips, obediently turned over so that she was lying on her stomach and Stanley advanced purposefully towards the couch.

'Elinor ... Are you sure? I mean ... Do you really want to go through with this?' Laura asked with some concern.

'Yes. Get on with it,' Elinor growled. 'And let this be the very last time I hear my private business being discussed.'

Andrew and Laura sat together on the side of the jacuzzi and watched in respectful silence as Stanley stood behind Elinor, stroking his long brown hand down the whole creamy length of Elinor's spine, parting her rounded buttocks and arranging her knees wide apart, exposing the puckered opening of her back passage, getting her ready for penetration.

Elinor lay without speaking, her mouth resting on the back of her hand, waiting to have her beautiful arse possessed by a man for the very first time. Stanley applied another dollop of the herbal oil to his fingers and slipped one finger into her tight entrance, making Elinor writhe and struggle against his hand. Her body's first natural response was to reject this intrusion into her private passage and he whispered hoarsely to her to relax and let him in and then it wouldn't hurt. Elinor bit into the skin on the back of her hand and breathed heavily, seeming to comply. She presented her bottom passively, while, ever so gently and slowly, Stanley eased more of the herbal mixture into her opening. Then he removed his fingers and parted her cheeks to reveal her silky crease and wet entrance, guiding the tip of his gleaming cock to the enlarged hole. The first few thrusts were as gentle as his fingers, but after that, he had no mercy on her. He shafted her up to the hilt, grasping her hips and pulling her towards him as he thrust himself into her until his penis disappeared between her buttocks. Now he had one hand underneath her, pleasuring her between her legs until, against her will, she groaned and writhed with pleasure under him, her knees trembling, hardly able to support her. Stanley didn't allow himself to come until Elinor was absolutely sated and gave an involuntary cry of pleasure. Only then did he silently and rapidly increase the speed of his thrusts and satisfy himself.

It was an awe-inspiring sight for Laura and Andrew and they remained silent as Stanley withdrew himself and went to the shower room, leaving Elinor in a crumpled heap. Gradually, she sat up and drew her robe around her while Laura asked solicitously if she was all right.

'Yes,' Elinor replied immediately and, after picking up her clothes, she went to her cabin without another word, walking away with some difficulty and trying to preserve her dignity.

Neither of them spoke for a few moments and then Andrew said, 'Well, I guess we won't have any more trouble from her.'

'Yes, that's for sure.' Laura grinned. 'That was a side of my boss I've never seen before. But she didn't seem too upset about it, did she?'

'I'm sure the "cabin boy" gave her every satisfaction,' he said. Then, thoughtfully, 'Stanley's gay himself as it happens, so maybe he understands her needs better than we do.'

'I never knew that,' Laura said. 'About Stanley, I mean. In fact, Fiona and I thought he was quite fanciable. We'd no idea.' She kept quiet, of course, about her own tryst with the Goan. It didn't do to let Andrew know *everything*.

Andrew smiled. 'Well, perhaps he could be bi, but enough of this. What about you and me? We need to go to my cabin and complete our unfinished business. It's my ambition to make you a happy and satisfied woman before I turn into a pumpkin at midnight.'

Laura laughed out loud with sheer relief at the freedom from the nervous tension of the evening's events. 'That suits me,' she said, and gathered her things together, conscientiously locking the door behind them as they left the salon. They walked hand in hand to the lift and up to Andrew's cabin. The ship was unnaturally quiet. Most cruisers were busy watching the climax to the Gala Variety Show. Only a few were taking the opportunity to gamble in the casino. She thought affectionately of Eileen and Reg and hoped fleetingly that their night of love and passion was going well and then she completely forgot about them because they'd arrived at Andrew's door.

He kicked it to behind them and grasped her wrists in the warm steel of his strong fingers, pulling her towards him. He bent his face over hers, his dark eyes gazing deeply into her own, and for a few seconds Laura's heartbeat faltered and she was utterly breathless with her longing for him. Before she could say a word, he'd pulled her against him with such force that she felt her breasts flatten painfully against the taut male hardness of his chest.

All he could say was 'Laura ... Laura' and then his lips were on hers, and his hands were dealing with the fastening on her jeans, pulling her T-shirt out and pushing it upwards with the utmost gentleness and sensuality, as he once more found her breasts. This time there were no spectators. They had absolute privacy and were able to let go of all restraints.

She discovered what a skilled lover Andrew was, as she'd guessed he would be. She realised how well he knew the workings of her body as he continued to undress her slowly, as though he had all the time in the world. He kissed her deeply and passionately and stroked her long blonde hair, winding his fingers through it and tugging it gently to pull back her head and at the same time pushing her gently on to the bed. He started to remove his own clothes and paused for a moment at the foot of the bed to look at her. Laura lay back and opened her legs provocatively to give him a tantalising glimpse of her hot wet pussy, as he pulled off the rest of his clothes, still holding her gaze and getting on to the bed at the side of her.

'You don't know how many times I've thought about

'making love to you, properly, since we first met,' he whispered, with his mouth once more on hers.

'I know.' Laura smiled and moved slightly to make more room for him. 'We seem to have had so many false starts. The course of true love never does run smooth. I'd begun to think it wasn't to be.'

'Oh, but it is, Laura. It's definitely meant to be,' he said very seriously, as he continued to look at her intently. 'As soon as I met you, I knew you and I could be an item, destined for each other. When we get home I'm taking you to Farnham for the weekend to meet my mother.'

While this was sinking in, he traced a line of white hot desire down each of her breasts, then down even further over her flat belly to find her sex. His eyes feasted on her face and body, taking in the beauty and symmetry, and Laura, not fully taking in the significance of his words, instinctively bent her knees slightly, pulling back her pussy lips and holding them open so that he could see every detail of her wide-open sex, moist and perfumed with the subtle scent of her arousal. Wishing only for fulfilment, she pressed herself closely against him, warm and trembling, raising her hips from the bed.

She was inviting him to enter her in the most direct way she knew, by pushing her silky mound against his erect and ready penis and rubbing herself hard against it. He pressed his pointed tongue into her open mouth, exploring it all over again, tantalising her and making her frantic to have more. The saltiness of his come was still on Laura's lips and their passionate open-mouthed kissing transferred it to his own, making her re-live the pleasure of his cock all over again. His hands were on her breasts, his nails gently scratching at her swollen nipples, making her mad for him. She wanted to feel him inside her. She was absolutely desperate for him to penetrate her and satisfy her. But she could sense that he was taking his time, holding back until he was sure she was ready for him. At last, when she sensed that he was unable to wait any longer, Laura grasped his cock in her hand and guided it into her hot wet entrance herself. For a moment, they both lay still, his cock not moving, revelling in this feeling that, at last, they were conjoined so intimately and sexily.

'Oh that's so good,' Laura sighed with relief. 'It's what I've wanted for so long, almost like coming home.'

He was still looking into her eyes, as if he were searching her soul. His own eyes expressed a passion that Laura had never expected. Then he started thrusting into her, at first slowly and steadily but as he gradually increased the momentum, he began to rub her clit with his thumb, very gently and insistently until she thought she'd be unable to hold off her climax for a moment longer. Her whole body throbbed and burned with urgency. Now he increased the intensity and speed of his fucking and at last Laura exploded with the force of her orgasm, letting the waves of exquisite pleasure overwhelm her. For a few moments she was incapable of any speech or movement but, feeling his cock pulsating, she held him closer as he came strongly and powerfully, shouting her name and pumping his warm seed inside her. They both finally surrendered into each other's arms, utterly spent, and lay together, relaxed and satisfied.

Laura held him, feeling a luxurious sensation of post-coital tenderness, and Andrew stayed inside her for so long that she thought he might have fallen asleep. She herself was feeling drowsy and only came to when his gradually softening cock finally slipped out of her and she felt the love juices leaking sneakily down her thighs. It must be getting quite late now, she thought languidly, and she turned to kiss him once more. She was almost on the verge of sleep herself and not expecting him to continue with further lovemaking.

But he was sitting up between her still open legs, and he arranged them so that they were now high as well as wide. Laura's limbs were as relaxed as rubber and he held her easily in this position as he bent over her, his tongue lapping softly and steadily to spread their combined love juices over the whole of her wide-open and relaxed sex. He licked at her fragrant pussy, his tongue wide and flat as though licking an ice cream, spreading the lubricating fluids to the tight little bud of Laura's anus. Now he pointed his tongue stiffly to stimulate her private entrance, and moisten it ready for his probing index finger.

After the first shock of this intrusion, Laura let herself relax until he'd slid his finger inside her up to the knuckle and began to twist it gently round and round to give her the most exquisite sensations she'd ever experienced. Meanwhile, he was massaging her pussy with his other hand, with first two, then three fingers in her already sensitised passage. Laura lay back groaning with pleasure as he bent once more between her legs and flicked at her hard red clit with his stiff tongue until she began to orgasm once more, breathless and sweating with the intensity of feeling. Andrew was by this time stiff again, but lying back exhausted against the pillows, with the last echoes of her climax gradually ebbing away, Laura sighed that they should really take a break.

He grinned. 'Can't stand the pace, eh?' he said. 'OK. I've got a drop of your favourite wine in the fridge. Let's chill out for a bit.'

He brought the wine and some tissues for her and they lay back in a comfortable silence. Laura wondered what it would be like living with Andrew. Pretty good, she thought, if tonight was anything to go by. She sipped her wine and turned to look at him, her face soft and glowing with a pleasure that was more than just sex.

'So I'm to meet your family, am I?' she said playfully, but she was aware of a feeling inside her that was deadly serious. For the first time in her life, Laura Barnes felt unsure of her own supreme capabilities to run the universe as she wished it to be run and she felt attracted and somewhat humbled by the idea of a partnership of equals. He was as strong as she was herself. She felt instinctively that a future with Andrew would be secure, loving and exciting.

He answered her seriously. 'Yes,' he said. 'If you think that you want it as well, I'd like us to get together, Laura.'

She looked deeply into his warm brown eyes and knew that he was sincere. He was looking slightly less than confident now, almost anxious in fact, as he waited for her reply. He leaned forward and kissed her, then reached out for the wine bottle and poured them both another glass.

'Well, what do you say? We're working together. How would you like us to be living together?'

As she looked into his clear eyes and handsome face, Laura thought fleetingly of the spotty youth who'd been her first teenage boyfriend in north Manchester. She didn't even need to think about it. She put her arms round his neck.

'Why not?' she said. 'That seems like a very good idea.'

13

Elinor never found out how Fiona got to know of the goings-on in the jacuzzi, but get to know she did, and she marched smartly to Elinor's cabin, her small young face red and angry. She was absolutely transformed by the tension of her fury and burst in on her lover after a very cursory knock, her usual rather mouse-like personality changed beyond all recognition. Elinor was sitting at the side of the bed, filing her beautiful nails. Her momentary irritation at the intrusion turned to affectionate welcome when she saw who it was, but then her loving smile disappeared at Fiona's furious onslaught and turned to shocked surprise.

'So you like to spy, do you, Elinor?' Fiona glared at her and clenched her small hands into hard little fists.

'No, of course not,' Elinor faltered. 'I don't know what you mean.'

'I mean,' Fiona hissed, 'that you've been hounding my friend Laura and threatening to report her.'

'I thought ... something was going on ... I'm ... I'm responsible if there're any irregularities ... I thought ...'

'You thought wrong then,' Fiona sneered, and stepped closer to her.

She reached out and grasped Elinor at each side of her neck, slipping her fingers into the crisp white overall and rubbing her thumbs lasciviously against Elinor's collar bone and then, very deliberately, she moved them down to rub her full breasts with her thumb pads.

Elinor's head jerked up and she instinctively thrust

herself towards Fiona's searching hands. Her nipples were now hard projectiles, clearly outlined through the white fabric of the bra beneath her starchy uniform and she unconsciously opened her legs a little. Her eyes were locked into Fiona's and it was obvious to the younger girl that her actions were getting her friend excited. Elinor's immaculately glossed lips were parted and her eyes heavy and sensual as Fiona began none too gently to pinch her stiff nipples through the white uniform. She was still speaking in an angry voice, but much more softly now.

'You Jezebel. You false friend,' Fiona said very theatrically. 'What did you think you were doing, interfering in Laura's business like that, trying to humiliate her in front of clients?'

'I'm ... I'm sorry, darling,' Elinor mumbled, uncharacteristically humble. 'I didn't realise ... Fiona, I –'

'Shut up,' Fiona ordered curtly. The two women had now completely reversed their usual roles and Fiona was quite definitely in charge. Without taking her hands off Elinor's nipples, she leaned forward and thrust her mouth against the older woman's eager lips and began to tongue her thoroughly and insultingly until Elinor gasped with pleasure and drew back a little, her nipple ends quivering and pulsing with excitement at the change in her normally gentle lover.

'Stand up,' Fiona said, 'and take your shoes off.' She pulled Elinor to her feet and Elinor obediently kicked off her shoes, her eyes luminous with anticipation as the two women faced each other in the small cabin.

'Undo your uniform and pull your bra up,' she ordered. 'I want your tits bare.'

Elinor swallowed audibly and removed the elasticated belt of her salon overall. She undid her top buttons down to the waist and pulled up her white cotton sports bra with trembling fingers, standing meekly in front of her young lover, her overall unfastened and her naked breasts on display.

'Now put your hands on your tits and keep them there,' Fiona ordered her. 'I'm going to teach you a lesson you won't forget in a hurry and you deserve it, don't you, you dirty little tell-tale? Don't you?' she asked again when Elinor didn't reply straight away.

'Oh yes, mistress,' Elinor breathed adoringly, and clasped her hands over her deep rounded breasts, her palms pressing obediently against the hard pointed nipples.

Fiona could tell by the way Elinor's eyes swivelled towards the door that she was aroused by the idea of her punishment and ready to be humbled. She locked the cabin door quickly and kneeled down in front of her, moving Elinor's feet a little way apart and sliding her hands slowly and sensuously up Elinor's legs, feeling the smooth nylon of her tights and making her shudder with pleasure as she finally reached her crotch. She slid her hands across Elinor's firm belly, slipping her thumbs into the waistband of the prim panti-hose then peeled them down. Both women knew what was going to happen and there was an air of suppressed excitement about both of them as the tights were finally unrolled around Elinor's ankles. Fiona pulled them off completely and tossed them on to the chair. She looked up and saw the submission in the flickering of Elinor's eyes and in the way she bent her head as she obediently pressed her hands against her tits and waited passively for Fiona to give her orders.

'Now I'm going to punish you and let you know what a bad girl you've been,' Fiona said softly. 'So bad that you deserve to have your clitty slapped. You don't like that, do you, Elinor? It makes you squirm and struggle, doesn't it?'

Elinor nodded mutely, her eyes still lowered. They'd played this game before.

'I'm going to let you keep your panties on for this,' Fiona said. 'It always stings more through the nylon and you deserve to sting, don't you?'

She noted the soaking crotch of Elinor's knickers and smiled up at her. 'Later, I'm going to torment your wet little pleasure button for a long time, Elinor,' she went on. 'But first things first.' She pushed her rather unceremoniously on to the bed and went into the tiny bathroom to wet one of Elinor's hand towels.

'Now, slave, what do you remember about the rules?' she said.

'I must keep my hands on my tits,' Elinor said dutifully.

'And what else?' Fiona asked sternly, and she rolled up Elinor's immaculate overall until it was round her waist.

'I don't know,' Elinor said, pretending innocence.

'Come on now. Make yourself know or I shall have to tell you.' Fiona twisted the damp towel until it was a thick rope.

'I ... don't remember, mistress.' Elinor faltered.

'Well then, slave, I'll have to jog your memory. The best way to do that is to mark your mound for you,' Fiona said firmly, and she parted Elinor's legs slightly, getting her ready for her punishment. She slapped the hard wet towel against Elinor's mound, not once but several times until the sensible white knickers were all wet and transparent. Through the nylon, Fiona could see that Elinor's copper-coloured pubes were splayed out and darkened with the force of the slaps. Soon, the red mound would be visibly pink through the thin wet fabric. She gave a much firmer slap and Elinor gasped and squirmed, momentarily taking her hands from her tits. Fiona steadied her with one hand on Elinor's abdomen.

'Oh dear, that wasn't very clever of you, was it? You know what happens to disobedient girls, don't you? Say yes, mistress.'

'Yes, mistress,' Elinor said, and obediently put her hands back on her breasts, tensing herself for the next slap. 'I . . . I get punished even more.'

She leaned back uncomfortably; her mound felt enlarged and had begun to tingle pleasurably. She kept her hands on her breasts and arched her back, thrusting herself upwards as though inviting more strokes and Fiona obligingly flicked the towel between her legs again and again, stinging her until she groaned with pleasure.

'The other thing you have to remember is that there's to be no shouting out, no whingeing, no cries or groans while I'm giving you your punishment. Is that understood?'

'Yes, mistress,' Elinor whispered.

'I'm sorry, I didn't hear that, slave.' She gave another stinging flick to Elinor's sore mound and got an immediate response.

'Yes, mistress. No cries or groans, mistress,' Elinor said loudly, and her eyes met Fiona's with the utmost complicity.

'You can turn over then,' Fiona said sternly. 'I'm going to wet your bum first, and give it a good warming up before I give you your proper spanking and then I'll expect you to be an obedient slave and never do anything so naughty again.'

'Yes, mistress,' Elinor said again, and turned herself over on the bed, exposing her rounded curvy bum covered by the white knickers, ready for her punishment.

Fiona primed Elinor's arse with the wet towel until the nylon knickers stuck to her bum, outlining every curve and crack. Concentrating fiercely, Fiona twisted the towel again and began to methodically pound Elinor's bottom, punishing each cheek in turn until both Elinor's shapely orbs shone through the white material and turned a glistening pretty rose pink. Elinor never said a word. She lay obediently on her front, grasping her breasts and pressing her sore mound against the bed sheet. She was quivering slightly as the comfortable warmth of the chastising towel made her glow with pleasure and lust. Fiona threw the towel down at last and reached across to the dressing table for the hairbrush.

She felt her own love juices running between her legs as she looked down at the shining contours of Elinor's behind through the white panties and felt a rush of tenderness for her lesbian lover. Elinor was the only lover she would ever want. If anything happened to part them, she'd be utterly bereft, she thought.

Aloud, she said, 'Right, let's have these knickers down now.' She edged Elinor's pants down over her glowing arse and caressed the exposed wet buttocks, reddening them a little further as she pulled the knickers down her legs. She slipped her hand under Elinor's body to find her wet mound, winding her fingers through Elinor's pubic hair and then tugging at it gently, but hard enough to sting, letting her know that she'd been out of order spying on Laura and Andrew, letting her know that the spanking she was going to get would hurt. Before she began, she rubbed the smooth back of the brush over the area to be spanked and Elinor grunted with pleasure at the feel of the cool plastic against her hot behind.

Elinor's buttocks twitched a little as the hairbrush came down with some force.

'Aah!' Elinor gave a cry of pain and Fiona stopped what she was doing immediately.

She said sternly, 'No crying out, remember? Now I'm obliged to make you pay a forfeit. It'll be three extra strokes for every groan you make. Is that understood, slave?'

'Yes, mistress,' Elinor gasped, and clenched her buttocks as well as her teeth, as Fiona turned her attention once more to the pink bare bottom, bringing the hairbrush down again, toasting first one cheek then the other until they were no longer wet and they'd both turned bright red.

'Mmm, you're nice and red now,' Fiona said, and she put the brush down to stroke the hot arse and slipped a hand underneath her again to feel Elinor's soaking wet pussy.

'Dear me, Elinor, you're so damp, you must be an absolute slut to have such sexy feelings without my permission. You'll have to have extra strokes for this. Three extra, at least.'

'Yes, mistress. Very good, mistress,' Elinor said meekly. 'I deserve to have my arse punished more.'

'Yes. At least six more,' Fiona said. 'The first three are for spying on Laura and threatening to report her and the second three are for being such a dirty little madam, oozing sex like that in the middle of your punishment.'

She laid on six more strokes, the hairbrush coming down hard and fast, but Elinor made no further groans, cries or shouts and when the spanking was finished, Fiona helped her to slide off the bed and stood tenderly fondling Elinor's heated backside.

'Say you're sorry,' she whispered.

'I'm sorry,' Elinor said.

'Say what you want now,' Fiona said to her, and began to rub her fingers down Elinor's crack and then into her wet pussy, flicking her clit and teasing her until the normally cool Elinor was beside herself with lust.

'You know what I want,' Elinor muttered thickly.

'I'm sorry,' Fiona said teasingly, 'I didn't hear that. What is it you want, slave?'

'You know what I want,' Elinor said again. Her normally pristine overall was a creased wreck, gaping open at the front and revealing the sports bra all rucked up underneath her neck. Her immaculate hair was tousled beyond recognition and her make-up had smudged with the sweat running down her brow.

'Let's have these clothes off first,' Fiona said softly. She began to undo the rest of the buttons and slipped the overall off Elinor's shoulders, unhooking the bra and removing it so that her lover was completely naked. Elinor's deep breasts stood firm, the tips red and glowing. She whimpered as Fiona started to pinch and nibble at her voluptuous flesh, taking the nipples one by one between her sharp little teeth and biting them like a mouse nibbling cheese. Elinor groaned aloud and begged for more and Fiona slid her hand down the older woman's belly, stroking the soft skin between Elinor's legs, carefully avoiding the sore mound, just concentrating on Elinor's thighs and groin. Elinor reached down and tried to push Fiona's hand towards her raging slit, but Fiona resisted, teasing her unbearably.

'Where do you want me? Is it your slit that's hungry? Is it your bumhole? Do you want me to make you come in your bumhole, or are you too sore?'

'No. No,' Elinor moaned. 'I want you inside me. Right up into my cunt. I want to come there while you suck me off.'

Fiona continued to stroke her hand up and down Elinor's twitching thighs.

'And what is it you want pushed up your hot little

flu?' she tantalised her. 'Is it two fingers? The vibrator? Black Johnny? What can I torment you with that'll make you beg for it?'

'Anything,' Elinor almost sobbed. 'Whatever you want. Do it to me.'

'Ram something up you, you mean? Fuck you hard and fast till you come on your back and then turn you over and let you come doggy fashion?' Fiona said. 'Very well. On the understanding that after I've let you come, you're going to return the compliment and beg to make love to me in any way I desire. Is it understood?'

'Yes. Yes,' Elinor moaned again. 'Do it to me. Oh please.'

Fiona stopped stroking Elinor to take her own clothes off. Then she reached into the bedside drawer and took out two small wicked-looking vibrators, one cigar-shaped and one shaped like an egg.

She began to move the vibrating egg just at the entrance to Elinor's sex, rotating it round and round her soaked hole and then briefly touching her lover's erect clit with it, until she found the spot that made Elinor's breath quicken and made her cry, 'Oh yes. There. Do it just there.'

Fiona pressed the vibrating egg a little deeper into Elinor's hole and left it there while she primed the silver cigar, pushing it in and out of her own pussy lips until it was shining and lubricated with her own copious love juice. She began to push it gently and deliciously into Elinor's bumhole, opening the twin cheeks of Elinor's bottom until she'd got it firmly in place. Only then did she switch on the battery, thrusting gently in and out until Elinor moaned and whimpered with lust as both her openings were stimulated at once. She pushed it in deeply, leaving it to hum and vibrate in Elinor's throbbing back passage while she fingered Elinor's clit, circling it with her finger until she was close to coming, but all the time keeping her on the edge. Elinor began to sob with lust, attempting to direct the tormenting finger herself, but Fiona still wouldn't let her come. The muscles in Elinor's thighs were twitching and tight with longing. Fiona slapped her hand down firmly and moved up Elinor's body, straddling her until her pussy was over Elinor's mouth.

'No more rubbing for you,' she said, 'until you've sucked me off.'

Elinor clamped her lips to the younger girl's hot wet sex, and murmured words of adoration and subjugation. Fiona reached backwards and began to casually finger Elinor's clit once more. Elinor gripped Fiona's hips in both hands, pulling her closer and tonguing her fiercely, until her mouth was covered in Fiona's pearly love juices. Fiona's arms and legs went stiff and her eyes closed as she shuddered and relaxed against Elinor's shoulder, pulling out the cigar and the egg as both of them climaxed and lay still. They were fabulous together, Fiona thought. The sexual chemistry between them was incredible. They caressed each other and kissed again and again as they lay in each other's arms.

14

After every action, there's reaction, and as she slowly made her way along the quiet corridors in the early hours of the morning, Laura wondered if Fiona had spent the night in Elinor's bed and whether she ought to give an explanation about her own whereabouts during the night. She needn't have worried. Fiona didn't appear until they met in the salon and then she behaved as though she'd noticed nothing. Elinor was as cool and hard edged as always and everything at the Shangri-la was in order. Tomorrow, they would reach Southampton and so today many of the clients were keen to book appointments for facials and hairdos ready for the evening to come. They would all want to look their best for the Captain's black and white farewell dinner party and everyone at the Shangri-la was pulling out all the stops. Tips and gratuities were rolling into the staff's communal funds and most of the cruisers were busy checking their drinks bills against their bar receipts.

Laura knew that Steve and the bar staff would have to be available in case the purser wanted to check any of these computerised till receipts. Some of the more elderly winos were brilliant at convincing themselves that they'd consumed a lot less than they had, in spite of the evidence of the printout. She also knew that on the last trip to the Caribbean, a rogue bar assistant had been printing his own till receipts. Printing was the operative word as well, she thought, because this young idiot had merely printed the names of the imaginary customers. He'd made no attempt to forge authentic signatures. Needless to say, Captain Browning had put him ashore at St Kits and he was out of a job. All this meant a lot of extra work for the staff, even though most of the passengers were more than willing to face up to the damage of their wine bill.

Things were busy in the salon as well. All the ordering of extra supplies had to be documented; every surface, cupboard and wash basin had to be prepared for the massive clean-up and anti-bacterial sterilisation that would ensue as soon as they reached Southampton and every towel, cloth and overall had to be laundered. The long-drawn-out disembarkation and customs regulation procedures were all still to come tomorrow morning. For the moment, though, Laura had work to do and was pleased to see Eileen, who came for her cleanse, tone and nourish treatment at eleven o'clock, looking radiant and sounding distinctively upbeat. It was obvious that things were now going well between her and Reg.

'We're both looking forward to the party tonight, Laura,' she said happily. 'And tomorrow we'll be heading back to South Yorkshire. It'll be nice to get home again, although we've enjoyed the cruise, of course.'

She kept up a bit of the inane chatter until Imogen, the young assistant, was out of earshot and then she lowered her voice to confide more seriously.

'We're so lucky, Laura. To have each other, I mean, and to have met you on this cruise. You and your friend, that is. You've saved our marriage, darling. Really, you have.'

She grasped one of Laura's hands and halted the progress of the toning gel as she said fervently, 'I don't know what I'd have done without you. No, really, I mean it. It was all up with Reggie and me. I didn't know what I was going to do. I know he needed a holiday, but the rest of it . . .' Her voice trailed off. 'Well, anyway, it's all worked out all right. After all this time, Reggie and I are on course again. Just like a couple of silly newly-weds in fact. And it's all down to you, Laura. No, really,' she said again, squeezing Laura's hand hard. 'It's true. Without your help we'd still be down in the dumps. You've saved our marriage. And I'm grateful. Truly grateful.'

'That's nice,' Laura said rather inadequately. 'What about this evening? What are you wearing for the black and white dinner?' And she turned the talk to more mundane things as she worked on giving Eileen a glamorous makeover for the evening to come.

At four o'clock, Steve came to the salon to seek her out. He was obviously in a state of barely concealed excitement and was holding a letter confirming his successful application for the *Borealis*.

'I've made it, Laura,' he gasped. 'I've got the job. Senior organiser for the upper bars on Sun, Lido and A deck on the *Borealis* cruise ship.'

It was obvious to Laura that she'd come nowhere in her application for senior administrator of the Northern Lights Health Spa.

'Sorry about that,' Steve said. 'It says here that while your qualifications are beyond question, unfortunately your experience has only been with the *Jannina* and they've received applications from so many experienced and well-qualified people, they were spoilt for choice.'

Laura nodded. 'I didn't think I'd have much of a chance,' she admitted. 'But I'm pleased for you, Steve. It's the opportunity you've been waiting for. Well done, you.' She gave him a big hug and a kiss.

'It means we'll be apart from now on though,' he said soberly.

'I know, but you've got to take your chance when it's offered and we can keep in touch.'

He breathed deeply and took her hand with a regretful sigh. 'Yes. We can keep in touch. I'll miss you though,' he said.

'And I'll miss you,' Laura assured him, and she covered his hand with her own. 'But it's what you want to do and we agreed . . .'

'I know we did,' he said. 'But that doesn't make it any easier, Laura.'

'I know. I know,' she said inadequately.

They looked at each other for a few long moments. All sorts of memories, regrets and shared pleasures were in Laura's mind, but she recognised that this was the parting of the ways: goodbye to her old love, a new start for both of them.

'I'll never forget you, Steve,' she said at last.

'And I'll never forget you,' he said sadly. 'You'll always be in my thoughts.'

'Keep in touch,' she said. 'I'll be thinking of you.'

'Yes. Keep in touch,' he said and, folding up the letter from the *Borealis*, he turned and walked away.

Laura had another two hours' work in the salon and plenty of time to reflect on the ending of her affair with Steve. Tomorrow, they'd be in Southampton and, ordinarily, she'd be speeding home to north Manchester and her lovely warm mum. Now, Andrew had added another dimension to the idea of her end-of-cruise leave. The thought of meeting his family in Farnham was both stimulating and intimidating. One half of her wanted to meet the exciting challenge head-on; the other half was nervous about the thought of what his formidable mother might be like. Well, she thought, she can't eat you, but even then she wasn't so sure.

It needed all Andrew's skilled powers of persuasion to convince her that the weekend would be a success and that his mother would love her instantly.

'I've sent a fax,' he said. 'Mum and Dad and my sister Jane are looking forward to meeting you. They'll fall in love with you as soon as they see you.' He was adamant that they'd have a lovely time. 'And then,' he said, 'we've got the music trip to the Mediterranean. Two sopranos, an ensemble and a moody Italian pianist. Could life hold more, I ask myself.'

Laura laughed and admitted that it couldn't.

The salon was closed. Andrew was free for an hour until the farewell dance. They were lying naked on Andrew's bed. Laura was feeling very relaxed with him, almost lazy, in fact. She lay with her mouth in his neck; he had his arm around her, quietly and soothingly stroking the small of her back. It was quiet after the hurly-burly of the salon and the mental tension of working with Elinor and Fiona.

'But it was all OK,' she murmured to Andrew. 'Elinor kept completely out of my hair today and I honestly don't think Fiona knew a dicky bird about Stanley and the jacuzzi. And Stanley would never say anything anyway.'

'And Reggie certainly didn't.' He grinned. 'I saw him and Eileen just now and you'd think they'd just invented sex. They were so pleased with things.'

'What about that poor old pervy Evans?' Laura said. 'Do you think he found out about Stanley's little session with Elinor?'

'I doubt it,' Andrew said.

But he was wrong.

Bob Evans had been nosing around the beauty spa, hoping to engineer a meeting with Laura and, in typical peeping-Tom fashion, he'd been able to catch a glimpse of the goings-on, without being observed himself.

The delicious image of the tall handsome Goan thrusting his long brown cock mercilessly into Elinor's body had sent him almost out of his mind. His delirious pouchy eyes were mesmerised by the scene in front of him until he'd finally reeled out of the spa, when it became obvious that he might get caught. Tired of being a voyeur, he hurried to his cabin and, flushed and perspiring, threw himself on the bed, his hands trembling as he pulled out his own stiff cock and began to wank himself frantically. The sight of Elinor's tight bumhole being repeatedly stretched and punished by Stanley's strong dark shaft had excited him unbearably. He was determined that the first time he got his end away with that supercilious blonde bitch, Laura Barnes, he'd have her arse. He'd have her face downwards on the bed and pump into her until he'd utterly subdued her. He'd show that stand-offish tart what a real man could do for her.

He'd wait until she was absolutely broken before he allowed himself to fill her up with the huge flow of his orgasm. He'd make her whimper while he punished her sore backside with his powerful organ. Evans knew that Laura didn't really like him and this made his fantasy of humbling her all the more potent. When he'd satisfied himself, he'd turn her over and fuck her silly, he decided. He'd soon show Laura Barnes where to get off.

With mounting excitement, he changed hands and rubbed himself even more fiercely, as his excited imagination took complete hold of him. He was breathing in shallow rapid gasps now and his hand flashed faster and faster up and down his cock. His left shoulder and arm began to ache unbearably but, feeling his orgasm was about to erupt, he just ignored the pain and finished in a gushing wet climax.

For a few moments, he lay panting and utterly spent, still unable to catch his breath or calm his breathing.

Although his hands and limbs were relaxed, the discomfort in his arm seemed to get worse. It moved across his chest, first like an aching spasm of indigestion and then, suddenly, in a tightly gripping agony. A terrible rending pain, as though a giant's hand was tearing his heart out of his body, squeezing and squeezing it pitilessly, without mercy, until he lost consciousness.

It was Stanley who found him, of course. Receiving no answer to his knock when he went to service the cabin, he inserted his swipe card and saw the stressed-out exec lying back on the bed, trousers undone, penis now limp and withered, hands fallen uselessly to his sides. It was obvious that he was ill and Stanley took a spare blanket from the wardrobe and covered him up before summoning the ship's doctor.

Later, he went in search of Laura and tapped on her cabin door. Fiona was nowhere to be seen.

'Mr and Mrs Walton, Tom and Emma, that is, have invited me round to 36B for a farewell drink, Laura,' he said. 'The dance isn't really their scene and they asked me to ask you if you'd join us.'

His dark eyes were smiling into hers and he said, 'I'll go if you will.'

Why not? She wasn't doing anything and they'd all be disembarking tomorrow, Laura thought. She liked both of them. She'd probably never see Stanley again. Thelma had told her that Stanley wouldn't be rejoining the ship. Despite his bisexuality, he was marrying a village girl back home and wouldn't be going to sea again.

'What time is the party?' she asked cautiously.

'About ten o'clock,' he said. 'But it's a movable feast. I'm on duty till nine, Laura, but I can make it for ten. If you can, that is.'

'Well, why not? I'll have done my packing by then and I've no deadlines to meet. I'll see you there then, Stanley.'

'Good,' he said. The smile in his eyes now reached his mouth and he left her to get on with her packing, his step light, his slim sinuous hips moving gracefully as always.

Laura looked at her watch. Plenty of time to freshen her make-up and put on one of her smart but casual cruise dresses. She took a deep breath, feeling suddenly calm in spite of her heart beating so hard. She remembered how much she'd enjoyed her last meeting with Tom and Emma. This had certainly been an eventful voyage, she thought. And it wasn't over yet. She felt in control of her own fate and that excited her. She supposed that she should feel a little guilty at the idea of enjoying this party without Andrew, but the truth was, she didn't. She just felt excited anticipation at seeing Tom and Emma again. All passengers had to leave their luggage in the corridor before midnight, because tomorrow everything would be unloaded, every cabin emptied and cleaned out. All the cruisers would disembark and set off on their onward journey. She snapped her suitcases closed and took a last look at her watch. Five to ten. Just right. She stowed the cases in the corridor and walked purposefully to the lift.

The door of 36B opened as soon as she knocked. Emma and Tom's luggage was already in the corridor and they'd opened the door to the bedroom and the balcony so that it made the best of the space. Emma had rung cabin service and had got a tray of champagne glasses and nibbles. Tom was pouring out the champagne and Laura noticed Stanley had already arrived and was wearing a casual white T-shirt and pale grey slacks, which did a lot for his sexy bum and long legs. The daylight was almost gone and Emma switched on the wall lights, which cast a soft glow all round the cabin.

'Welcome,' Emma said. She was wearing a flowing black kaftan and Tom was in a black silk kimono dressing gown, tied at the waist.

Tom handed her a glass of champagne and sat down beside her. 'Hello again,' he said and smiled. Laura felt her clit beginning to throb as she looked into his handsome face and met his sparkling blue eyes. Any doubts she might have had about accepting the invitation had now disappeared and she felt totally relaxed.

There was a little silence as they sipped the ice-cold champagne and smiled round at each other. Tom was the first to speak

'Well, God bless all here,' he said. 'We've really enjoyed meeting you two this trip and we'll always remember the *Jannina*. I never expected a cruise to be so interesting. Emma and I have decided that the theme for our last evening should be living out our fantasies.'

He paused to let this sink in while they all looked at him and he went on a little less confidently, 'In the past, my favourite fantasy has always been to be a spectator when my wife makes love to another woman and she's indulged me in this loads of times and I've found it an utter turn-on. It's improved our sex life no end. So far, though, I've never seen Emma make love to another man and I just want to try it with someone trustworthy and discreet.'

He paused again and then said, 'Emma's already told me what her favourite fantasy is.'

Eyes shining, lips parting in a smile, Emma said, 'I've always wanted two men to come on to me at the same time.'

Tom looked questioningly at Stanley. 'And I've always

wanted to make love in a threesome, either two women or a couple, at the same time,' Stanley said modestly.

Laura was last. 'I've always fancied the idea of putting on my own auto-erotic sex show,' she said slowly. 'Of giving myself a good screw in public, but of course it wouldn't ever happen like that. It would have to be in private, in front of a selected audience.'

She glanced round at the others. She could see that this idea was a turn-on for the other three and she felt turned on herself.

'Well,' Tom said, 'if we're all agreed, I'll be the MC and arrange the programme. Laura's auto-erotic thingy seems a good starting point and, after that, we'll play it by ear.' He replenished everyone's glass and Laura took a gulp of champagne to soothe her stretched nerves, as the other three looked at her expectantly. She just hoped she hadn't bitten off more than she could chew.

Emma produced a small flight bag from the wardrobe. 'We've got quite a nice little collection of sex toys in here if there's anything you fancy, Laura.' She giggled. 'Take your pick. It's your choice.'

Laura coolly selected a wicked-looking cream plastic phallus and walked over to the bed.

'As the MC,' Tom said, 'it's my special role to help the artistes tonight.' He came so close to her that she could smell his lemony aftershave as he put his hands on her shoulders. 'Stand still a minute,' he said. 'Turn round while I unzip you.'

Obediently, Laura turned her back on him and he undid the long zip at the back of her dress, letting the material slide down her body and over her hips till it fell on the floor. He stooped to pick up the dress and put it on a chair and Laura stood revealed before her audience. Her long tanned legs didn't need tights and she was just wearing minuscule black satin panties and a lacy underwired bra to match. She knew that the bra made the most of her magnificent breasts, but the panties were of the briefest imaginable. Just two black satin triangles, one covering her mound and the other high up over her buttocks. A little wisp of black lace joined the triangles together at each side. She looked and felt magnificent.

Her body was trembling with arousal as Tom ordered her to sit on the bed. 'Now lie back,' he said. 'I need to put some cushions under you, so we can all see everything.'

Laura lay back against the pillows and he fetched cushions from the settees to raise her hips and support her bottom.

'Make yourself comfortable, Laura, and start when you're ready,' he said, and he stepped back to sit with the others, leaving her feeling exposed and vulnerable, but at the same time sexy and powerful.

She reached both hands behind her back and undid her bra, slowly drawing it off in front of her and pulling it away from her body, baring her breasts and rubbing them slowly and sensually with the palms of her hands. She didn't give eye contact to any of them, but just gazed at a distant view while she tweaked and pinched her nipples, rotating the globes of her breasts with her palms and then tweaking again, shocking her nipples into stiff swollen points, then rotating her globes again and again until her flesh was flushed and excited. She let her hands slide down to her belly, closer and closer to her wispy panties, but not yet removing them. Instead, she opened one leg and, holding it open, exposed her thick wet lips and trembling clit to her audience. Every sensation was heightened as the spectators greedily watched the movement of her probing finger, circling round and round her sex, making herself moan and shudder as she stretched herself open. She spent time spreading her cream up and down her crack, massaging her clit and bumhole until she was ready for the sex toy. Only then did she take off the tiny panties, easing them down her hips and discarding them with the black bra. She spread her legs wide apart and bent her knees, angling herself upwards on the cushions so that they could all see everything. She switched on the plastic phallus and ran her hand down between her legs holding her pussy lips wide as she touched the entrance to her sex with the tip of the dildo. As the sex toy began to hum steadily, she nudged it in and out of her opening, trying to grip and hold it as she moved it deeper and deeper into herself, as far up as it would go. She was only vaguely aware of the heavy breathing and absorbed concentration of the others as they watched avidly. She rolled her head from side to side as the dildo vibrated strongly. She was filled right up, completely stretched, ready to come. As the vibrations touched every one of her sexual nerve endings, she touched her clit again with her fingers and immediately her body was racked and shaken with her orgasm then she lay still.

There was a significant silence for a few moments and then Tom said rather unsteadily, 'That was fabulous, Laura. Well done. A hard act to follow.'

Emma passed her a towelling robe and whispered, 'That was wonderful, darling. A real turn-on.'

Laura saw that Stanley was gazing admiringly at Emma, his tight trousers already bulging and it was Stanley who made the next move. He put his glass down and went into the bedroom and lay down on the king-sized bed. There was no mistaking the invitation that he was signalling with his eyes to Emma and she went and joined him almost immediately.

Laura and Tom could both see what was happening through the open door and the atmosphere in the cabin suddenly became charged up again. Stanley lifted the skirt of Emma's kaftan and revealed her elegant shapely legs. Taking her cue from her first encounter with Laura, Emma had nothing under it but a pair of glossy stockings and he began to kiss her ankles through the fine nylon, rolling up the kaftan until he reached her knees, licking the shining nylon and wetting it with his mouth all the way up to the white lace stocking tops. He licked the lace and kissed the area of soft vulnerable flesh above the stockings opening her legs a little so that he could press his mouth into her groin. And then he left Emma lying there, with everything exposed, while he tugged off his trousers.

Emma's breath became short and panting as he got back on to the bed. Stanley had left his T-shirt on and his huge golden cock stuck out from under it, lifting it up at the front. He carried on kissing her, burying his lips into her pubic hairs, licking them until they were slicked back with his saliva and Emma's juices as his lips roved higher to brush her soft belly. Emma looked at his beautiful near naked body and pulled the kaftan up even further, trying to present him with her pert breasts. Stanley immediately pulled it down again to where it was before. He had his own agenda and was determined to take things at his own pace. He opened her legs wider and lay between them, supporting himself on his elbow and only gradually rolling the kaftan up above her perfect breasts. Then he used the hem of the black gown to press it right across Emma's eyes, holding it down tightly at either side of her head, until she was in effect blindfolded. She lay passively, a prisoner in the dark, held by his strong grip and she offered absolutely no resistance as he bit and licked her breasts, flattening his long tongue against her sharp red nipples and then taking each one into his mouth and sucking them so strongly that they were pulled out and elongated by the force of his lips.

It was obvious that Emma was revelling in his ministrations, adoring the piquancy of feeling anonymous behind the blindfold and the lack of responsibility for what was happening to her willing body. She shifted slightly on the bed, opening her legs even further and moaning with longing, indicating that she was ready to take in his thick golden brown shaft. The gesture wasn't lost on Stanley, who lifted his T-shirt up to give his prick some freedom of movement and pulled the skirt of the kaftan away from her eyes so that he could push his cock into her mouth. Emma's juices were making snail trails down her inner thighs and this was when Tom threw off his robe and came to kneel between her legs, pushing his face close to her sex, letting her feel the warmth of his breath against her wide-open pussy lips. The whole of her sex was glistening as Tom stroked and smoothed her belly and pubic hair and kissed the inside of her thighs while she sucked on the huge cock that Stanley was thrusting remorselessly in and out of her mouth. Tom scissored her labia apart, stretching the silky wet lips, getting her ready for the onslaught of his own stiff cock. As Stanley rhythmically pounded into Emma's mouth, Tom moved inside her strongly and steadily until her whole body stretched and strained with need and she gasped and whimpered and threw her head back. Tom reached down and caressed her clit with the lightest possible touch, but it was enough to push Emma over the edge and her clit jerked uncontrollably as she thrust herself closer to him and her orgasm burst over her suddenly. The two men climaxed almost simultaneously, Stanley discharging his come into her mouth and throat in quick hot spurts and Tom groaning aloud as he pumped his spunk into her throbbing sex.

After a moment, Stanley withdrew himself from Emma's mouth, leaving behind his hot seed which had filled her mouth and flooded into her throat. He climbed gracefully off the bed and came to join Laura, standing in front of her, looking at her with his unfathomable dark eyes.

'God, I'm aching all over,' he said. 'I'm flying home tomorrow, Laura.'

'I know,' she said, and reached up to kiss him on the lips, still looking into his eyes. He looked magnificent, even though his cock was softening, as he walked gracefully to the shower room, and Laura watched him go with regret.

Tom gently took Emma in his arms, holding her close and whispering endearments as he stroked her soft hair. As for Laura, she too felt suddenly weary and longed for bed. She lay back in the comfort of the towelling robe and closed her eyes.

She opened them to see Emma standing in front of her. 'God, I'm absolutely bushed,' she said, and she went to join Stanley under the swiftly running shower, leaving Tom and Laura alone. He wrapped himself in a *Jannina* robe and sat beside her.

'That was really something, Laura,' he said. 'We've only known you for a fortnight, but we'll never forget you. Emma and I both hope we'll be friends forever.'

They smiled at each other. 'Come on,' he said, and took her hand, pulling her to her feet. 'I think those two have finished now. Let's have a shower.'

15

The weekend really was the success that Andrew had promised her, and his family gave her a genuinely warm welcome. In spite of their obvious affluence and upmarket lifestyle, his parents and sister seemed totally without pretension and Laura quickly relaxed and started to enjoy herself.

After dinner they were tactfully left alone with their coffee and Andrew leaned over to her and grinned wickedly as he whispered to her, 'Ma's just an ordinary Surrey girl at heart, and she's put you in the guest bedroom. She's reached that age when she can't bear to think of her little boy doing anything naughty, so we'll have to set something up.'

Laura grinned back. 'What had you in mind?' she asked cheekily. 'Your place or mine?'

'Oh mine,' he said. 'You may have got an en suite, but I've got a big bed.'

She felt a delicious sense of anticipation and naughtiness as midnight approached and the house gradually grew dark and quiet. There didn't even seem to be any traffic noises as she opened her door noiselessly and crept along the landing to his room, dressed modestly in a satin dressing gown.

Andrew had one lamp on at the side of his bed and was lying back on his pillows, his cock already hardening as he waited for her to throw the dressing gown on to the floor and get into bed. Laura sighed softly and lay back beside him, spreading her legs and putting her hand on her tingling crotch.

He put his hand on hers. 'Here, let me do that for you,' he said softly. 'Lie back while I stroke you.'

She was only too happy to obey. She lay still and let him stroke her, revelling in the feeling of being alone with him at last. The disembarkation procedures and the journey to his home had been tiring enough, but the tension of meeting his family for the first time was even more exhausting. There's nothing more shattering than entertaining and being entertained, she thought, and she leaned her head against Andrew's shoulder.

'I've looked forward to this all evening. I've been fantasising about you like mad, ever since we left the ship,' he said softly.

'Oh?' she whispered back. 'Tell me about it,' and she stroked his long hard shaft very gently.

'Well, in one fantasy,' he said slowly, 'I'm with another man. I have my cock in your mouth, while he licks and fingers your delicious little bumhole until it's so hot and ready that you're writhing about, begging to come. But we won't let you get off like that. I keep taking you to the edge and then withdrawing, tormenting you until you're frantic and us two men can't hold off any longer. Only then do we both fuck you together, front and rear, filling you up until you come everywhere. Would you enjoy that? Do you fancy threes up?'

'Oh yes,' Laura breathed, and she curled her fingers round the tip of his prick. She wondered who the other man would be now that Tom and Stanley were gone, but cross that bridge when we come to it, she thought. Perhaps Andrew already had someone in mind.

'My threesome is always with another woman,' she said. 'We're sex slaves and you're the very stern slave owner, who disciplines us before we're allowed to climax.'

She probed gently beneath his foreskin, pulling it back a little and bending her head to lick the first trembling dewdrop of his love juice. She sensed that this particular scenario had really got him going and she sucked a little harder, swallowing a drop of salty liquid and licking her lips.

'And who's your oppo in all this?' he asked rather hoarsely.

'Oh, Fiona perhaps,' Laura said. 'I think she's good slave material, don't you?'

'Definitely,' he said, groaning softly as she rubbed him with her hand again, the saliva from her mouth making him glisten.

'I'd love to be a sex slave,' Laura continued dreamily. 'We'd have to take it in turns, of course, one watching while the other one is bent over his knee and the slave owner is giving us exercises to make us more submissive.'

'What sort of exercises?' Laura could feel his stiff cock lengthen as he thought about it.

'Well, usually punishments for bad behaviour. Maybe a spanking with a strap, followed by an apology from the slave and then a reward with his cock or a special dildo when she persuades him that she's obedient and submissive.'

'Jesus, Laura,' Andrew whispered. 'I could live with that.'

His cock was now massive, rearing up against his belly. He stood up suddenly, holding it in one hand as he moved swiftly across the room. Laura heard a drawer open and close and then he was back again.

'Come on, then,' he said, and sat down on the edge of

the bed. 'We haven't got a third party and we've no strap, but we can improvise with a ruler. We don't need a dildo, we've got this.' He stroked his huge stiff shaft.

'Now, get across my knee, you bad girl,' he ordered.

'Yes, master,' Laura said eagerly, and she obediently bent over his knee, exposing the beautiful twin swellings of her shapely arse in the glow of the bedside lamp.

Andrew eased her away from his cock, making himself more comfortable, and then said with mock seriousness, 'I've been far too lenient with you lately and you've taken advantage of me, running off to Farnham for a dirty weekend and then jumping into bed with someone.'

Laura twisted round trying to look at him. 'But, sir, I didn't know . . .'

'Silence. Don't answer back. If you pretend you didn't know then I'm going to *make* you know,' he growled angrily, and he held her firmly in the middle of the back, pressing her against his thighs so that she was absolutely helpless and had to gaze at the floor. 'You must learn, my girl, that bad behaviour has to be punished.' Then he whispered, 'Do you know what happens to naughty girls?'

'Yes, sir,' Laura answered in a little girly voice.

'Go on then,' he prompted. 'How many smacks do you get for sneaking into someone's bedroom?'

Laura pretended to think about it, then she said, 'Whatever you decide, master.'

'Right first time and remember, slave, no wriggling or crying out. Any movement or sound on your part will result in further punishment.'

'Yes, master. Whatever you say, sir.' Laura licked her lips in anticipation.

'What a lovely naughty white bum you have,' Andrew said softly, and he stroked each cheek of her helpless bottom. Laura wriggled under his caressing hand.

'It's a pity it's so disobedient.'

'But I can change, sir,' Laura said.

'I've heard that one before. The only thing that'll make *you* change is a good hiding.'

'Not too hard ... please,' she begged him.

'Quiet,' he ordered. 'It's got to be hard or you won't have learned your lesson.' He tapped firmly with the ruler across one pale cheek of her bottom.

Then he stroked the hard edge of the ruler down her spine and between her legs, caressing her very lightly and then stroking it upwards again towards her shoulder blades.

'Remember,' he said, 'I can punish you anywhere I like with this. Not just on your naughty wilful little bottom. I could use it on your shoulders or the backs of your legs. I could use it on your hard little clitty and spank it till it behaves itself.'

'Oh no, not that. Please, Mr Gibson, sir.'

'Silence, slave. A slave isn't allowed to say what she wants or doesn't want. Very well, just for now, I think twenty firm strokes, just to warm you up and then we'll get on to the hard stuff.'

Laura shivered a little with excitement as he gave her a stroke on the other side. In the soft glow of the bedside lamp, two pink lines had appeared on her buttocks and Laura was enjoying the sound of it, followed by the sensation of sexy warmth as he counted out the strokes and she began to writhe with pleasure.

'No wriggling,' he said, 'or you'll get extra.'

'Sorry, Mr Gibson.'

'Sorry, Mr Gibson, *sir*, if you don't mind.'

'Right, sir. Sorry, Mr Gibson, sir.'

'That's better. Now stay still and take your punishment without speaking.'

Her bottom was now a uniform shade of pale pink both sides and felt deliciously hot and ready, in contrast to the cool night air from the open window. Each time the ruler hit her toasted bottom, she rubbed her crotch longingly against his hard thighs.

'Wriggling already?

'Please, sir, let me go now, sir,' she pleaded. 'Let me have your cock inside me. Please, sir.'

A wave of red-hot longing rushed from her swollen sex lips and centred agonisingly on her clit. She only needed a few strokes of his cock and she'd come. She tried to reach behind her to his rock-hard shaft and gasped out, 'I want . . .'

'What? A bit of nipple nipping?' He began to nip the ends of her tips, tormenting them into a state of unbearable rapture until she begged again to be allowed to come.

'Oh please, Mr Gibson, sir, let me kneel in front of you and suck you off. I –'

'Silence, I said, or I shall spank you harder. How many strokes have you had now?'

'I think it's twenty, master.'

'Rubbish. It's only fifteen. You've still five to go.'

'Oh, no. Mercy, *please*, sir.'

'Yes. You've got to have another five on your naughty sore little bum.'

'Thank you, master. I'll be so obedient after this,' Laura promised.

'You'd better be,' he growled, and gave her the next five slightly harder, so that she was really red and glowing and felt even more horny.

'I'm glad you've decided to be good,' he said, 'because now we're going to play the Chinese torture game. I'll touch you in here for a while.'

Still holding her across his knee, he eased two of his fingers a little way into her dripping opening and spread some juice up to her bumhole. With his two fingers still in place, he massaged the opening of her tight secret hole with his thumb and began to circle it gently round and round until Laura began to moan softly and squirmed to try to push herself on to his tormenting hand.

'Please. Oh please,' she moaned softly. 'Please let me come now, sir. I'll be good, really I will.'

He looked at her bent head and twitching thighs. 'Well, I suppose I could let you have a little bit more, if that's what you want,' he said.

'Yes. I want it now,' Laura begged frantically, and tried once more to bear down on his teasing fingers.

He immediately withdrew his fingers from her aching holes and gave a warning slap on the already red arse. 'But "I want" never gets. Manners are just as important as obedience to a slave master, aren't they?'

'Yes,' she gasped. 'I'm sorry, master. Please give me some more. Please. Put it in for me.'

'All right,' he said with feigned reluctance. 'As you asked so nicely, I suppose I can give you a little bit more.' He put the two fingers back in place. Once more, Laura writhed and wriggled vainly to try to get him to go deeper, but he ignored her heaving buttocks and soft whimpers and coolly continued to circle her cunt and bumhole, slowly and deliberately. 'Shall I give you a bit more? Could you take another extra inch?' he whispered tauntingly, and Laura could only gasp in reply, her thighs taut and trembling with desire. He put three fingers inside her now and pushed them all the way up to the knuckles. 'How's that?' he whispered. 'Ask nicely if you want more.'

'Please. Oh *please*,' was all that Laura could manage.

'I'm sorry,' he murmured. 'I beg your pardon, but I didn't hear you.'

'More, please, master.'

'Good girl,' he said. He knew she'd reached the point of no return and now he pushed his fingers all the way in and brushed the end of her clit with his thumb. The added tension of having to be quiet, so that no one would guess what they were up to, made her even more aroused. She clenched her teeth together, determined not to cry out as she climaxed, her body shuddering and heaving under his firm skilful hands. Then she lay motionless and utterly relaxed over his knee until he gently helped her back on to the bed.

'It's hard work being a slave master,' he joked as he bent over her. He gazed down at her naked breasts and softly rounded belly as he eased her down on to the pillows. Laura relaxed her buttocks and shoulders against the wide comfortable bed.

'This is heaven, Laura, having you underneath me like this and knowing we've got all night.'

He stroked her bare breasts and belly and, in spite of her relaxed state, Laura began to tingle all over again. Her nipples had remained excitingly erect, her lips still puffy and swollen from his earlier kisses.

'Heaven,' he said again, and kissed her deeply.

Laura made no reply, but pressed her lips even closer to his, their breath mingling as he sucked her mouth and stroked the softness of her inner thighs. She sighed; her eyes closed as he moved his hands back to her breasts. Laura was still in the mood for submission and felt almost light headed with pleasure as she arched her back so that her breasts were thrust towards him. He took them in his hands, squeezing them and massaging the firm white globes, and crushing her nipples hard in his palms. No one had ever played with Laura's breasts so skilfully. No other man had ever been able to excite her so unbearably by mouthing her nipples. She knew he could make her get off just by concentrating on her breasts and she was content to linger on the sensual edge of orgasm again. She could feel his thick rod pressing insistently against her thigh and she opened her eyes.

'What wonderful titties, Laura,' he said. 'They're the best I've ever seen.'

'Oh yes?' she whispered, smiling. 'So how many have you seen?' She fastened her eyes on his rigid cock and reached down to stroke it, making him growl softly with ecstasy as her fingers went up and down his finely veined tool.

'Quite a few magnificent pairs,' he admitted rather breathlessly, 'in my misspent youth of course. But none to compare with these.'

Laura knew he was bent on arousing her all over again and spread her legs for him. Andrew traced a long slow line with his finger, from her bumhole to her soaking wet pussy, and Laura sat up on her knees and leaned forward, still holding his cock and licked the glittering drop of come which was trembling on the tip of his tool. She held the base of his prick firmly and licked again, more firmly. The swollen purple tip was wet with spit and she moved her tongue further down his shaft, enjoying his cock until it rippled and throbbed against her tongue. He was now twitching dangerously and he began to breathe heavily, delirious with pleasure, his tool dribbling thick love juice which Laura licked away. She dipped her fingers into her cunt and smeared her own juices over his tightly packed balls, squeezing them gently until he writhed and jerked, pushing his tool further into her mouth. She wetted her finger again and slid it gently between his buttocks, moistening his tight arsehole until he groaned and pushed her hand away, laying her back on the pillows and holding her wet pussy.

'Oh shit, Laura,' he whispered. 'I can't wait any longer. I've got to be inside you.'

He forced open the delicate wet lips of her pussy and held her wide open while he pushed his rock-hard cock halfway in and then stopped, trying to regain some control.

'Oh, that feels lovely,' Laura said softly. She wanted to take all his hardness into her tingling warm sex, but Andrew was intent on fighting to keep control and he paused for a few seconds, breathing hard and concentrating on holding back. Then he thrust deeply into her, moving in and out slowly and steadily at his own sure pace.

Laura pressed her mouth into his naked shoulder so that her cries and sobs of ecstasy were muffled. She began to move to his rhythm, her body bathed in sweat and love juices, as his prick plunged into her tight wet pussy. Her arse was still tingling from the spanking and that sensation heightened her pleasure even further. Her body screamed and cried out to come again and she moved her pelvis more quickly against him, encouraging faster and deeper thrusts. He reached down and touched her silky clit and Laura climaxed, recovered and climaxed again, sobbing silently with relief against his shoulder as she felt his cock pump its come into her red-hot opening.

They lay still for a few moments, unable to move or speak, and then Andrew leaned across her to switch off the lamp. 'Christ,' he whispered, 'you really excelled yourself this time. We'll have to sleep in my bedroom again if it inspires you like that.'

'*You're* the one who was inspired,' Laura murmured sleepily. 'I don't know where all that spunk comes from. It's all over your mum's clean sheets.'

'Perhaps I'll have to be punished for it.' He grinned. 'After all, it must be *my* turn now, mistress.'

It was dawn before Laura made it back to the spare bedroom and the virginal guest bed. The sheets were tucked in tightly and it felt very cold after the heat of the one she'd just left. Never mind, she thought as she stretched her legs down the pristine bed, it'll soon warm up, and she closed her eyes and thought of Andrew.

16

In spite of their late night lovemaking, when Laura opened her eyes, Andrew was sitting on the side of her bed, in pale grey boxer shorts, putting a tray of coffee on her bedside table.

'Good morning, Miss Laura, ma'am,' he said with a smile and a tolerable imitation of Stanley's soft lilting tones.

'Oh, good morning,' Laura said, and she stretched lazily, smiling at him, pleased with the coffee and even more pleased with the sight of her lover.

'When does madam want her bath?' he continued. 'Would you like me to run it for you now?'

'Yes please, slave,' Laura said languidly. 'Get on with it, or it'll be the worse for you.'

He disappeared into the en suite and she heard the taps running while she sipped her coffee and stretched her legs down the bed for a few minutes, luxuriating in the idea of a refreshing bath. Andrew turned the water off and came back to her.

'Finished the coffee? Good,' he said. 'Your bath awaits, ma'am. There's a power shower as well,' he added with a wickedly sexy grin.

She stepped into the bath and he took his boxers off, dipping his hands into the water and squeezing body wash on to his palms. He rubbed his hands together to spread it around and then began to soap her body with it, starting at her neck and working downwards, paying particular attention to her breasts, caressing them from the front and then from underneath her arms, worshipping her voluptuous flesh with both hands and pulling and pinching at her nipples until they were as long and tender as last night. Laura leaned her head back against the end of the bath as he moved his hands further down, soaping her belly and mound, then opening her legs to thrust them between her thighs. He picked up each of her legs in turn and massaged her feet and ankles, making her shiver with the sensual pleasure of his palms on the soles of her feet, so close to tickling, it was almost unbearable. She lifted her hips a little as he moved up her legs again, trying to expose her sex to his questing fingers.

'I can't reach you,' he said. 'You'll have to kneel for me.'

She turned over immediately, kneeling obediently on all fours so that he could slip both hands underneath her, sawing up and down her clit with one hand and using his other hand to ease two fingers into her, juicing her sex and puffing out the already big lips even further.

She looked over her shoulder and had a shock of pleasure as she saw his handsome erection. 'Are you going to fuck me like this, Andrew?'

'Yes,' he said. 'I can't do it any other way. Sex is impossible under water,' and he climbed into the bath behind her.

She felt a shiver of pleasure as his tip entered her and then the whole of his cock shot into her so forcefully that she had to put her hands on the edge of the bath to steady herself.

'Yes, I am going to fuck you, Miss Laura, ma'am,' he said rather breathlessly. 'Like this ... and this ... and this ... and this ...'

He shafted into her, using all his strength to pound his cock in as far as it would go, his balls slapping up against her body until her sex began to clench around him.

He opened her buttocks wider, grasping them hard so that he could pull her back towards him and penetrate even further. Laura's body was on fire with the pounding she was taking. Sweat beaded her brow and a lock of hair fell over her eyes.

'Oh God, Andrew,' she moaned. 'I want to come now. Let me come now. Oh please.'

For answer, he slid one hand down to her wide-open sex lips and found her clit, pushing it this way and that, making it jump and dance to the movement of his finger, until all her feelings were concentrated in that one pleasure zone and her orgasm came like an explosion, shattering her to fragments as wave after wave of ecstatic feeling convulsed her and spread everywhere.

She felt Andrew's cock throb and shudder. Then it jerked backwards and she felt his hot come jetting inside her.

'Jesus,' he groaned. 'You don't know what you do to me, Laura.'

'I think I've got a pretty good idea.' They remained motionless for some minutes and then Andrew reluctantly eased himself off her body so that he could use the shower.

'Stand up,' he said, 'and I'll sluice you off.'

She stood in front of him as he switched on the jet of hot water, rinsing down his body and hers and reviving the temperature of the bath water. He switched it off and she looked round for some towels.

'No, don't get out yet,' he said. 'There's something I've been wanting to do ever since our night in the jacuzzi.'

'Oh? What is it?'

But she knew what it was and licked her lips with anticipation.

'Lie down again.'

She lay down in the warm water and he opened her legs as wide as they'd go, propping her feet on the lip of the bath. Then he switched on the shower again, directing it straight between her legs and on to her clit and increasing the power until she gasped and clung to the sides of the bath as the jet found her sore clit and made it sting. Gradually, the force of the water turned the stinging sensation into a thrilling sexy tingle and spread into a glowing heated climax which made Laura continue to moan softly long after the delicious sensation had died away.

He turned off the water and reached for a towel. As Laura stepped out of the bath, he blotted her body all over, drying her thoroughly and then towelling her shoulders and breasts, vigorously rubbing her nipples harder and harder until she was nearly ready to come again. She stood satisfied and glowing, happier than she'd ever been in her life.

'Well?' he said. 'What do you think to the staff here?'

'Marvellous,' she sighed. 'Five star.'

'And the room service?'

'Fabulous,' she said. 'It couldn't be better.'

Epilogue

The first day back at work was often rather fraught and tense, but Laura's visit to her prospective in-laws had proved a great success and Andrew's lovemaking more than fulfilled her expectations. It had been all that Andrew had promised. They'd even had time to race up to Manchester and take Wendy out for a Chinese before joining the ship for the music lovers' cruise.

The passengers were much of a muchness, Laura reflected as she and Fiona took their places once more behind the Shangri-la's reception desk. It didn't seem to matter whether they were music lovers, sun worshippers, antique collectors or just culture vultures. All the clients wanted the same thing, namely to relax, to pamper themselves and to indulge in whatever took their fancy. After all, Laura thought, that's what they're paying for and that's what they'll do. She smiled to herself as she remembered Eileen Grimshaw and hoped things were going well with her and Reggie. The last news they'd had of Bob Evans was that he'd recovered from his heart attack and was convalescing in Bournemouth. She doubted if they'd ever see him again.

There were other quite significant differences on this cruise, she thought. For a start, there was no Steve. She'd had the presence of mind to write to her mum before they docked at Southampton, rather than phone. She reasoned that this would give it time to sink in, that Steve was no longer on the scene and that she was in Farnham with the new man in her life. In spite of her bewilderment, Wendy had taken it very well.

Now, when Laura spread out her beautifully kept hands on the appointments book, the clients couldn't fail to notice the large solitaire diamond on her ring finger, flashing and winking in the sunlight. Surprisingly perhaps, this didn't fill any of the golden oldies with envy for the beautiful girl on the brink of a long liaison with a handsome young officer. On the contrary, most of them seemed to be recalling their own youthful dreams of love and desire as they looked at her with expressions of approval and admiration.

Stanley had not joined the cruise ship this trip. His forthcoming marriage to a girl in his own village had now been arranged for him and would be taking up all his energies. With the dowry and his own savings from his cruise work, Stanley had enough to become part-owner of a fishing boat. They would live with his parents for a few years and work towards building their own modest home.

Laura wondered fleetingly about the young bride. She'd be an innocent young village maiden, and a virgin, of course. She hoped Stanley's bisexuality would not be a source of unhappiness to the young girl, but might even give her some freedom from the traditional rigid structures of the marriage. She was sure that Stanley would treat his bride with absolute love and respect. She wished them both well.

A major change this voyage was that Laura had been allocated a single cabin, so sharing with Thelma wasn't necessary. Fiona was with Elinor, naturally enough, and was looking both radiant and much more relaxed. Poor kid, Laura thought. I bet she was really tensed up on the last trip. Elinor herself seemed to be actually blooming and much more approachable and friendly now that she'd got Fiona to herself.

She'd noticed one or two promising young hunks

already and she and Thelma had even caught a glimpse of the very handsome Latin, who was obviously the concert pianist on this trip. She dealt with the immediate queue of passengers wanting appointments and then, suddenly, Elinor was in front of her.

'Hi. How are you doing?'

'Oh, OK,' Laura said cautiously. 'Looks like we're going to be as busy as usual this trip. How about you?'

'The same,' she said. For the first time since Laura had known her, Elinor smiled with no trace of her usual bitter waspishness, just a friendly open grin showing the perfect, even teeth, which made her seem very attractive and approachable.

'Maybe we could get together for a spa and massage session one night,' Elinor went on. 'Fiona, you, me and Andrew, is it? We'll probably be in need of a little warmth and massage if it carries on being as busy as this.'

Again, she gave a warm open smile and Laura hesitated, surprised.

Then she said, 'Why not? That sounds like a good idea, Elinor. I'd like that and I'm sure Andrew would as well.'

'Right. We're on then. Champers and nibbles in the spa tomorrow night, ten thirty?' she said.

They looked at each other for a long minute.

Laura nodded.

'See you then,' Elinor said.

'Yes. See you,' Laura said with a smile.

Here's a turn-up for the books, she thought, but even so, she was going to make sure that she and Andrew were up for it.

Elinor had excelled herself. The champagne was a good one and was already on ice when they arrived, bearing a second bottle, well chilled and enclosed in an insulated sleeve. Elinor had provided some very sophisticated nibbles, canapés and olives, along with paper plates and napkins and plastic wine glasses, so that all safety rules were observed. Even the towels were special – bath sheet size and warm and fluffy, straight from the laundry room.

Andrew grinned when he saw the set-up. Although they were at the stage of their relationship when he wanted Laura all to himself, he'd had no hesitation in accepting the invitation. Both of them were conscious of a new gentleness and urbanity in Elinor, which must obviously be because of her happiness with her young lover. She and Fiona were obviously as delighted as Andrew and Laura with the new arrangements. The four of them were more like honeymooners than ship's crew.

Elinor and Andrew elected to go and get changed in a cubicle, but the two young women were quickly undressed and sipping champagne by the time they returned. Elinor was at first very much in charge and arranged herself on one of the toning tables, tipping the back so that her shapely legs were slightly higher than her head and arranging cushions behind her head so that she could still manage her wine. Laura smilingly watched these proceedings, very conscious of Andrew's admiration as he gazed at her own stunningly beautiful nude body. He was more laid back than Laura had ever seen him and seemed quite prepared to do anything that Elinor had planned for him.

'Doesn't she look lovely?' Fiona said to the other two, and the others agreed that Elinor did.

'I feel we should raise our glasses in celebration of the Shangri-la,' Elinor said, and they all obeyed.

Laura's mind wandered a little as she looked round the room. She was glad that she now had Elinor as a friend. She wondered what Steve was doing now and if he missed her. She'd send him a postcard when they got to Kusadasi. Stanley would have reached his home by now, probably preparing for his wedding night, she thought, and she smiled at the vivid memory of his strong brown cock.

Fiona was bending over Elinor, unable to take her eyes off Elinor's sumptuous tits and big nipples. Fiona had become surprisingly assertive in her worship of her lover's body. Laura was amazed at the way the younger girl had gained in confidence in the salon, and in handling Elinor, of course.

The four of them seemed to get on extremely well together, Laura thought. It wasn't even as though any of them were alike – except in their sexual interest, that is. They were already quite a tightly knit little group, although they could always introduce new people, she supposed. Who knows? There might be another Tom and Emma among the musicians.

She looked again at Elinor, lying back on the toning table unashamedly rampant, while Fiona gazed at her adoringly. Her eyes flickered to Andrew, sipping his champagne and trying to contain his massive hard-on. He was more than ready to celebrate the Shangri-la Health and Beauty Spa. They smiled and raised their glasses to each other.

At that moment, Thelma walked in and there was silence in the Shangri-la as she was given a glass of champagne and went into a cubicle to strip off. Her body was as sexy as Laura had imagined it. Long limbed and deep breasted, she came out of the cubicle unselfconsciously, gracefully naked and tanned all over. No white bits at all. She walked confidently up to Elinor, holding up her glass and smiling round.

'Wicked,' she said to them. 'Well, cheers, maties. This

has got to be a first for the Shangri-la. Well, here's to health and beauty.' She took a sip of champagne. 'Now it seems to me, sports, that we oughta put the champers aside for a minute and see what we can do for those lovely boobs of Elinor's,' she said.

Andrew grinned at her. 'Yes,' he said. 'Why not? That sounds like a good idea.'

Visit the Black Lace website at
www.blacklace-books.co.uk

FIND OUT THE LATEST INFORMATION AND TAKE
ADVANTAGE OF OUR FANTASTIC **FREE** BOOK OFFER!
ALSO VISIT THE SITE FOR . . .

- All Black Lace titles currently available
  and how to order online

- Great new offers

- Writers' guidelines

- Author interviews

- An erotica newsletter

- Features

- Cool links

**BLACK LACE — THE LEADING IMPRINT
OF WOMEN'S SEXY FICTION**

**TAKING YOUR EROTIC READING
PLEASURE TO NEW HORIZONS**

LOOK OUT FOR THE ALL-NEW BLACK LACE BOOKS – AVAILABLE NOW!

All books priced £6.99 in the UK. Please note publication dates apply to the UK only. For other territories, please contact your retailer.

WOLF AT THE DOOR
Savannah Smythe
ISBN 0 352 33693 5

Thirty-year-old Pagan Warner is marrying Greg, a debonair and seemingly dull Englishman, in an effort to erase her turbulent past. All she wants is a peaceful life in rural New Jersey but her past catches up with her in the form of bad boy 'Wolf' Mancini, the man who seduced her as a teenager. Tempted into rekindling their intensely sexual affair while making her wedding preparations, she intends to break off the illicit liaison once she is married. However, Pagan has underestimated the Wolf's obsessions. Mancini has spotted Greg's own weaknesses and intends to exploit them to the full, undermining him in his professional life. When he sends the slinky, raven-haired Renate in to do his dirty work, the course is set for a descent into depravity. **Fabulous nasty characters, dirty double dealing and forbidden lusts abound!**

THE CAPTIVE FLESH
Cleo Cordell
ISBN 0 352 32872 X

Eighteenth-century French convent girls Marietta and Claudine learn that their stay at the opulent Algerian home of their handsome and powerful host, Kasim, requires something in return: their complete surrender to the ecstasy of pleasure in pain. Kasim's decadent orgies also require the services of Gabriel, whose exquisite longing for Marietta's awakened lust cannot be contained – not even by the shackles that bind his tortured flesh. **This is a reprint of one of the first Black Lace books ever published. A classic piece of blockbusting historical erotica.**

Coming in August

DIVINE TORMENT
Janine Ashbless
ISBN O 352 33719 2

In the ancient temple city of Mulhanabin, the voluptuous Malia Shai awaits her destiny. Millions of people worship her, believing her to be a goddess incarnate. However, she is very human, consumed by erotic passions that have no outlet. Into this sacred city comes General Verlaine – the rugged and horny gladiatorial leader of the occupying army. Intimate contact between Verlaine and Malia Shai is forbidden by every law of their hostile peoples. But she is the one thing he wants – and he will risk everything to have her. **A beautifully written story of opulent palaces, extreme rituals and sexy conquerors. Like *Gladiator* set in a mythical realm.**

THE BEST OF BLACK LACE 2
Edited by Kerri Sharp
ISBN O 352 33718 4

The Black Lace series has continued to be *the* market leader in erotic fiction, publishing genuine female writers of erotica from all over the English-speaking world. The series has changed and developed considerably since it was launched in 1993. The past decade has seen an explosion of interest in the subject of female sexuality, and Black Lace has always been at the forefront of debate around this issue. Editorial policy is constantly evolving to keep the writing up-to-date and fresh, and now the books have undergone a design makeover that completes the transformation, taking the series into a new era of prominence and popularity. *The Best of Black Lace 2* will include extracts of the sexiest, most sizzling titles from the past three years.

SHADOWPLAY
Portia Da Costa
ISBN O 352 33313 8

Photographer Christabel is drawn to psychic phenomena and dark liaisons. When she is persuaded by her husband to take a holiday at a mysterious mansion house in the country, unexpected events begin to unravel. Her husband has enlisted the help of his young male PA to ensure that Christabel's holiday is eventful and erotic. Within the web of an unusual and kinky threesome, Christabel learns some lessons the jaded city could never teach. **Full of dark, erotic games, this is a special reprint of one of our most popular titles.**

Coming in September

SATAN'S ANGEL
Melissa MacNeal
ISBN O 352 33726 5

Feisty young Miss Rosie is lured north during the first wave of the Klondike gold rush. Ending up in a town called Satan, she auditions for the position of the town's most illustrious madam. Her creative ways with chocolate win her a place as the mysterious Devlin's mistress. As his favourite, she becomes the queen of a town where the wildest fantasies become everyday life, but where her devious rival, Venus, rules an underworld of sexual slavery. Caught in this dark vixen's web of deceit, Rosie is then kidnapped by the pistol-packing all-female gang, the KlonDykes and ultimately played as a pawn in a dangerous game of revenge. **Another whip-cracking historical adventure from Ms MacNeal.**

I KNOW YOU, JOANNA
Ruth Fox
ISBN 0 352 33727 3

Joanna writes stories for a top-shelf magazine. When her dominant and attractive boss Adam wants her to meet and 'play' with the readers she finds out just how many strange sexual deviations there are. However many kinky playmates she encounters, nothing prepares her for what Adam has in mind. Complicating her progress, also, are the insistent anonymous invitations from someone who professes to know her innermost fantasies. **Based on the real experiences of scene players, this is shockingly adult material!**

THE INTIMATE EYE
Georgia Angelis
ISBN 0 352 33004 X

In eighteenth-century Gloucestershire, Lady Catherine Balfour is struggling to quell the passions that are surfacing in her at the sight of so many handsome labourers working her land. Then, aspiring artist Joshua Fox arrives to paint a portrait of the Balfour family. Fox is about to turn her world upside down. This man, whom she assumes is a mincing fop, is about to seduce every woman in the village – Catherine included. But she has a rival: her wilful daughter Sophie is determined to claim Fox as her own. **This earthy story of rustic passion is a Black Lace special reprint of one of our bestselling historical titles.**

Black Lace Booklist

Information is correct at time of printing. To avoid disappointment check availability before ordering. Go to www.blacklace-books.co.uk. All books are priced £6.99 unless another price is given.

BLACK LACE BOOKS WITH A CONTEMPORARY SETTING

☐ THE TOP OF HER GAME Emma Holly	ISBN 0 352 33337 5	£5.99
☐ IN THE FLESH Emma Holly	ISBN 0 352 34498 3	£5.99
☐ A PRIVATE VIEW Crystalle Valentino	ISBN 0 352 33308 1	£5.99
☐ SHAMELESS Stella Black	ISBN 0 352 34485 1	£5.99
☐ INTENSE BLUE Lyn Wood	ISBN 0 352 34496 7	£5.99
☐ THE NAKED TRUTH Natasha Rostova	ISBN 0 352 34497 5	£5.99
☐ ANIMAL PASSIONS Martine Marquand	ISBN 0 352 34499 1	£5.99
☐ A SPORTING CHANCE Susie Raymond	ISBN 0 352 33501 7	£5.99
☐ TAKING LIBERTIES Susie Raymond	ISBN 0 352 33357 X	£5.99
☐ A SCANDALOUS AFFAIR Holly Graham	ISBN 0 352 33523 8	£5.99
☐ THE NAKED FLAME Crystalle Valentino	ISBN 0 352 33528 9	£5.99
☐ CRASH COURSE Juliet Hastings	ISBN 0 352 33018 X	£5.99
☐ ON THE EDGE Laura Hamilton	ISBN 0 352 33534 3	£5.99
☐ LURED BY LUST Tania Picarda	ISBN 0 352 33533 5	£5.99
☐ THE HOTTEST PLACE Tabitha Flyte	ISBN 0 352 33536 X	£5.99
☐ THE NINETY DAYS OF GENEVIEVE Lucinda Carrington	ISBN 0 352 33070 8	£5.99
☐ EARTHY DELIGHTS Tesni Morgan	ISBN 0 352 33548 3	£5.99
☐ MAN HUNT Cathleen Ross	ISBN 0 352 33583 1	
☐ MÉNAGE Emma Holly	ISBN 0 352 33231 X	
☐ DREAMING SPIRES Juliet Hastings	ISBN 0 352 33584 X	
☐ THE TRANSFORMATION Natasha Rostova	ISBN 0 352 33311 1	
☐ STELLA DOES HOLLYWOOD Stella Black	ISBN 0 352 33588 2	
☐ SIN.NET Helena Ravenscroft	ISBN 0 352 33598 X	
☐ HOTBED Portia Da Costa	ISBN 0 352 33614 5	
☐ TWO WEEKS IN TANGIER Annabel Lee	ISBN 0 352 33599 8	
☐ HIGHLAND FLING Jane Justine	ISBN 0 352 33616 1	

☐ PLAYING HARD Tina Troy   ISBN 0 352 33617 X
☐ SYMPHONY X Jasmine Stone   ISBN 0 352 33629 3
☐ STRICTLY CONFIDENTIAL Alison Tyler   ISBN 0 352 33624 2
☐ SUMMER FEVER Anna Ricci   ISBN 0 352 33625 0
☐ CONTINUUM Portia Da Costa   ISBN 0 352 33120 8
☐ OPENING ACTS Suki Cunningham   ISBN 0 352 33630 7
☐ FULL STEAM AHEAD Tabitha Flyte   ISBN 0 352 33637 4
☐ A SECRET PLACE Ella Broussard   ISBN 0 352 33307 3
☐ GAME FOR ANYTHING Lyn Wood   ISBN 0 352 33639 0
☐ FORBIDDEN FRUIT Susie Raymond   ISBN 0 352 33306 5
☐ CHEAP TRICK Astrid Fox   ISBN 0 352 33640 4
☐ THE ORDER Dee Kelly   ISBN 0 352 33652 8
☐ ALL THE TRIMMINGS Tesni Morgan   ISBN 0 352 33641 3
☐ PLAYING WITH STARS Jan Hunter   ISBN 0 352 33653 6
☐ THE GIFT OF SHAME Sara Hope-Walker   ISBN 0 352 29935 1
☐ COMING UP ROSES Crystalle Valentino   ISBN 0 352 33658 7
☐ GOING TOO FAR Laura Hamilton   ISBN 0 352 33657 9
☐ THE STALLION Georgina Brown   ISBN 0 352 33005 8
☐ DOWN UNDER Juliet Hastings   ISBN 0 352 33663 3
☐ THE BITCH AND THE BASTARD Wendy Harris   ISBN 0 352 33664 1
☐ ODALISQUE Fleur Reynolds   ISBN 0 352 32887 8
☐ GONE WILD Maria Eppie   ISBN 0 352 33670 6
☐ SWEET THING Alison Tyler   ISBN 0 352 33682 X
☐ TIGER LILY Kimberley Dean   ISBN 0 352 33685 4
☐ COOKING UP A STORM Emma Holly   ISBN 0 352 33686 2
☐ RELEASE ME Suki Cunningham   ISBN 0 352 33671 4
☐ KING'S PAWN Ruth Fox   ISBN 0 352 33684 6
☐ FULL EXPOSURE Robyn Russell   ISBN 0 352 33688 9
☐ SLAVE TO SUCCESS Kimberley Raines   ISBN 0 352 33687 0
☐ STRIPPED TO THE BONE Jasmine Stone   ISBN 0 352 33463 0
☐ HARD CORPS Claire Thompson   ISBN 0 352 33491 6
☐ MANHATTAN PASSION Antoinette Powell   ISBN 0 352 33691 9
☐ WOLF AT THE DOOR Savannah Smythe   ISBN 0 352 33693 5

BLACK LACE BOOKS WITH AN HISTORICAL SETTING

☐ PRIMAL SKIN Leona Benkt Rhys   ISBN O 352 33500 9   £5.99

☐ DEVIL'S FIRE Melissa MacNeal   ISBN O 352 33527 O   £5.99

☐ WILD KINGDOM Deanna Ashford   ISBN O 352 33549 1   £5.99

☐ DARKER THAN LOVE Kristina Lloyd   ISBN O 352 33279 4

☐ STAND AND DELIVER Helena Ravenscroft   ISBN O 352 33340 5   £5.99

☐ THE CAPTIVATION Natasha Rostova   ISBN O 352 33234 4

☐ CIRCO EROTICA Mercedes Kelley   ISBN O 352 33257 3

☐ MINX Megan Blythe   ISBN O 352 33638 2

☐ PLEASURE'S DAUGHTER Sedalia Johnson   ISBN O 352 33237 9

☐ JULIET RISING Cleo Cordell   ISBN O 352 32938 6

☐ DEMON'S DARE Melissa MacNeal   ISBN O 352 33683 8

☐ ELENA'S CONQUEST Lisette Allen   ISBN O 352 32950 5

☐ THE CAPTIVE FLESH Cleo Cordell   ISBN O 352 32872 X

BLACK LACE ANTHOLOGIES

☐ CRUEL ENCHANTMENT Erotic Fairy Stories   ISBN O 352 33483 5   £5.99
     Janine Ashbless

☐ MORE WICKED WORDS Various   ISBN O 352 33487 8   £5.99

☐ WICKED WORDS 4 Various   ISBN O 352 33603 X

☐ WICKED WORDS 5 Various   ISBN O 352 33642 O

☐ WICKED WORDS 6 Various   ISBN O 352 33590 O

BLACK LACE NON-FICTION

☐ THE BLACK LACE BOOK OF WOMEN'S SEXUAL   ISBN O 352 33346 4   £5.99
     FANTASIES Ed. Kerri Sharp

To find out the latest information about Black Lace titles, check out the website: www.blacklace-books.co.uk or send for a booklist with complete synopses by writing to:

Black Lace Booklist, Virgin Books Ltd
Thames Wharf Studios
Rainville Road
London W6 9HA

Please include an SAE of decent size. Please note only British stamps are valid.

Our privacy policy
We will not disclose information you supply us to any other parties. We will not disclose any information which identifies you personally to any person without your express consent.

From time to time we may send out information about Black Lace books and special offers. Please tick here if you do <u>not</u> wish to receive Black Lace information. ❑

Please send me the books I have ticked above.

Name ....

Address ....

....

....

....

Post Code ....

Send to: Cash Sales, Black Lace Books, Thames Wharf Studios, Rainville Road, London W6 9HA.

US customers: for prices and details of how to order books for delivery by mail, call 1-800-343-4499.

Please enclose a cheque or postal order, made payable to Virgin Books Ltd, to the value of the books you have ordered plus postage and packing costs as follows:

UK and BFPO – £1.00 for the first book, 50p for each subsequent book.

Overseas (including Republic of Ireland) – £2.00 for the first book, £1.00 for each subsequent book.

If you would prefer to pay by VISA, ACCESS/MASTERCARD, DINERS CLUB, AMEX or SWITCH, please write your card number and expiry date here:

....

Signature ....

Please allow up to 28 days for delivery.